A Lone Wolf

J. C. Fields

Cover Design – Niki Fowler

Publishing Coordinator – Sharon Kizziah-Holmes

Paperback-Press
an imprint of A & S Publishing
A & S Holmes, Inc.

ISBN -13: 978-1-945669-84-2

ACKNOWLEDGMENTS

I want to say thank you to all the individuals who lent their talents to the creation of this new novel.

Sharon Kizziah-Holmes, owner of Paperback Press, has enthusiastically reinforced my desire to create a new series. Her support has been unwavering from the beginning and I am indebted to her efforts on my behalf.

Colonel Mark "Buzz" Masters, USAF (ret) and a recently retired pilot for Southwest Airlines, provided background and offered hints on how someone could fly across the country without coming under TSA scrutiny. But remember, this is just a work of fiction.

Jeff Vaughn, standup comedian and man of leisure, provided a few of his jokes and his permission for a cameo appearance in Chapter 10. I had the pleasure of listening to his routine several years ago, plus, he has enjoyed reading the Sean Kruger series. At least he says he enjoys them. He's a comedian.

To my new developmental editor, Holly Atkinson. Thank you for joining the team. I look forward to working with you over the course of more novels.

Alisa Trotter, thank you for your fine tuning of the manuscript. It is amazing what one final read through will find.

Niki Fowler, a graphic artist extraordinaire, continues to create images for my books garnering praise and establishing continuity for the series. This cover produced accolades by everyone who previewed it.

Paul J. McSorley has narrated every installment of the Sean Kruger Series for Audible.com. His talent is such there is no way I would entrust one of my novels to anyone but him. While there is always a bit of sadness when I complete a new book, the excitement returns when Paul starts producing it for audio.

And again, last but not least, my wife Connie. She is and always will be the love of my life and my largest supporter. Not sure where I would be without her.

AUTHORS NOTE

The itch to write a story without Sean Kruger started right after I finished *The Imposter's Trail* in July of 2017. Well, two years and two additional Kruger novels later, here it is. After numerous discarded first drafts I looked back at a short story I penned in 2015, *The Ghost in the Mirror Affair*. It was the perfect background for the book you hold in your hand.

For those that are interested, I am offering the short story as a free PDF download on my website: www.jcfieldsbooks.com.

Numerous references found in *A Lone Wolf*, are dealt with in more detail in the short story. However, you can enjoy the novel without reading it.

While there are three characters from the Sean Kruger universe within these pages, (Kruger is not one of them), they are minor players within the story and will not appear in future episodes. As additional tales for this new series are developed, a new supporting cast will be introduced. You will discover several of them within these pages.

For readers who are concerned Sean Kruger will finally retire, fear not. He is a long way from fading away. As long as I continue to enjoy creating stories with his character and can develop fresh new ideas, he will be around for a while.

I hope you enjoy *A Lone Wolf*; I've had an absolute blast writing it.

Peace
J.C. Fields – Summer 2019

PART ONE
Two Years Ago

CHAPTER 1

BARCELONA, SPAIN

The sniper peered through Zeiss Victory HT binoculars as the woman wandered purposely northwest on the historic street in Barcelona. Taking her time, she remained 800 meters from her final destination. Eventually, the woman would arrive at the tapas bar with sidewalk seating on the northeast side of the street called La Rambla. An unoccupied apartment five floors up and two buildings northwest provided the sniper an unobscured view of the tables.

As she stopped at various boutique shops along the street, she pretended to gaze at goods in the windows. The sniper knew the exact purpose of these frequent stops. The woman was not looking at merchandise in the window, she was checking to make sure no one followed her.

He glanced at his wristwatch. She was an hour early. He continued to watch as she strolled along the crowded street.

The woman appeared slender and of average

height. He could tell she was beautiful even from his observation point 400 meters away. Her long dark brown hair flowed unbound, allowing the soft breeze to rustle it gently around her neck and shoulders. She wore tight jeans, flat canvas shoes and a white silk blouse. It was open at the collar with the top three buttons undone. The sniper knew the leather bag, carried on a long leather strap over her shoulder, contained a Walther PPK. She was a Mossad agent assigned to meet a contact who supposedly possessed information about a terrorist attack aimed at the Knesset.

When she reached the restaurant, her instructions were to sit at a table near the sidewalk and wait for someone to ask for directions. The sniper's briefing did not provide too much additional information, except the person asking the question would be a male. Both the woman and the man were his targets.

Now with the woman in position and sipping an espresso at the table, the sniper got behind his suppressed Kalashnikov SVK sniper rifle. He centered the crosshairs just below her breast bone, controlled his breathing and waited.

Nadia Picard sipped her coffee and casually surveyed the pedestrian traffic in the crowded area known to tourists as Las Ramblas. A mild concern tickled the back of her mind, but she remained calm. The concern stemmed from the fact she did not possess a description of her contact. Her instructions were to wait for a man to ask directions to a specific restaurant. She would reply it was closed and the contact would say, "Too bad, I was hoping to take you there." The conversation would be in French, her native language.

Her circuitous approach to her current location took most of the morning. Glancing at the clock feature on her cell phone, she saw it was fifteen minutes before the designated rendezvous. As she waited, she watched the crowd meandering on the street filled with tourists from all parts of the globe. The din from Las Ramblas grew louder as she carefully kept an eye out for threats and her contact. She finished one espresso and ordered another.

Before the new coffee arrived, she saw a man moving rapidly toward her location. His stride seemed familiar as did his appearance. She stiffened as he approached and placed one hand inside the purse lying on the table next to her. Her eyes did not divert from the man's face. She knew every feature of it and every contour of his body. When he stopped next to her table, she looked up with surprise. "What are you doing here?"

The sniper's dark complexion, average height, slender build, black hair and neatly-trimmed beard allowed him to fit in anywhere in Europe. Political and religious affiliations were of no concern to him. His loyalties were to any person or organization with the most money.

Considering the fee for successfully completing his current task, his concentration was total. Pressure on the rifle's trigger increased slightly as he observed a change in his target's demeanor. She had straightened and concentrated on something to her left. He saw her hand slide into her purse, ever so nonchalant.

Keeping his breathing slow and steady, he mentally walked through his next steps; wait for the woman's contact to sit and then squeeze the trigger. Before anyone would be able to react, another bullet would be on its way.

Suddenly, the situation changed as the woman looked up and said something. Feeling his chance of completing the assignment slipping away, he applied additional pressure to the trigger.

Michael Wolfe did not answer the question. Instead, he grabbed her arm and jerked her out of the seat, leading her into the mass of people on the street. Almost immediately, he heard the unmistakable sound of a bullet striking the concrete behind where Nadia had sat. The next sound was the cry of a waiter as pieces of the now-shattered projectile embedded in his upper thigh.

Wolfe did not panic as he led Nadia into the throng of tourists. Disappearing from the sniper's line of sight became his only concern.

CHAPTER 2

SOMEWHERE IN SOUTHERN MISSOURI

Joseph Kincaid navigated down Missouri Highway 90, slowing for the obscure turnoff leading to his final destination. The individual he would be meeting knew him as Charlie Rose. It was the *nom de guerre* he used when dealing with CIA assets.

Joseph maintained a persona of a mystery inside of an enigma. Few individuals were aware of his real background or what duties he performed for the CIA and the United States government. The man he planned to meet knew the more obscure ones, having worked for him at various times in the past.

Joseph was a tall slender man in his late sixties. His normal attire consisted of a navy blazer, white button-down oxford shirt, khaki cotton pants, shiny loafers and boldly-colored socks. His striking resemblance to the actor Morgan Freeman irritated him occasionally due to the constant requests for autographs. But on occasion he used it to his advantage.

Following the barely-passable road composed of exposed dirt, ruts and the occasional patch of river rock, he guided his Range Rover through a dense area of trees and underbrush until it opened into a clearing. He parked his SUV in front of a grassy earthen berm and surveyed the surroundings. A grove of birch trees dominated the left side, conifers and oaks to the right. The sloping terrain appeared natural, although Joseph knew different.

After exiting the vehicle, he noticed a man of average height and build, arms folded, leaning against a large white oak. A week-old beard, revealing more gray than brown, adorned the oval face. Narrowed green eyes under a knitted brow studied him.

The man standing by the berm was a former employee of the CIA and the owner of the property, Michael Wolfe.

Joseph raised one hand in greeting. The other held a 10-inch Samsung tablet. "Michael, good to see you. What was the emergency?"

Without saying a word, Wolfe motioned with his head for Joseph to follow.

As they approached the south side of the mound, Joseph marveled at how the entrance to the earthen structure seamlessly merged into the landscape. A bedrock gray concrete overhang blended into the limestone sedimentary stonewall surrounding the entrance. A flat, pea-gravel porch led to the interior guarded by a massive ornately carved oak door reinforced with a layer of Kevlar between two solid sheets of oak planks. Michael opened it and stood aside as Joseph entered.

The space behind the door was open. A comfortable sitting room blended into an oversized gourmet kitchen on the left side. Rough-hewed oak columns and beams supported the weight of the roof. Natural light illuminated the interior from two large bulletproof double-pane windows on either side of the oak door aided by skylights strategically placed within the ceiling. Toward the rear right side of the room, stairs led to an upper chamber. Charlie remembered this part of the house contained Michael's bedroom, bath and study.

Once inside, Michael turned and seemed to contemplate his guest before speaking. "I apologize for the theatrics used to get you here, but I need to make sure this place is concealed from prying satellites."

"I understand." He offered the Samsung, which Wolfe took and activated.

Joseph watched as the other man swiped the screen to study the images displayed.

Four minutes elapsed before Wolfe looked up, offered the device back and gave him a slight smile. "I like the way the wind turbine looks like a tree and the solar panels resemble a pile of rocks. Thank you, Charlie."

Nodding, he accepted the tablet back. "My friend is very good at what he does. I've asked him to continue to monitor images on Google Earth and any taken by the National Reconnaissance Office."

"I appreciate it."

"Now, do you mind if I ask…"

The appearance of a woman walking down the stairs lent Joseph pause. He knew the woman, having worked with her in a far-away land on the opposite side of the world. Nadia Picard was out of place in this rural, rustic setting. She wore a white cotton robe covering a tall athletic body. Her dark brown hair, damp from a recent shower, streamed around an oval face highlighted by an upturned nose and emerald green eyes. As she ran a comb through her hair, she stepped over to Wolfe's side.

Joseph smiled. "Hello, Nadia. Nice to see you again."

She smiled but only nodded.

"We were set up, Charlie." Wolfe's words conveyed a genuine concern.

"Set up? What do you mean?"

Wolfe's jaw tightened as he placed his arm around Nadia's waist. "Trapped, compromised, ensnarled, ambushed, cornered—you name it. We barely escaped."

"Whoa, slow down. When? Where? Give me details."

Wolfe's eyes narrowed. "You don't know. Do you?"

"No, I don't. What happened?"

Wolfe took a deep breath and glanced at the woman. Returning his attention back to Joseph, he said, "We both thought the CIA was behind it. I've known you a long time, Charlie. You don't startle easily. Apparently, our theory was wrong." He paused, his expression softening, and gave his ex-boss a smile. "Would you like coffee?"

"Yes."

"Last I knew, you two parted ways several years ago." Joseph accepted the mug handed to him.

Wolfe poured a cup for Nadia and one for himself. "We did. Uh—circumstances presented a necessity to work together again."

Joseph chose not to respond. He sipped his coffee, grimaced, set it down and added a little sugar.

Nadia responded, "Retreating to this place seemed the prudent thing to do."

Smiling, Joseph took another sip. "You're both

9

dancing around something. What happened?"

After studying his coffee mug for a moment, Wolfe looked up. "I was offered a job."

"Where?"

"Barcelona."

"Okay, for what?"

"Eliminating an opposition leader of the Catalonian Coalition."

Joseph tilted his head. "Who hired you?"

"As usual, I was not told. Initial contact was made the normal way. Funds were transferred from a bank in Madrid to one of my accounts in Zurich. Nothing seemed out of the ordinary, so I didn't question the source."

"SOP. Go on."

"I was told the target was female and would be at a specific place, at a specific time."

"That seems unlike you, Michael, considering your normal security protocols."

Wolfe blushed and his mouth twitched. "It was mistake number one."

"Okay, go on."

"Mistake number two was continuing the job without being given any background information or a photograph."

Joseph offered another frown, but remained quiet.

Wolfe took a deep breath. "At the time, I didn't think it was a big deal. Guess I'm getting old."

"I'm not buying that. Why did you accept the job?"

Wolfe ran his fingers through his hair. "A lot of money and I got cocky, okay?" He crossed his arms and stared hard at Joseph.

"Cocky will get you killed."

"I know." Closing his eyes, he shook his head. "Maybe a little lazy, too."

"For someone in your line of work, those are two

lethal attributes."

"Once I realized who the target was, I knew it was a set up."

More silence met the comment.

Nadia spoke with her Parisian-accented English. "Michael got us safely out. It took four days, but we managed to arrive here without anyone knowing— until you arrived."

"Good. What do you need from me?"

"I need to know who set us up and why."

Joseph nodded. "I, too, would like to know who set you up." He turned to Nadia. "Why were you there?"

"I was supposed to meet someone for an information exchange."

Raising an eyebrow, Joseph cocked his head to the side. "Information exchange? What kind of information?"

She sipped her coffee and gave him a half-smile.

"Okay, forget I asked."

Nadia nodded slightly.

"Who assigned you?"

"My controller."

Joseph crossed his arms and turned his attention to the windows next to the front door. The view was of a flat pasture south of the home. "He or she?"

"She."

"How long has she been your controller?"

"She made contact with me a month ago and knew all the right contact procedures."

"Have you tried to get in touch with her since the incident?"

She responded with a nod.

"And?"

"She has not returned my query."

Joseph turned back to Wolfe. "Michael, how many people know about this location?"

"You, me, now Nadia and my contractor."

"Who's that?"

"Someone I trust."

Rose narrowed his eyes. "Are you sure?"

Wolfe gave him a parental nod. "Yes, Charlie, I'm sure."

"How were you contacted?"

"Normal method, email to a blind mailbox. This place is off the grid. I only access the internet off-site."

"Good. I can have my colleague monitor the box."

There was silence as Wolfe sipped his coffee. "What do you think?"

"I don't have enough information at the moment."

Nadia took her coffee cup and walked to the window. She stared into the distance for several minutes before she turned. "I don't think it was anyone from my employer. My concern is that Mossad's been compromised."

"Why do you say that?"

"We've had several of my fellow members disappear over the past year. We didn't think anything about it, because..." She hesitated. "You know, things happen."

Joseph nodded.

"What if they were set up, just like I was? Could you check on your side to see if anyone's gone missing this past year?"

Wolfe and Nadia watched the man they knew as Charlie Rose. A blank expression met their gaze as he mulled something over in his mind.

Wolfe spoke first. "You know something, don't you?"

"Yes. Before I answer I need to know one more thing, Nadia."

"Okay."

"Who is missing?"

She stole a quick glance at Wolfe, who nodded. "Do you know Asa Gerlis?"

With a grim smile, Joseph nodded.

"He was my controller until he..."

"I'm aware of what happened."

"The missing agents all worked for him."

"Hmmm..."

She sipped her coffee again, gave it a frown and headed toward the kitchen. As she poured more coffee into her mug, she looked at the now-silent Joseph. "You are puzzled?"

Wolfe picked up on the change in Joseph's attitude. "I've seen that look before, Charlie."

"I need a fresh cup of coffee. Is there any left, Nadia?"

She smiled and nodded. "Help yourself."

Standing, he proceeded to the coffeemaker, his silence growing louder by the second. After pouring a fresh cup, he took a sip and looked back at Wolfe and Picard. "There have been—uh—a few incidents over the past year."

"Just what the hell does, 'a few incidents', mean?" Wolfe put his hands on his hips and glared.

"It means just that, a few incidents."

"Ours was not an incident."

"What would you call it?"

"A blatant attack."

Taking a seat on a bar stool next to the kitchen island, Joseph looked at Nadia and then at Michael. "The agency has lost three in the past eighteen months. Mossad lost two. The circumstances you described were similar in all five incidents.

Wolfe blinked a few times and walked closer to Nadia. "Where?"

"Istanbul, Prague and Budapest."

"Mossad?"

"Ankara, Turkey and Cyprus."

"Any suspects?"

Joseph shook his head. "Made to look like accidents."

CHAPTER 3

SOMEWHERE IN SOUTHERN MISSOURI

Wolfe lay in bed, his hands behind his head, staring at the dimly-lit ceiling. This section of the house lacked windows. The available light came from a digital clock on the nightstand. He heard the shower shut off and smiled. Nadia refused to go to bed without taking a shower first. It was a personality trait older than their friendship. At one time they had been lovers, but that was many years ago. Now they were partners in the task of determining who wanted to kill them. He heard the bathroom door open and then felt her slip under the sheets next to him. She smelled of rose petals and vanilla.

"Are you awake?" Her voice soft, barely above a whisper.

"Yes."

She snuggled up to him. He automatically put his arm around her bare shoulder, the heat from her body comforting as she placed an arm over his chest. He felt bare skin against his.

"Why did you leave Israel, Michael?"

He did not answer for a few moments. "I felt my presence was endangering your life."

"How?"

"Someone told me, in no uncertain terms, our relationship was not good for your health."

"Who told you that?"

"Asa Gerlis."

She was quiet as her fingers combed through the hairs on his chest. "He never said anything to me about it. When did he tell you?"

"The night you flew back from France and I met you at Ben Gurion Airport."

"I wondered why you were quiet that night."

"He explained how my services to Israel were no longer needed and I should return to the States. He didn't give me any options."

She slipped a hand toward his flat stomach, not stopping until it was beneath his boxer shorts. He turned his head and kissed her brow. "What are you doing? I thought we agreed to take it slow until we figured out what to do about Barcelona."

"We did take it slow. Now I want to speed it up. Make love to me, Michael. I need you tonight."

He moved his other hand from behind his head and embraced her tightly.

She sang a song in her native French while she looked for eggs in the refrigerator. As she bent to retrieve them, her robe rose to the middle of her tanned thighs.

"Nice view from back here."

She smiled as she flipped up the back of the robe,

exposing her bare bottom.

"Be careful," he said. "I might repeat last night."

She turned. "I would like that. But first, I am starved. You have not had a proper French omelet for a long time, I am sure."

"Not like you make them."

"Good. Are these eggs fresh?"

He nodded. "I have chickens."

Before cracking the egg, she raised one eyebrow. "Who takes care of these chickens when you are away?"

"A friend."

"Who?"

"The guy who helped me build this house and who takes care of it while I'm gone."

Folding her arms, she glared at him. "Michael, I do not see you trusting anyone enough to know about this place."

"He's an old military friend, diagnosed with PTSD. I help him and he helps me."

"And where does this person live? I did not see a house for miles when we first got here."

"At the far end of my property is an old cabin left over from the original homestead back in the 1800s. I gave him a couple of acres surrounding it and we added a few modern touches, like plumbing and electricity. He's doing better now."

"Do you trust him?"

"With my life."

She relaxed and went back to cracking eggs for their omelets.

Wolfe busied himself making coffee as she prepared their breakfast. As the water started passing through the grinds, he looked at her and grinned. The semi-closed robe exposed most of her breasts. "I am enjoying the view."

She looked down, grinned and partially closed the robe.

He leaned against the kitchen island. "Do you like it here?"

Her green eyes sparkled as she flipped her hair over her shoulder. "Yes. I have not been able to relax like this in years. I like the solitude."

"I finally figured out why Asa told me to leave Israel."

"Oh..."

"He was jealous."

"He was married."

"Doesn't stop some men from being jealous."

She frowned and returned her attention to the omelet. Her silence told him all he needed to know.

"When did he try to get you into bed?"

"The night he told me you had left."

"Comforting a broken heart. How gallant of him."

She shot him a fierce glare. "He was disgusting."

"What did he tell you about my departure?"

"Not much—just that you returned to the States."

She plated the perfectly folded omelet in her normal fashion. With her momentary anger gone, she offered him the plate. "Tell me how good it is."

Accepting the plate, he watched as she started another one.

As she cracked more eggs, her voice grew soft. "Has there been anyone else in your life since me, Michael?"

He studied the dark liquid in his coffee mug and shook his head. "No."

She did not respond immediately, her face brightened. "I have been alone as well."

A comfortable silence occurred as he watched her prepare the next omelet.

"What did Asa tell you?"

Taking a deep breath, she plated her own omelet. "He said you had an emergency and would not be returning to Israel."

"No explanation."

"No, no explanation."

He watched as moisture pooled in the corner of her eyes. "I'm sorry. He lied to both of us."

"Yes, I am sorry too." She blinked several times. "But now we know the truth and the incident is history. Eat your omelet before it gets cold."

"I was waiting for you."

They sat next to each other at the breakfast bar and ate quietly. He stole several glances at her to find her looking at him as well. Finally, Wolfe broke the silence. "Better than I remembered. I've missed your cooking."

Placing a hand on his arm and leaning her head on his shoulder, she smiled. "I have missed you too."

He took her hand and led her back to the bedroom.

As they lay in each other's arms, savoring the moment, Nadia broke the silence. "How much do you trust this Charlie Rose person?"

"It's not his real name. He was my controller while I worked for the CIA. He's always been a little on the mysterious side, but he's never lied to me. So, I guess I do. To a point."

She grew quiet, her thoughts miles away. "What is his real name?"

"Joseph Kincaid."

She raised herself up on one elbow. "I wondered how he knew my name. I now remember where we met—he attended several meetings with Asa in Tel Aviv before you and I were together."

"I don't doubt it. I've always been amazed at how many individuals Joseph knows or has worked with."

They lay in each other's arms again, her head on his chest, both lost in their own thoughts. Finally, she said. "Joseph will be back tomorrow with this JR person. Who is he?"

"From what Charlie—uh—I mean Joseph told me, he's one of the best computer hackers in the world. Some years back, he apparently got into trouble after hacking into the computer of a Wall Street executive and diverting a lot of money. He got caught. The executive decided it was simpler to kill him than turn him over to the police. He escaped, changed his identity, and is now a very successful businessman."

"What about the executive? Did he pursue the matter?"

"No. Turns out he was running a Ponzi scheme with his investors. It didn't end well for him."

She snuggled against him. "How is he going to assist us?"

"Several ways. He is going to create two new identities we can use to travel. And then he will create the illusion we are dead."

"Yes, I know that. But how?"

"Not sure. Guess we'll find out tomorrow."

CHAPTER 4

W here the hell are you taking me, Joseph?"
JR Diminski held the Range Rover's grab-
bar above the front passenger door as the
vehicle swayed back and forth on the so-called road
leading to Michael Wolfe's home. He stared ahead as
he tried to keep his slender five-foot-ten frame from
bouncing off the seat.

"Michael's property is, uh... Let's just say,
secluded."

"I would say secluded is an understatement." He
paused "Is this the property you wanted hidden from
prying satellites?"

"Yes."

Diminski frowned. "Not sure anybody would look
for a home this far into the boonies."

Joseph glanced at his friend. "You might be
surprised."

"You want me to help them disappear?"

"You've done it before."

Diminski bounced in his seat after a particularly deep pot-hole and thought back to the circumstances surrounding his meeting the man currently driving the Range Rover. JR Diminski was not his birth name. After his past transgressions caught up to him, Joseph helped him create a new life.

Now the owner of a successful computer security company, he understood how to protect companies from hackers like himself. He also knew how to subvert the vast majority of computer security measures currently in use across the country. Over the past five years, this knowledge had allowed him to assist Joseph on numerous projects.

"Do they have multiple IDs?"

Joseph smiled.

"I'll take that as yes."

"Take it how you want."

"Do they know you as Charlie Rose or Joseph?"

"Rose."

"Okay. I'll try to remember that."

"No big deal—they know it isn't my real name. I was Michael's CIA control until he started working for Israel some years back. He reminds me of you in ways and I have a lot of respect for him. We've kept in contact."

"Why?"

He shrugged. "I like him."

JR chuckled. "He still works for you, doesn't he?"

There was no reply, only a slight grin.

"Thought so. He works for your network."

"He hasn't for a while, but I'd like to see him come back."

"Got it. What's his story?"

"His resume is pretty impressive. Decorated Marine sniper during Desert Shield and Desert Storm. Left the military and earned a degree in International

Business Management at Georgetown University. He spent several years working for me at the CIA. During this period, he met a woman from Israel, got married and moved there. After she was killed in a Palestinian terrorist attack, he did a little work for the Mossad."

"What kind of work?"

Joseph did not respond.

"Okay, got it. What else?"

"Now he calls himself an international business consultant. He's handy with languages, fluent in French, German, Hebrew and passable in Spanish and Arabic."

"Impressive."

"He's an impressive individual. Kind of like you."

JR shot Joseph a quick glance. "How so?"

"He's as good a marksman as you are a computer hacker."

"Really?"

Joseph nodded.

"How good?"

"He took out a target at over 1600 meters on a windy beach in Madagascar in 2014. Headshot."

JR whistled.

"Yeah, he's good."

"I'm looking forward to meeting him."

"Curb your enthusiasm. He has an issue with trusting people."

"As do I."

Michael Wolfe shook the hand of JR Diminski as Joseph introduced them. They each stared at the other without comment. He presented Nadia next. She smiled but kept her distance afterward.

Wolfe spoke first. "You did nice work on the

satellite image. Thank you."

JR nodded but did not reply. He adjusted his wire-rim glasses and glanced around the living room. "Now that I see the terrain at ground level, I can adjust the image better. The entrance can be made to look more natural."

Smiling, Wolfe turned to Joseph. "Now what?"

Gesturing in JR's direction, Joseph walked toward the coffeemaker on the kitchen island and poured a cup. "JR can assist with the issue we discussed yesterday."

Turning his attention to JR, Wolfe tilted his head. "Charlie indicated you've done it before."

JR nodded. "I have."

"What do you need from us?"

"A set of IDs. Ones you will never be able to use again."

Nadia spoke for the first time. "We can use our Spanish ones. After all, we were in Barcelona when everything went sideways."

Wolfe nodded. "Makes sense. Then what?"

"A contact in Mexico City will handle the rest. Cost is ten thousand per, so twenty thousand."

"Okay."

"I do the rest."

"How much?"

"My part is free, Joseph..." He hesitated and shot a glance at his friend. "I mean Charlie and I go back a few years. I owe him."

Smiling, Wolfe raised his hand and waved off the comment. "I've known his name was Joseph Kincaid for years. I've just always called him Charlie."

Joseph shook his head and pursed his lips. "So much for trying to keep a secret."

Wolfe folded his arms and returned his attention to JR. "How's this going to work?"

"We have to establish a sighting of you two in Mexico City, without you actually being there."

"How?"

"Simple, really. If you were to go to Mexico City from, let's say, Spain. Where would you go?"

Wolfe remained quiet.

Nadia gave JR a decisive nod. "There's a small apartment in the La Juarez area, we have—uh—frequented."

JR nodded as he opened his laptop.

"I don't have internet." The comment came from Wolfe.

Looking up from the computer, JR frowned. "Forgot. I'll have to do it a little different." He took out his cell phone and checked to see if he had a signal. It was weak, but would work. After a few minutes, he started typing on his laptop. When he finished, he looked up. "What's the address?"

Nadia walked over to Wolfe's side. "30 Calle Milan. Northwest corner of the intersection of Calle Milan and Calle Lucerno, second floor apartment."

JR beamed. The directions were perfect. He pointed to his computer screen. "Is that it?"

Moving to get behind JR, Nadia glanced at the computer and nodded. "Yes. How did you do that?"

Chuckling, JR said, "Google Earth. It's amazing how many street level views you can find."

Keeping his attention on her, JR asked, "How frequently are you two there?"

Nadia frowned. "Never together. It is what you would call a safe house for the company I worked for."

Joseph sipped his coffee while leaning against the breakfast bar. "JR, that would be Mossad."

"Got it." He started typing as Nadia glared at Joseph.

Wolfe put his hand on her arm. "It's okay, Charlie—

uh—Joseph knows more about us than you think."

Her face tightened as she nervously flipped her hair over her shoulders.

Looking up from the computer again, JR turned his attention to Nadia and Wolfe. "I'll need a supply of blood from each of you."

Chuckling, Wolfe nodded. "Our blood in the apartment, but no bodies, correct?"

"That's the plan. Bodies disappear in Mexico City all the time. Your IDs will be discreetly hidden, but findable, within the apartment. Since it's a safe house for the Mossad and you've both worked for them, they will have your blood type and DNA profile. They'll assume you two are dead."

"Is this man you know in Mexico City reliable?" Wolfe's eyebrows pinched together.

"Actually, I don't know if it's a man or a woman. I've never met them. But we've both, at times, been associated with a like-minded group of computer hackers."

Joseph said, "Michael, he's talking about Anonymous."

"Thought they were a myth perpetuated by the media."

JR nodded. "The group exists, but the public persona is a little more nebulous. To answer your question, yes, the hacker is very reliable." Retreating into a focused fury of typing on his laptop, JR concentrated on his next task.

Joseph motioned for Wolfe and Nadia to join him at the breakfast bar. "When he's concentrating like that, he won't communicate with anyone."

Wolfe went to the kitchen cabinet and removed two coffee mugs. In one, he placed a tea bag retrieved from a canister underneath. After filling it with water, he placed the cup in the microwave oven above the stove. While the tea heated, he filled the remaining cup with coffee. When the microwave signaled the end of the cycle, he removed the tea and handed it to Nadia.

She accepted it, and with a half-smile, checked the tag on the tea bag. "How did you have the type of tea I like?"

"I like Earl Grey, too."

"You hate tea, Michael."

"I don't hate tea. I prefer coffee."

"I've never known you to have tea on hand."

He shrugged and sipped his coffee.

Nadia swept the back of her hand across her eye.

Joseph asked, "Michael, who did you get your assignments from?"

"My broker."

"What's his name?"

Hesitating, Wolfe raised the coffee to his lips, but before taking a sip, he put the cup down. "A retired MI6 chap I met in Tel Aviv."

"Name?"

"Geoffrey Canfield."

Hiding his surprise, Joseph took a deep breath. "When was the last time you heard from him?"

"He's the one who told me about the Barcelona contract."

"How many times has he contacted you in the past year?"

"About three. Why?"

"Geoffrey Canfield died of a sudden heart attack about a year and a half ago."

Wolfe was silent as he studied the contents of his coffee cup. Nadia drew closer to him and put her head on his shoulder, an arm around his waist.

"Whoever contacted me knew the correct protocols." He paused; his eyes glued on Joseph. "The contacts were no different from past ones."

"Except the details on Barcelona?"

Nodding, Wolfe put his arm around Nadia. He looked at her and then turned his attention back to Joseph. "What's going on here?"

"That's what we need to determine. When was the last time you saw Canfield?"

"About three years ago in a London pub."

"How did he look?"

"The same. Geoffrey never seemed to age—he always looked like a university professor."

"Yes, that he did."

"You knew him?"

"Very well. He and I worked together in Africa for a while. I don't like the coincidence of Asa Gerlis and Geoffrey Canfield dying so close in time to each other."

Nadia raised her head. "Asa's body was never found."

Tilting his head, Joseph raised an eyebrow. "I wasn't aware of that."

She nodded.

Joseph studied the floor for a few moments and then looked back up. "The more I think about it, the more I believe Canfield's heart attack was not natural. I saw him just before it happened. He looked fine, but seemed preoccupied."

"Did he still have contact with MI6?" asked Wolfe.

"I believe he did. He and I performed similar functions for our respective governments."

Wolfe frowned. "I didn't know he still worked for MI6?"

"He didn't. He worked for the Prime Minister, same as I work for the President."

"Huh."

"If you don't want to tell me, that's fine, but what

kind of assignments did he give you?"

Pinching his eyebrows together, Wolfe took a deep breath. "Mundane stuff, really. Until the last three." He paused and sipped his coffee. "Normally I'm asked to find individuals classified as terrorists."

"Makes sense. What made the last three different?"

"Just two actually. I turned one down."

"Why?"

"Money and country weren't right."

Joseph frowned. "Where?"

"Russia."

Joseph nodded. "What about the other two?"

"First was Turkey. The second was the Barcelona gig."

"So, after years of being assigned individuals who were known terrorists, he suddenly starts giving you political targets?"

"When you put it that way—it doesn't make sense. Guess I got complacent."

"Dangerous, Michael."

"Yes, I'm very much aware of that, Joseph."

JR lifted his head from the laptop. "Okay, everything is ready. I'll need a few days to get the details worked out. I'll be back—uh, let's say Thursday."

CHAPTER 5

SOMEWHERE IN SOUTHERN MISSOURI

Two Days Later

Wolfe opened the envelope JR handed him and peered inside. He extracted the contents and placed them on the kitchen table. There were several documents, each looked official. He saw a birth certificate and a social security card, one set for himself and the other set for Nadia. He also saw a marriage license. All were issued by the state of Missouri. Two sheets of paper showed a computer printout of driver's licenses, one for each of them. While their first names were the same, the last name on the IDs read, LYON.

Michael smiled as he looked at JR. "Where did you get the photos?"

JR shrugged.

Nadia picked up the sheet with her license and chuckled. "This is my old Israeli driver's license photo."

Michael looked at his. "Now I recognize it. It's the picture from my CIA ID. How did..."

Joseph said, "I told you he was good."

After placing the sheet back on the table, Michael folded his arms. "This is all well and good, but these are not useable as identification."

"The birth certificates, marriage license and social security cards can be. The printout of the driver's license tells anyone checking the database you have a DL on file. All you have to do is go to any Missouri Department of Revenue office, present your birth-certificates and social security cards and tell them your licenses were stolen. Or if you prefer, lost. They will find the ones on file and be happy to replace them. For a fee, of course."

"Goes without saying."

JR pointed to the documents. "Everything I've given you exists in the system as of yesterday. You both have a work history within the Social Security database and you've been married for ten years. You've even been filing and paying your taxes on time, all very official, all very real in the digital world."

Wolfe looked from JR to Joseph. "What does the IRS think I've been doing?"

Joseph removed an envelope from the breast pocket of his navy blazer. He handed it to Wolfe. "Read this."

Extracting a document from the envelope, he read it quickly and then passed it to Nadia. "Hedge fund manager? I don't know the first thing about hedge funds."

Shrugging, Joseph gave him a mischievous grin. "Neither will anyone you talk to. You have a degree in International Business Management. It's a perfect background for a fund manager. If asked, just say you felt burned out and left. No one will question you. It's an obscure field normal people don't understand. Plus, positions like that produce a lot of cash, which will help explain your lack of employment at the moment."

Wolfe shook his head and stared at all the documents he and Nadia were given. "These are better than forged documents."

JR nodded. "Every day of the week because they're real. No one can or will question them."

Nadia frowned as she stared at her birth certificate. "This says I was born in Kansas City. How do I explain my accent?"

Joseph answered, "First of all, never explain it. Second, if someone does question you, tell them your father was a diplomat and you grew up in France. Simple. Your English is impeccable. Most people from around here will think you're from the east coast."

Michael frowned. "What about passports if we need to travel abroad?"

JR pointed to the documents. "Simple. Use those and your new DLs to apply for an official one. There will be one in the system for Nadia as a child, but it expired long ago. The background checks will pass. Trust me."

Turning his attention back to JR, Wolfe said. "This is better than I could have hoped for. I have to owe you something."

"You don't owe me a thing. I enjoy screwing the system. They've made it completely digital but haven't figured out how to keep it from being manipulated."

Wolfe nodded. "Very well, but I owe you."

Joseph folded his arms. "Tell them about Mexico City."

"I need a sample of your blood."

Nadia tilted her head. "How much?"

JR reached into his ever-present computer bag and

withdrew four vials and a blood collection kit. "Two each, six milliliters per vial."

Wolfe chuckled. "Who precisely can do that in this room?"

"I can." Nadia offered. "I am a trained EMT."

Everyone in the room smiled.

After Nadia finished drawing blood, she handed the vials to JR. "Now what?"

"These will be sent, along with the Spanish passports you gave me, to an address in Mexico City via Fed Ex. I've already made a wire transfer that can't be traced to my contact there. He will handle it."

"I can't let you pay for that, JR." Wolfe frowned.

"You didn't."

"What do you mean?"

"Let's just say your former employer gave you a severance package. Did you know the CIA had a hold on your bank accounts in Zurich?"

Wolfe's eyes widened. Through clenched teeth, he said, "No, I didn't."

"They don't anymore. In fact, your accounts in Switzerland no longer exist. I'll give you the access codes before I leave. You're solvent again."

"Where is my money?"

"Untraceable and residing in very safe banks in Dubai and Hong Kong."

Closing his eyes and nodding, Wolfe asked, "When were they seized?"

"The day you two escaped from Barcelona."

"Who did it?"

Joseph answered. "A man named Gerald Reid."

Wolfe blinked several times, his gaze still on JR.

JR continued, "I assumed you had access to cash."

"When I work, I always make sure I have enough to get back without leaving a paper trail."

"Very wise."

Nadia asked, "So you think we were set up by the CIA?"

Joseph shrugged. "While I don't have any proof, I don't believe so. Reid was reacting to an alert from the Centro Nacional de Inteligencia in Madrid about your activities."

Wolfe nodded. "Covering their asses."

"Pretty much."

"So, the CNI set us up?"

Shaking his head, Joseph paused for a moment before answering. "My source doesn't think so. CNI was reacting to a tip they received via the Turkish National Security Service."

Wolfe was quiet as he stared out one of the front windows. "Apparently my accepting the job in Turkey started a cascade of events."

"I would agree with you. I'm still confused as to why you accepted the Turkey job. It's not like you, Michael."

Nadia held his arm and placed her head on his shoulder. "Tell them."

Wolfe looked at her and nodded. He turned his attention to Joseph. "How much do you know about my activities after I left Israel?"

"Sketchy. Just what you've told me, which wasn't much."

"I'll start from the beginning. This piece of land belonged to my grandfather. Since my parents were gone and I was his only grandchild, he left it to me when he passed. Because of my situation overseas, I set up a trust fund to pay the taxes each year and then forgot about the land. That is, until I returned to the States after leaving Israel. The first time I saw it, I fell in love and decided it would be my home. Any desire to be around my fellow man was gone, so I sequestered myself."

Nadia took his hand. He gently squeezed hers and continued.

"I was ordering building material one day at the Meeks Lumber Yard in West Plains when I noticed an old Marine buddy stacking lumber in the yard. He looked horrible, so I asked one of the sales guys handling my order about him. They told me he was a temp who came in when they needed extra help. So, after he got off work, I took him to a restaurant and bought him dinner. He briefed me about his situation, which was not good. I made a decision while we sat there and presented it to him. If he would help me build my place, I would give him some land, a cabin and help him get back on his feet. He's the one who suggested we build an earth-sheltered home. In fact, most of the designs in this structure are his."

JR asked. "How's he doing now?"

"Extremely well. Thank you for asking."

"I understand the connection."

Wolfe tilted his head slightly. "Were you in the military?"

"Yes, but this is your story."

Wolfe continued. "Anyway, it took a year to build this place, but as you can see it was worth it. I can hide in plain sight and no one will know I'm here unless I tell them."

Joseph stood and went to the coffeepot. "Michael, that still does not explain why you took the job in Turkey."

"I'm getting to it."

Joseph nodded.

"After we completed construction, I reached out to Canfield and told him I was ready to get back to work. That's when he started giving me assignments. All the targets were classified as terrorist by European governments."

"How did he communicate with you? There's no internet service here."

"Sat phone."

Nodding, Joseph sipped his coffee but remained quiet.

JR pursed his lips and said, "Figure out how to get internet here and I'll show you how to mask your location."

Wolfe looked at JR with a frown. "How the hell can you do that?"

The hacker gave him a toothy grin.

Nadia squeezed his arm. "Go on, Michael. Tell them about your last three contracts."

He took a deep breath and let it out slowly. "There was a lull in the assignments for six months. Then I got one in early February. My phone pinged, which is my signal an email landed in a blind email account I keep. To receive the email, I have to travel to a Wi-Fi location and log into the account. I try to rotate the locations for each access."

JR nodded. "Good."

"I think this one was a McDonald's in West Plains. Anyway, Canfield always identified his emails with a specific word in the subject line. When I reviewed this email, it had the correct word but was different from most of the other contracts I've been offered. Normally, it's from an intelligence agency identifying someone associated with a known terrorist network. This one was for a Ukrainian First Vice-Premier. The money wasn't that great and the risks were unacceptable."

Joseph tilted his head. "Why?"

"The contract called for completion inside Russia."

"Ah—got it."

"I turned it down."

"Wise."

Wolfe glanced at Nadia and returned to his narrative. "The next communication was in May. I really don't remember the date, but it took two days to retrieve the email. The money was triple the amount offered in February and the location was acceptable—Istanbul. Bulgaria is close and so was the eastern peninsula of Greece. I accepted the assignment."

"Why?" Joseph's tone held a note of concern.

Shaking his head, Wolfe pursed his lips. "I don't know. The money was good, the ingress and egress were non-problematic, so why not?"

"In other words, easy money."

"Yeah."

JR asked, "Who was the target?"

Wolfe stared at the ceiling for a few moments. "A leader of the Republican People's Party, which is the main opposition group in Turkey."

"And you agreed?" Joseph's tone was now accusatory.

"Yes."

"Why?"

"Like I said earlier, I hadn't heard from Canfield in almost six months prior to the job in Russia. I thought I was being eased out of the rotation."

Joseph chuckled. "Okay, I get it. Go on."

"The job went off without a hitch. I was in and out of Turkey and back in the states in two days. Easy money. The next time I heard from Canfield, or whoever it was by then, was in July.

"This was another political target, a female opposition leader in the Catalonian movement. I was given a date and location. The money was five times my normal fee."

"Didn't that set off an alarm, Michael?"

Wolfe did not answer immediately. "It should have, but with business down, I looked at the money first.

The location was non-controversial and the site very public. Easy in and easy out, just another Istanbul. I didn't question it."

Neither Joseph nor JR commented.

"When Nadia appeared in my crosshairs, I realized something was horribly wrong. My first reaction was to get to her as quickly as possible. When I got there, she stared up at me and said something, I don't remember what because I was too busy getting her out of the chair. That's the only reason the bullet didn't hit her. It hit the sidewalk behind her as we ran."

The room was silent as Wolfe stared at Nadia. She bowed her head and nodded. "He saved my life."

"Okay, Nadia, why were you there?"

She looked at Joseph. "An assignment by my new controller."

"Who was he?"

"He was a she. I was never introduced. I was told someone would be in touch and I would know who by the contact procedures."

"Did you ever see her?"

"No, I only had one phone conversation. It was short and she didn't elaborate."

"Is that normal?"

"What's normal? I am not exactly in a normal business, Joseph. It was within standard parameters of contact. Her contact protocols were precise and she answered the challenge questions correctly."

Joseph nodded. "Okay, what then?"

"She explained I needed to be in Barcelona to meet an undercover agent who had knowledge of an ISIS attack on Tel Aviv."

"How were you supposed to know this agent?"

"He was to ask directions to a specific restaurant."

"No picture?"

"No."

"I take it no one at the rendezvous asked about the restaurant."

She shook her head. "No. Next thing I know, I see Michael running toward me. When he got there, I stared at him and asked what he was doing. He grabbed my arm and pulled me into the crowd. I felt the sting of the bullet and heard it ricochet behind me."

"Was there another shot?"

"I have no idea. I followed Michael and we ran. If he had not grabbed my arm and pulled me away..."

"I understand." Joseph turned to Michael. "I take it you realized something was wrong when you saw Nadia?"

He nodded. "Yeah, by the time I got to her, I knew we'd been set up. I knew where the shot would come from. I knew when the shot would be fired and I realized I had been played. The shot would not come until I was in the range of the scope. That was why I pulled her out of the chair so hard. It was the only thing I could do to disrupt the plan."

Wolfe took a deep breath and closed his eyes. Nadia hugged his arm.

He continued. "With that one rifle shot, the fog clogging my brain after leaving Israel melted away. My reactions were back and the ability to anticipate the moves of my opponent heightened. I awoke from a three-year nightmare and was not going to let anyone take Nadia away again."

JR noticed tears pooling in Nadia's eyes. He asked, "If both of you were so miserable about being apart, why did you allow it?"

Wolfe shook his head, "I felt my presence in Israel was endangering Nadia. She was told a similar lie."

"Glad you figured it out."

"We were manipulated by an individual or

individuals with ulterior motives."

Joseph frowned. "Motive of the state or personal motives?"

Nadia looked at Joseph. "We don't know."

"Do either of you believe the set up in Barcelona was because of your personal relationship?"

Wolfe glanced at Nadia. Both shrugged. He said, "We don't know. Asa Gerlis was dead by that time and so was Geoffrey Canfield, though I didn't know it at the time."

Joseph smiled and tilted his head. "Are you sure Asa Gerlis is dead?"

Nadia crossed her arms. "Do you know something we don't know?"

"Maybe."

Wolfe narrowed his eyes and glared at Joseph. "Don't start lying to me now, not after all these years."

"There's a rumor, mind you, it's only a rumor, that Asa was not beheaded in the video circulated by ISIS."

"It looked real to me." Wolfe frowned. He turned to Nadia. "Did you see it?"

She shook her head.

He turned back to Joseph. "What evidence do you have it wasn't Asa on the video?"

JR answered, "Computer graphics."

"How?"

Joseph turned to JR. "Want to show them?"

With a grin, JR opened his laptop and pressed the enter key. After several moments of typing, he turned the computer around so that Nadia and Wolfe could see. There was no sound as the video started. The masked figure dressed in black stood behind a kneeling subject, his knife pointing at the camera as his mouth moved. Suddenly, the knife went to the kneeling man's throat and the video froze. JR turned the computer around and typed furiously. Smiling, he turned it around again. The same video played, only this time, the person kneeling was Asa Gerlis. Nadia gasped and Wolfe leaned over to study it closer.

JR turned it back and said, "It took me less than a minute to change the face of the victim. What if I took my time to make it more realistic?"

Wolfe nodded and Nadia's face grew crimson. "They faked his death," they said in unison.

JR turned his attention to them. "I believe someone did. I haven't looked at the original video, but it would be easy to do. I would even venture a guess the video wasn't circulated by ISIS."

"What do you mean?" This from Nadia.

"Why would ISIS help a Mossad agent fake his own death?"

Wolfe nodded. He was quiet for a few more moments. "You're right—it doesn't make sense. But what if he was an ISIS mole?"

JR shook his head. "Gerlis was in Israel long before ISIS was even a concept."

"Well, there is that."

Joseph stood and walked to the breakfast bar. After seeing the coffee pot was empty, he started preparing a new batch. When he was done, he turned and leaned against the edge. "I spoke to one of my contacts with MI6. There is skepticism about Geoffrey's death as well. Apparently, he kept in touch with some of his old mates and told one of them he'd passed a stress test in September with flying colors."

Wolfe raised an eyebrow. "Is anyone looking into it?"

"Kind of hard. His family had him cremated."

"What do you think, Joseph?"

"I hadn't seen Geoffrey for a long time. The individual I spoke to had, however. He told me Geoffrey took care of himself, didn't drink to excess and had never smoked. He wasn't overweight and walked his dog every morning, rain or shine."

"If Asa Gerlis' death was fake and Geoffrey Canfield's death was suspicious, Nadia and I have a bigger problem than I originally thought."

Joseph nodded. "I would agree. What do you think, JR?"

Looking up from his computer, he said, "Whoever set you up in Barcelona knows you escaped. That's a given. Once we plant the seed you two were killed in Mexico City, it should give you a little freedom to move around. Particularly with your new status as citizens of Missouri."

Wolfe stood and walked toward the window in the front room. He stood there with his hands behind his back. Nadia did not follow him. Several minutes passed before he said anything. "What is the address on my driver's license, JR?"

"For lack of a better idea, I used a condo complex on Table Rock Lake."

"Good. We'll drive there tomorrow and find one to rent. Then we can change our address when we get the new licenses." He heard JR typing. "How hard would it be to set up a satellite internet connection here?"

"Easier than you think. Register it at the place you rent on Table Rock Lake."

Wolfe nodded. "Would you set it up?"

"Be happy to."

"I'm going to buy a new computer. We need to do some research." He turned, his eyes narrowed and his brow furrowed. "I'm tired of running and hiding. We'll let things settle down for a while, then we'll start looking for answers."

Nadia smiled and nodded ever so slightly.

CHAPTER 6

BRANSON, MO

Located in a strip mall on the north end of Branson, the local Department of Motor Vehicles licensing office sat next to a large grocery store. Operated by an independent contractor, long lines were the norm. This day was no exception. Wolfe and Nadia stood patiently waiting for one of the minimum-wage clerks to be available. Inching their way forward in the line, their wait lasted thirty minutes.

Delaying their trip to Branson for two weeks had given Wolfe time to grow a goatee and mustache. His hair was longer and he wore non-prescription glasses. Nadia had dyed her dark brown hair to a light brown and also wore glasses. While not drastic these small changes would help make subtle differences with their license photos.

The overweight clerk appeared to be in her early twenties. Sitting behind a chest-high counter with a computer screen and a keyboard in front of her, she looked at Wolfe and then at Nadia with bored eyes. "Renewal?"

Michael smiled. "No, we lost our licenses."

"Stolen?"

"No, lost."

"Name?"

Handing the woman his new birth certificate, he stated the name and smiled again.

The young woman stared at the document and then typed on her keyboard. "Okay." She looked at Nadia. "Name?"

Nadia followed the same procedure and stated her name.

"Yup, there they are." She typed again and then looked up. "I'll need your social security numbers and proof of residence. Do you want new license numbers?"

Both Wolfe and Nadia said yes and offered the utility bill provided by JR for the address currently on file.

"Okay. Sit over there and I'll take your pictures."

Ten minutes later, Michael and Nadia walked out of the DMV with brand new driver's licenses. Michael studied his and shook his head. "Amazing."

"Do you think getting new passports will be as easy?"

"I don't see why they wouldn't be. Joseph said JR's work is always solid." He stared at the plastic card and shook his head. "I still can't believe it."

The view off the back deck was breathtaking. A hundred feet below, the trees on the opposite side of the cove were brilliant in their fall golds, reds, and yellows. Michael leaned against the wood railing and stared out over the lake. It was the third condo on their list and this one felt right. He turned to Nadia, who was also spellbound by the view. "What do you think?"

"Is it always this beautiful here?"

"No, we have four distinct seasons in this part of Missouri. Fall is my favorite and I like spring, too. But summers can be brutal as are the winters. Winters are pretty on occasion with freshly fallen snow, but as a rule, it's brown and colorless."

Nadia turned toward him. "What if we forget about our past and move on with the identities JR created for us? If they think we are dead, they will not look for us." She paused briefly. "It is so beautiful here, Michael. I could get used to it."

He gave her a half smile. "Yes, so could I. But I really don't want to be looking over my shoulder for the rest of our lives."

"The rest of our lives?"

He nodded as he returned his gaze to the lake. "Yes, ours."

She smiled. "I like this one."

"So, do I. Let's sign the paperwork."

It took a few days to finalize the one-year lease. Now with the completion of the paperwork and buying furniture for the condo, Nadia and Wolfe sat at their kitchen table, listening to JR Diminski explain how to set up their satellite internet connection.

Nadia absorbed every word while it went right over Wolfe's head. His mind wandered while JR explained.

When Diminski finished, he asked. "Does that make sense?"

Nodding and looking at her notes, Nadia said, "It's simple when you think about it."

"Yes, it is. What about you, Michael?"

He did not answer right away as he stared out the sliding glass door leading to the deck. "As long as Nadia understands, we're good."

JR followed Wolfe's gaze. "Great location."

Wolfe nodded.

Nadia placed her hand on his. "What is wrong, Michael?"

He shook his head. "Nothing."

Crossing his arms, JR straightened in his chair. "Joseph heard from one of his contacts at the agency."

This brought Wolfe's attention back to the conversation. He looked at JR. "And?"

"The Mossad thinks one of their agents and a former member of the CIA met with foul play in Mexico City. They wanted to know if the agency knew anything."

"What else?"

"A Mossad safe house was ransacked and it appeared two individuals were shot while in bed. No bodies, but the blood was analyzed. That's how they knew who the victims were."

Wolfe smiled. "Twenty-two hollow point to the head? Not a lot of blood that way."

Diminski shrugged. "Don't know the details. Joseph was told the agency would be cooperating with Mossad in trying to find out what happened."

Returning his gaze to the glass door, Wolfe remained quiet for several moments. "Without bodies, they will have doubts. But it should slow their efforts to locate us for a while."

"Joseph believes it will stop the search completely."

"Why?" Wolfe looked at JR again.

"A couple of passports washed ashore a couple of

miles apart in the providence of Veracruz. They'd been in the Gulf for about a week."

"Ours?"

JR nodded.

Wolfe's smile returned. "Even better. It won't convince them completely, but it should help."

Nadia raised her eyebrows. "What about Asa Gerlis?"

Standing, Wolfe walked over to the glass door and watched a hawk soar above the condo. "He's the wild card. We know he faked his own death and more than likely orchestrated the events in Barcelona. He might not be so easily fooled by our ruse in Mexico City."

JR asked, "Why do you think he would fake his own death?"

"Don't know, unless he really was a double agent."

After thinking about Wolfe's comment, Nadia narrowed her eyes. "He said something the last time I saw him. I thought it strange at the time, but now it makes sense."

Turning to look at Nadia, Wolfe asked. "What did he say?"

"Something about the guardians of the state needed to be more vigilant because Israel was on the edge of a precipice."

"When was this?"

"Two weeks before he disappeared."

"We need to find out where he is."

Nadia frowned. "That would mean traveling overseas. I'm not sure I want to right now."

Nodding, Wolfe said, "I really don't want to either."

JR placed the laptop into his backpack and stood. "Want some advice?"

Turning slowly, Wolfe looked at JR. "Depends."

"Joseph thinks you should both forget what happened and move on. I disagree."

Nadia narrowed her eyes. "Why do you disagree?"

"Personal experience. If they're still looking for you, they will eventually find you, no matter how well you've covered your tracks."

"How will we know if they're looking for us?"

With a sly grin, JR tapped his backpack. "You won't. Without Joseph's knowledge, I've placed a few tripwires in a couple of high-level computers at Langley and in Tel-Aviv. If anyone uses your real names in an email or places them into a database search, I'll know about it."

Wolfe raised an eyebrow. "Thank you." He paused for a heartbeat. "Why are you helping us?"

The hacker shrugged. "I needed to disappear a few years ago myself. Couple of people helped me. It's time I paid the favor forward. Besides..." He gave them a sly grin. "The system is rigged against the individual. I enjoy making the odds better for the little guy."

Without another word, he slipped the backpack over his shoulder and left the condo.

CHAPTER 7

Gerald Reid watched the security camera video on the forty-inch flat screen monitor for the third time. "Play it again, slower this time."

Kendra Burges used a mouse to move the video's progress bar back and to slow the presentation rate. She then played the clip again.

Reid was concentrating on the screen when he held his hand up. "Freeze at 11:03:23."

"Yes, sir."

Leaning closer to the monitor, he pointed at the image. "He knows where the shooter is. Right there, he glances up to his left. Amazing. He knew what was going to happen. Go to the same timestamp on the bank camera video, please."

The scene was the same, just from a different perspective. "There, he knows."

"I would agree, Gerald."

Sitting straighter, Reid pursed his lips. "How did he know?"

"Training?"

Reid didn't answer. After several minutes, he crossed his arms and raised his right hand to his chin. "He knew because he was also there as a sniper. He knew where all the best hides were located. Someone set them both up. They knew Wolfe wouldn't shoot her—he'd run to her and both would be in the real sniper's crosshairs. His grabbing her arm saved her life."

Burges looked up from her laptop she was using to control the video. "Why were they set up?"

Reid shook his head. "A good question. I don't know. But I intend to find out."

As a twenty-five-year veteran of the CIA, Gerald Reid currently held the position of an assistant director in the counter-terrorism division. A graduate of West Point, he left the army after two years and joined the CIA just before the events of Operation Desert Shield. Currently, he faced the daunting task of finding a man who was well-trained at being invisible and hiding in plain sight: ex-CIA employee, Michael Wolfe.

Reid straightened his five-foot ten frame as he kept his hazel eyes focused on the monitor. "Kendra, who's on the desk tonight?"

"Not sure. I'll find out."

Reid heard the clicking of nails on a keyboard.

"Barry Tan."

"Would you mind giving him a call?"

"Just a moment."

Reid's mind raced as he determined what information he needed and in what order.

"Tan," a bored voice answered over speakers next to the big monitor.

"Good evening, Barry. Assistant Director Reid here."

The voice grew serious. "How may I be of assistance this evening, sir?"

"I need a bio and current location on an ex-CIA operative named Michael Wolfe."

"Yes, sir. Should I call you back or email the data?"

"This is an urgent request. Can you call us back?"

"Yes, sir. I will call you as soon as I have the information."

"Thank you."

The call ended as Reid continued to stare at the frozen image on the monitor glancing at the sniper hide above and to his left.

The return call came an hour later. Reid answered.

"Sir, it's Barry Tan."

"Yes, Barry. What did you find?"

"Not much, sir. I'll send the bio to your email address, but his only known address is a problem."

"How so?"

"Well..." The silence was deafening as Reid waited. "Uh—well, sir, the location is a homeless shelter in Canton, Ohio."

Reid laughed.

"Excuse me, sir?"

"Expected, Mr. Tan. Our Mr. Wolfe is good at subterfuge. Thank you for your efforts, son." The call ended and Reid nodded slowly as he paced the office space within the converted guest house.

Kendra Burges pushed her glasses up her nose. Ten years younger than Reid, she was a slender five-foot-seven and his assistant since she joined the CIA twenty-one years earlier. Both were unmarried and kept their personal lives quiet. Kendra, during work hours, wore blocky black glasses which did not enhance her oval face. Her brownish-blonde hair was thin and normally kept in a ponytail. She strived for plain and accomplished it with great efficiency. After hours, the glasses were exchanged for contacts and she used a touch of makeup. She emerged as a pretty woman—not gorgeous, but attractive.

As a well-trained Company analyst specializing in digital imagery, both still and motion, she assisted other departments when it became politically expedient for both of their careers. Both were ambitious and the relationship depended on Reid's rapid rise within the hierarchy of the agency. She liked Reid's status and he liked what she did for his career. They made a great team.

The building they occupied stood adjacent to Reid's rural Virginia estate. The property contained twenty acres with a four thousand square-foot residence and the separate guest house. After his parents passed away, Reid, being the only child, had inherited the property. Ten years later, and hundreds of thousands of dollars in renovation, the home reflected his personality and as time went by, reflected Kendra's, too.

After ten minutes of pacing, Reid stopped. Without looking at his watch, he turned to her. "Kendra, what time is it in Tel Aviv?"

"Five thirty-six a.m.:

"He's awake. I need to talk to my counterpart with Mossad."

"I'll find the number."

Using a secure landline, Reid called the number Kendra provided. The answer came on the fourth ring.

"Good morning, Gerald."

"Sorry to call so early, Uri."

"Nonsense. My day started an hour ago. What can I do for you this morning?"

Uri Ben-David ran the counter-terrorist division of Mossad. He kept his tone professional, Gerald Reid being an individual he did not care to interact with.

"I'm looking for someone: Nadia Picard."

Silence was his answer. Reid waited.

"So are we. What is your interest in her?"

"Actually, I'm looking for the man she disappeared with, Michael Wolfe. I was hoping you might have some insight into their whereabouts."

"It seems Wolfe was in the right spot at the right time in Barcelona. I take it you've seen the security camera recordings."

"Yes. What did you conclude from it?"

"Someone drew them together for a reason. Apparently to kill them."

"I concur. Who?"

"We have our suspicions, but no proof. Do you have any thoughts on the matter?"

"That's why I'm calling. We analyzed an assassination video and found it faked."

"Oh, whose assassination?"

"Asa Gerlis."

"Interesting. What makes you think his death was faked?"

"The pixel count was inconsistent where they joined the facial image and the body. The image was manipulated. At least that's the conclusion of our analytical team."

"Interesting."

"Any idea of why he would fake his own death?"

"I can't answer that question because we didn't question the authenticity of the video. We will have to re-examine it."

"Who would benefit from Gerlis disappearing?"

Once again, silence was the answer. After more than twenty seconds, Reid heard, "The only person I can think of would be Asa Gerlis."

"Why?"

"Without going into any detail, he was under investigation. That's all I can say at the moment."

"I see. That would be a good reason not to examine the video. Everyone wanted it to be real."

Unseen by Reid, Ben-David rolled his eyes and reminded himself of why he did not like interacting with the man. "No comment."

Reid chuckled. "I would feel the same way if the circumstances were reversed."

"I will have the video examined and get back to you."

"Thank you, Uri."

The call ended and Reid could not help smiling. "Apparently, your discovery of finding the video of Gerlis' death as a fake is going to be inconvenient for the Israelis."

Kendra stood and stretched. "It's late Gerald. I'm going to bed."

"I'll join you, my love."

Uri Ben-David knocked on the open door leading to the office of Mossad's director, Yosef Freidman. The man was standing next to a credenza pouring a cup of coffee from a carafe.

"Ah, Uri, come in. Would you like coffee? Ida just brought a fresh pot in."

"No, thank you."

"Very well. What was the urgent matter you called about?"

"There's been a development in the murder of Asa

Gerlis you need to know about."

"Oh, what is that?"

"His death was faked."

Freidman was about to take a sip of his coffee but stopped. He frowned and walked back to his desk. "What do you mean faked?"

"For lack of a better way to explain it, his face was Photoshopped onto the body of the real victim."

Freidman set the coffee cup on his desk and turned to look out the only window in the room. "When was this discovered?"

"My counterpart with the CIA called about it early this morning. We checked their work."

The Director remained silent.

Ben-David continued, "They are looking for Michael Wolfe and Nadia Picard. They believe, like we do, someone arranged for them to be in the same place at the same time in Barcelona—someone who wanted both of them dead."

"Who was Nadia's controller?"

"Asa Gerlis."

"I realize that, Uri. Who was assigned after Gerlis' supposed murder?"

"No one had been assigned because she was on personal leave. I checked on the reason."

"And?"

"The note in her file said she was in Paris caring for her ailing sister."

Freidman nodded.

"There's a problem with that, sir."

Frowning, the Director stared at the top of his desk. "Let me guess. She doesn't have a sister."

Ben-David shook his head. "No, she doesn't."

"Okay, Uri, what's going on here?"

"At this point, I would only be speculating."

"Speculate."

"Asa Gerlis faked his own death to avoid us completing our investigation into his extracurricular activities. Since he was supposedly dead, there was no need to expend further resources to investigate. The file was classified top secret and buried."

"What was found?"

"Uh, as you know, when he immigrated as a teenager to Israel, he had papers identifying himself as a Polish citizen. After completing his compulsory military duty, he joined the Mossad."

The Director nodded.

"He wasn't from Poland."

Freidman slowly massaged his temples. "Where was he from?"

"We think somewhere in northeastern Kazakhstan."

"You think."

"Yes, sir."

"You are not positive."

"No, sir."

"Was he Muslim?"

"No, he was Jewish, but he was also Russian."

The Director closed his eyes and sighed. "Are you telling me we've had a mole inside the Mossad for twenty years?"

"It would appear so."

"Do you think Gerlis is the one who set up Nadia and Wolfe?"

"Now that we know he's probably still alive..." He nodded.

"Why? Why would he go to all that trouble?"

"We don't have enough facts to speculate. However, there was another development overnight."

"What was that?"

"Blood found in one of our safe houses in Mexico City was been identified as Picard's and Wolfe's."

Friedman remained quiet.

"No bodies."

The Director sipped his coffee. "It's Mexico, Uri."

"Yes, I know. But, without bodies, it is hard to verify they are dead."

"I would agree."

"One more thing," said Ben-David.

"Yes."

"Their Spanish passports washed up on shore in Veracruz, a couple of kilometers apart."

Freidman's expression remained neutral. "Interesting. Picard is smart and well trained, as is Wolfe." He paused for a moment and sipped his coffee. "Make a note in her file she is missing and presumed dead. Tell no one of your suspicions, but assume they are alive. Go slowly, but find them. Find them before Gerlis does. Maybe Nadia knows something Gerlis wants kept quiet."

Ben-David nodded and left the Director's office.

CHAPTER 8

SOMEWHERE IN SOUTHERN MISSOURI

A Week Later

Nadia watched from the main window of the sheltered home as Wolfe drove the Jeep Wrangler south. She followed it until it disappeared over a rise nine hundred yards from the house. Closing her eyes, she wrapped the blanket tighter around her. Wolfe had quietly gotten out of bed at dawn to make the trip to his friend's cabin on the southern end of the property. Even though he'd tried not to wake her, his absence next to her in bed and the sound of his departure had disturbed her.

She stood another minute, watching the spot where the Jeep went out of sight. Her thoughts turned to the past two months. Smiling slightly, she walked to the kitchen and started a pot of coffee. Being around Michael had cured her of her preference for tea.

As the coffee brewed, she changed into jeans and a baggy sweatshirt to ward off the slight chill in the house. Fall had come and gone along with the beautiful colors in the surrounding trees. As Michael had told her, the coming of winter brought different shades of grays and browns over the landscape. During times when they were apart, her thoughts drifted back to the night Asa Gerlis had told her of Michael's departure. As she sipped the freshly poured coffee, she closed her eyes and remembered.

A knock on the apartment door startled her. Michael wasn't due for another hour. With caution, she approached the door. Instead of a peephole, Michael had installed a miniature wireless security camera in the door's eye-level hole. A video screen on the wall to the left of the door showed a fisheye camera view of the hallway. With a Glock 26 held in her right hand behind her back, she approached the monitor.

Anger and disgust set in when she saw who was there. Asa Gerlis.

Without opening the door, she said, "I have company coming, Asa. What do you want?"

"He's not coming, Nadia."

"Who is not coming?"

"Michael. May I come in?"

Her breathing grew shallow as she hurriedly unlocked the door to let her Mossad controller into the apartment. Face-to-face meetings were discouraged, but here he was. She kept the Glock hidden behind her.

Of average height for an Israeli male, Gerlis was shorter than Nadia, which allowed her to look down at him. His round face, short, prematurely gray beard and close-cropped hair made him appear older than his forty-five years. During the few physical meetings they'd had, she'd found his piercing gray-blue eyes predatory.

"What do you mean he's not coming?"

Gerlis surveyed the small apartment before he answered. "He left on a six-p.m. flight for Atlanta."

"He would not leave without telling me. You are lying."

The shorter man shook his head. "No, he will not be back. He tendered his resignation and left the country. I am sorry he did not tell you."

She remained quiet, trying to determine the truthfulness of what he told her. "Why did he resign? He never mentioned anything to me about it."

Gerlis shrugged. "Maybe he is not the person you think he is. He is a dangerous man, Nadia. Men like Wolfe are impulsive and narcissistic and will do what they want when they want."

Now she knew Gerlis was lying. But if Michael had actually left the country without telling her, maybe she didn't know him as well as she thought.

"So why are you here?"

"To offer comfort." He spread his arms, inviting her into an embrace.

Her revulsion brought the Glock from behind her back as she pointed the pistol at Gerlis' face.

"Get OUT."

"Nadia, I am here as a friend."

"You are not my friend. GET OUT."

With a slight grin, Gerlis nodded and walked toward the door. As he was about to open it, he turned. The Glock was still pointed at him. "You will find I am not lying. He is gone, Nadia. Get used to it."

Michael's entrance through the front door ended her reminiscing.

"I hope I didn't wake you when I left."

She shook her head and took a sip of her now stone-cold coffee. She wondered how long she had been thinking about Gerlis' lies. "I made coffee. Would you like some?"

"Yes, it's cold out there."

She poured a mug and handed it to him. "How is Bobby?"

Wolfe grinned. "I think he has a girlfriend."

"You think?"

The grin intensified. "I saw a few feminine touches in the living area of the cabin."

Nadia crossed her arms. "And how would you recognize a feminine touch?"

"A discarded bra next to the sofa."

She laughed. "Good for Bobby." She walked quickly to Wolfe and embraced him.

He returned the hug. "What's the matter?"

"Nothing. I just felt like it."

Smiling, he enjoyed the moment.

With the Jeep loaded with their luggage and Nadia's laptop, they prepared to leave the Howell County home. She sat in the passenger seat as Wolfe engaged the security system and locked the front door. Once behind the Jeep's steering wheel, he glanced at his wristwatch. "We should be there in plenty of time to meet Joseph."

She nodded. Her eyes did not leave the house.

"You like this place, don't you?"

"Yes, more and more each day." She turned to him. "What if we decide to live our lives under our new names and forget about Barcelona? No one is going to find us. If they try, JR will let us know."

He smiled and placed a hand on her thigh. "For now, we will do nothing. If JR determines someone is looking for us, we will return here and make plans."

She closed her eyes and nodded.

"I want to spend the rest of my life with you, Nadia. I also want it to be a long life."

She nodded and returned to staring at the house.

Joseph slid the contract across the small glass breakfast table where the three sat. Wolfe picked it up and flipped through the pages.

"This spells out your compensation and expense reimbursement. It hasn't changed since the last time we worked together. No one—and I mean no one except JR and me—will know where you live or where you are at any given time."

Wolfe skimmed the three-page document and returned his attention to Joseph. "US Marshal Investigative Services?"

"Yes."

"How's that going to work? Won't I have to report to someone?"

"It gives you the authority. It doesn't mean you actually work for them. You will be working under a Presidential Executive Order originally signed by the first President Bush. That order established my team. We were originally designated to work overseas, but since the military ramped up Special Forces, we aren't needed over there as much. However, our services are now better suited to working within the United States, where the military isn't allowed to function."

Wolfe nodded as he read the document again.

"How many of us are there?"

Joseph just smiled.

"Okay, got it. Need-to-know only."

"Yes."

"What will I be doing?"

"The tasks will vary. Mostly the same thing you did as a hired gun. You just won't need the rifle."

"Explain."

"Michael, you work best by yourself. You're a lone wolf, no pun intended."

Wolfe grinned but remained quiet.

"When we identify someone domestically that's dangerous to our country, you will be asked to find them. Once you do, you will contact me and I will send in an apprehension team."

After signing the last page, and then initialing the front two, he handed the document back to Joseph and smiled. "Thanks. It feels good to be legit again."

Nodding, Joseph took the signed document, folded it lengthwise, and placed it in the inside breast pocket of his sport coat.

Turning to Nadia, Wolfe said, "Guess all we need to do now is find something you would like to do."

Another grin from Joseph. "Actually, we don't have to. If she wants it, she has an interview with the Branson School District tomorrow for an opening in their foreign language department as a French teacher."

Nadia's smile lit up the room.

After details of her appointment were discussed, Joseph turned serious. "What's your connection to Gerald Reid, Michael?"

Wolfe's eyes narrowed. He stood and walked to the sliding glass door next to the breakfast table in the condo's kitchen and dining area. He clasped his hands behind his back and watched the lazy flight of three turkey vultures as they circled high above the dense trees on the opposite side of the cove. He was quiet for several minutes. Joseph and Nadia watched him.

After half a minute of silence, Joseph said, "You obviously know him."

"I know of him. None of it good. Geoffrey showed me a picture of the man taken by an MI6 surveillance team, oh, I guess it was several years ago. I can't even remember the reason he showed it to me. Apparently, they worked together at one time in the past. Geoffrey didn't care for the man. In fact, he went out of his way to tell me Reid was dangerous. Why do you ask?"

"He sent someone to the apartment in Mexico City."

Wolfe turned to look at Joseph. "How do you know that?"

Shrugging, Joseph didn't answer.

"I've never had any contact with him. Why would someone like Gerald Reid be involved?"

"I was hoping you could tell me. All I know is he's an assistant director in the CIA's counter-terrorism division. He's well connected within the ranks of CIA management and..." He let the sentence die.

"And what, Joseph?"

"I believe he is looking for you and Nadia."

Wolfe blinked a few times and glanced at Nadia. Her eyes were glued on him. "Did our ruse not work?"

"Officially, it did. Your CIA file identifies you as deceased."

"What about Nadia?"

"My contact in Israel told me it's the same, missing, presumed dead. It's their way of saying no body was recovered."

"So why is Reid still looking?"

"I was hoping you might have some insight on the matter."

Returning his attention to the view outside the condo, Wolfe shook his head. "I've got no idea. Hell, I've never even met the man."

Nadia asked. "Joseph, do you think anyone in Israel is looking for us?"

"I wish I had a good answer for you, but I just don't know." He hesitated for a moment, "Why all the fuss about you two?"

Turning, Wolfe displayed a grim smile. "That's the question no one's asked yet. Who and why were we set up in Barcelona? Now we learn someone in the CIA is looking for us? And, I bet if we dig hard enough, you'd find someone within the Mossad still looking for us, despite our official status."

Joseph pulled a cell phone out from his sport coat. "I can't answer those questions, but I know someone who can."

CHAPTER 9

After decades working for the CIA, Joseph Kincaid knew more so-called "spooks" than most people in Washington. The correct title within the agency remained operations officer. But the now former CIA employee he was calling earned his living as a consultant, a fancy way of saying he charged a lot of money for information other people needed.

The man who answered grumbled. "What did I do to earn a call from you, Joseph?"

Standing on the back balcony of Wolfe's apartment, Joseph grinned. "Just checking up on you, Will. Wanted to see how you were doing."

"Bullshit. You want something. It's the only time you call."

"That's not fair."

William Fischer, better known as Will to his friends, did not look like the stereotypical Hollywood spy. On the contrary, Fischer possessed unruly dark rusty brown hair, bushy eyebrows he refused to trim, a round face accented by a broad nose and a red walrus mustache. Dark green eyes saw the world through the smudged lenses of his black horn-rim glasses. His normal wardrobe could best be described as thrift shop chic—rumpled corduroy sport coat, khaki pants two inches too long, scuffed loafers and a wrinkled white oxford shirt.

"It will cost you."

"Normal fee?"

"Yeah, a pint of Guinness."

"You drive a hard bargain. Agreed."

"Okay, what do you need?"

"Background."

"On who?"

"Gerald Reid."

There was silence on the other end. Joseph took a quick glance at his phone to see if the call had been dropped. Finally, he heard a mumbled, "Why?"

"Curiosity."

"Uh, boy. You know that killed the cat, don't you?"

"I've heard that, but I'm still curious."

"He's a dangerous man. Do not get in his way up the ladder—he'll throw you off and laugh as he watches you fall."

"Do you know him?"

"No one knows Gerald Reid. No one wants to know Gerald Reid."

"Okay, now you've really piqued my curiosity."

"I really don't want to discuss this on a cell phone. Call me from a landline. Here's the number."

It took an hour for Joseph to return to his secluded

home forty miles north of Wolfe's condo on the lake. Using protocols learned from JR, he initiated the call from his computer, the location masked by programming he did not understand nor care to.

Fischer answered with a hesitant, "Hello".

"It's Joseph, Will."

"Where the hell are you? Caller ID indicates you're calling from Oregon."

"A little magic and a lot of technology. I'm assured this is more secure than an encrypted landline."

"Huh, okay."

"So, tell me what worries you about Gerald Reid."

"It's not really a worry." Fischer paused. "The problem is he believes the world revolves around him and him alone. His is a world without shades of gray, only stark contrasts of black and white. You and I both know that's an unrealistic view."

"Odd for someone so high up in the CIA, but I guess it's possible."

"Have you ever been around him?"

"I'm retired, remember? That's why I'm calling you."

Joseph heard chuckling over the phone.

"That's funny, you retiring. Bullshit. You're still up to your armpits in this crap."

With an amused expression, Joseph replied. "Okay, I still keep my toe in the water. How's that?"

"Still funny. Anyway, Reid is like a laser-guided missile. Once he has an objective targeted, he won't let up until it is destroyed."

"Go on."

After a brief period of silence, Fischer said. "Remember the sudden retirement of Bernadine Frazier last year?"

"Yeah."

"That was orchestrated by Reid."

"How so?"

"The how is still unknown, but my source indicated Reid wanted her job, so he went after it."

"Huh."

"That's an understatement."

"So, one instance does not make a person dangerous, Will. What else?"

"That's how he's climbed the ladder at the agency— one destroyed career after another. He takes no prisoners and leaves carnage in his wake."

"What does the director think?"

"Don't know, but he hasn't stopped him. Kind of tells you where his mindset is."

"Yeah."

"One other thing. I'm told he lives and breathes the job. Works fourteen to eighteen hours a day. He has an assistant that follows him to every new position at the agency." Fischer paused for a moment. "Why do you want to know all this stuff?"

"I have my reasons."

"Joseph, don't go self-righteous on me. We go too far back. Why do you want to know?"

"He's looking for one of my old operatives."

"Why is he looking?"

"That's what I'm trying to determine."

"Well, if the guy's alive, Reid will find him."

"Thanks, Will. I'll keep that in mind."

The call ended and Joseph sat staring at the laptop screen. It was several minutes before a small grin grew into a wide smile.

"Do you think it will work?"

Joseph nodded as he sipped his coffee. The three individuals sat in a small café in downtown Ozark. He looked at Michael Wolfe and then at Nadia Picard. "The trick is to get bone DNA from both of you. All DNA is the same within a given organism. It's the cell structure that's different. The DNA determines the function of the body part so muscle tissue and bone tissue would have a dissimilar cell structure. However, they both have the same DNA. If we want this to work, we'll need bone cells for the DNA comparison."

"Bone marrow extraction?"

"Yes, that's what I'm thinking."

"Where do we get it done? It's probably more complicated than drawing blood."

"Don't know. I'm not a doctor."

Nadia frowned. "Even if we have the samples, how do we get them to Reid? He would demand to know the chain of custody. Otherwise, he won't accept it as real."

Wolfe smiled and looked at her. "You and I can handle that. We'd just have to know where to intercept the courier."

Joseph emptied his coffee cup and stood. "Let me handle the details. Did you two get new passports?"

They both nodded.

"Good. Be prepared to get on a plane at a moment's notice."

"I've got my own," replied Wolfe

Joseph raised an eyebrow. "You what?"

"I have my own plane in a hangar at the West Plains airport. Just let us know where to go and we'll be there."

"Michael, you never cease to amaze me."

His response was silence as Wolfe took a sip of coffee.

"Charlie Rose, or should I just call you Joseph?"

"Whichever you prefer, Uri." Joseph's call to Ben-David had been answered immediately.

"What's it been? Fifteen years?"

"At least. I left the agency ten years ago."

Ben-David laughed. "You no more left the CIA than I suddenly moved to Syria. Don't start lying to me after all these years, Joseph."

"Can you talk?"

His jovial mood dissipated. "Depends. About what?"

"The disappearance of Michael Wolfe and Nadia Picard."

"Oh, I didn't know they disappeared."

"Now who's lying, Uri? Michael worked for me at one time. He's someone I cared about and I need to know what happened to him."

"Are you on a cell phone, Joseph?"

"No, secure VoIP."

"Very well. We don't know much."

"The rumor is they were killed in Mexico City."

"Officially, that is the story."

Joseph was quiet for a brief moment. "But you don't believe it."

"Belief is a nebulous concept. Let's just say I haven't seen bodies or DNA evidence to support believing she and Wolfe are deceased."

"I see." Although Ben-David could not see it, Joseph smiled involuntarily. "Are you still looking?"

"Not actively, soft inquiries only. Why?"

"A promise I made a long time ago. Let me ask you a question."

A pause ensued before Ben-David answered. "Okay."

"I have, uh, someone in Mexico also doing soft inquiries."

"Thought you didn't work for the CIA anymore."

"Uri, do I have to explain?"

Ben-David chuckled. "No. Sorry I doubted you."

"If something comes of this inquiry, would your forensic team do the analysis?"

"You act like you already know something. Be truthful, Joseph, or this conversation will end."

"I really don't know anything at the moment. But you never know."

"Why not take this to the agency?"

"To be honest with you, Michael did not leave the CIA with many friends. I am one of only a few and simply want to know what happened to him. That's all."

"I'll remember that. We will talk again soon."

Joseph closed the lid to the laptop and looked up at Wolfe and Nadia. "At least we have a path now. I think getting your DNA to the Israelis is our best bet. They will inform the CIA and hopefully you two will officially be declared deceased."

A grim smile came to Nadia's lips. They were now at Joseph's secluded log home deep in the rolling hills of the Ozarks. She turned and walked to a sliding glass door, staring out toward a tree line over a hundred feet from the structure. "Uri Ben-David is not easily fooled. How do we get the sample to him and make him believe?" She turned, her attention on Joseph. "Who is this person in Mexico?"

The corner of Joseph's mouth twitched. "A young recruit of mine. He also happens to be an Ex-Navy Seal. Originally from southern California, he speaks Spanish like a resident of Mexico City. He arrived yesterday."

Michael frowned. "Do Nadia and I need to go to Mexico?"

"Not sure, yet. Like I told you earlier, be prepared

to leave at any moment."

Jimmie Gibbs possessed the physique of a swimmer—tall and slender with well-proportioned muscles. Swimming was a passion for the man who still held several Navy Seal records for endurance and distance.

After retiring from Team Six, he let his black hair grow long and kept it tied back in a ponytail that extended past his shoulder blades. As a native Southern Californian, his usual dress was surfer casual—cargo shorts, linen shirt and sandals. Today was no exception.

Having arrived in Mexico City on his first assignment for Joseph Kincaid, he looked forward to the new challenge. During his recruitment, he was told he would be joining a quasi-CIA specialty group, utilizing individuals possessing skill sets similar to his. So far, he had not met anyone else on the team. It really didn't matter—he was back in the game and loved it. However, on this particular day and in this particular city, he felt like he was dumpster diving. After visiting seven city morgues in two days, his frustration level grew with each failed search. He extracted his cell phone and dialed. The call was answered on the third ring.

"Did you find it, Jimmie?"

Gibbs knew not to give details on a cell phone. "Nah. Not yet. You sure it's here?"

"No, I'm not sure it will be, but we have to look. It's important."

"I know, but I am running out of locations to search."

"How many more left?"

"Three."

"Call me back when you've completed your task."

The phone went dead. Gibbs, not one to complain about an assignment, took a deep breath and continued his task.

In the ninth morgue, he found what Joseph needed him to find. After placing a claim on the two corpses, he slipped the mortician an American hundred to seal the deal.

At his hotel, Gibbs used his laptop, provided by his new employer, to make a more secure VoIP phone call.

Joseph Kincaid answered immediately. "I take it you found something."

"Yeah. Just what you ordered. A man and woman, neither of them possessing their heads."

"Condition of the bodies?"

"Rough. Been in the elements for a while."

"Excellent. Where?"

Gibbs gave him the location and the claim number he'd received from the morgue. "What else do you need from me?"

"Keep an eye on the location. Someone will be there within twenty-four hours to secure the bodies. At that time, you're done."

"That was easy."

"Not all your tasks will be as such."

"Good."

The call ended and Gibbs checked out to find a hotel closer to the mortuary.

By one o'clock in the afternoon the next day, activity at the normally obscure morgue was ablaze with activity. Gibbs watched from the interior of a small café across and several doors down. Four Mercedes sedans and a black Suburban, all with diplomatic plates, were parked up and down the street. Men in suits and others dressed in surgical scrubs entered the mortuary. After thirty minutes, the men in scrubs wheeled two gurneys to the back of the Suburban. Two black body bags were off-loaded into the rear of the large SUV and it sped away.

Gibbs picked up his phone and dialed. When the call was answered he said two words, "Package received." Per his instructions, he terminated the connection without waiting for a response.

He paid his bill, left the café and drove through the congested traffic to the Mexico City International Airport for his return to the United States.

Joseph sat next to JR in a cubicle on the second floor of a building in the southwest part of Springfield, Missouri. The building contained the computer security company owned by the hacker. JR pointed to an email. "This is the main email account for the Israeli Mossad case officer operating at their embassy in Mexico."

Joseph shook his head, "I won't ask."

"Good, I wouldn't tell you. He is indicating the bodies are too decomposed for fingerprints to be validated. Looks like they will use bone marrow samples for the DNA test and leave the bodies in Mexico."

"What part of the body are the samples being extracted?"

"Hip."

"Kind of what we thought. That's where we extracted it from Wolfe and Picard." Joseph rubbed his chin. "What airline will they use to transport the samples?"

"Looks like Delta to Tel Aviv." JR smiled and turned to Joseph. "With a layover at JFK."

"Perfect, we can make the switch there. I'm assuming they are not treating this with a high degree of urgency or secrecy."

"No. Flight isn't until tomorrow. It will be transported via a diplomatic pouch in the cargo hold."

"No refrigeration?'

JR shook his head. "None needed. Bone DNA has a half-life of 521 years."

"Didn't know that."

A nod was his reply. JR clicked on a JPEG file attached to the email. It showed a picture of the pouch, the test-tubes containing the DNA and their markings.

Joseph bent over and studied the photo closer. "They are making this too easy."

"Not really. The email was encrypted."

"Then, how did..." Joseph paused, smiled and just shook his head. "Never mind."

JR's fingers flew over the keyboard as his attention was drawn to the computer screen on the left. "I can access the luggage routing from here. However, someone is going to have to physically switch the packages at JFK when it lands."

"That's not a problem, they are ready. We just needed to know when and where."

Three weeks later, Uri Ben-David read the final report about the DNA samples sent from Mexico. They showed a positive match to Michael Wolfe and Nadia Picard. He took a deep breath and let it out slowly. In a soft voice he said, "I will say Kaddish for you, Nadia. May you rest in peace."

He picked up the phone and dialed a number he had been given four weeks prior. It was answered on the second ring. "Good evening, Uri. Do you have news?"

"I'm afraid so, Joseph. The DNA from the bodies in Mexico match Wolfe and Picard."

Ten seconds of silence followed. "I was afraid of that. Thank you for following up on it."

"Did he have any family?"

"No. Both parents are gone and no siblings. Same with Picard."

"What happened to the bodies?"

"Mexican authorities cremated them a week ago, against our wishes. But they don't like taking orders from Israel."

Joseph's next request would need to be handled carefully. "How well do you know Gerald Reid?"

"Professionally, that's about it."

"Somehow he needs to be informed about the DNA results without him knowing I'm involved."

Uri chuckled. "We will send a memo to him as a courtesy. Your name will never be mentioned."

"Thank you, Uri. I'll light a candle for Michael."

"And I, for Nadia."

PART TWO
Present Day

CHAPTER 10

KANSAS CITY, MO

The comedy club occupied a renovated building north of the Kansas City Plaza on Broadway. During the week, it operated as a cocktail lounge and open mic nightclub for aspiring new comedians. Located near the UMKC Dental and Law Schools, the club catered to the student population living near campus. Three nights a week—Thursday, Friday, Saturday and occasionally Sunday, if someone famous was available—it drew crowds of multiple age groups depending on the acts featured. Tonight, the audience leaned toward Millennials and Gen-Xers. Tables for four dominated the lounge area, with the occasional two-top bistro table scattered around for those who did not like sitting in a group. The stage dominated the room opposite the bar.

Two members of the audience paid little attention to the comedian currently on stage. They were there to observe an individual who sat alone at a bistro table near the center of the room. The name on his driver's license identified the patron as Roger Garcia of Olathe, Kansas. His real name happened to be Samir Nassar, an Egyptian from Cairo, who was in the country illegally. This was his third visit to this particular club since Thursday; it was now Saturday. Tonight, the audience packed the club waiting for the featured act. Thursday and Friday's crowds had been considerably smaller.

Michael Wolfe and Nadia Picard sat in a darkened section against the outside wall of the showroom floor, making sure they kept Nassar within sight. They knew his real identity after having spent the last two weeks watching and tracking his movements. Both were concerned about his frequent trips to this particular club.

Wolfe leaned close to Nadia's ear and whispered, "I've got a bad feeling about tonight. I'm going to check his car. Text me if he gets up and tries to leave."

She did not look at him, but nodded, her attention still trained on the Egyptian as Wolfe left the expansive room. No act was currently on stage, but as Wolfe disappeared through the entrance door, the lights in the room dimmed and Nadia heard:

"Your feature act tonight tours comedy clubs around the nation. He is an accomplished actor having just completed a major motion picture with Academy Award winner Tatum O'Neal." There was a slight pause. "Please welcome to the stage—Jeff Vaughn!"

Enthusiastic applause and whistles ensued as the comedian approached the microphone. Nadia noticed that Nassar was not clapping, but looking around the room with a neutral expression. He appeared to be checking if anyone was paying too much attention to him. She kept him in her peripheral vision and joined the crowd welcoming the comedian.

As Vaughn started his set, Nassar returned his attention to the stage.

"As you can probably imagine, the first thing people notice about me is this 1970s porno-style mustache." Polite laughter could be heard in the room. "I get lots of comments on it, but I don't mind. I take them as a compliment. Although some people don't. The last time I complimented somebody on their mustache, it really pissed her off. I guess there's just no pleasing my mother-in-law."

The audience roared with laughter. Nadia smiled, her concentration remaining on Nassar.

The comic continued with his routine, but Nadia did not listen as Wolfe settled back into the chair next to her. He leaned in closer to her ear. "We have a problem."

She shot him a concerned look, but did not reply.

"Seems our Mr. Nassar has a trunk-full of assault weapons, handguns and a bulletproof vest."

Nadia stared at the stage for a few moments and then turned to Wolfe. "Do you think he'll try something tonight?"

"Yeah. Got any ideas?"

She smiled and nodded just as the comedian told another story.

He said, "How many of you out there are married?" Good-mannered applause could be heard in the auditorium.

Nadia gave Wolfe a mischievous grin as she clapped.

The comedian continued. "How many people here are divorced?" The audience responded louder and a few, "Yeah, man."

After a pause he said, "I'm married." He looked around timing his next words. "Actually, I'm married to my high school sweetheart." Another brief pause. "She'll be a Senior next year."

The room erupted into laughter and hand-clapping. Nadia noticed Wolfe chuckling for the first time since the comedian started his routine, but his attention stayed on the Egyptian.

Wolfe turned to her. "What was your idea?"

"I'll pretend to pick him up?"

Wolfe grinned. "You're kidding."

She extracted a small vial from inside her small purse. "Glad we remembered to bring this tonight. I've done it before. Remember that fat Iranian in Ammon, Jordan?"

Wolfe nodded and watched as she unfastened the top two buttons on her blouse, exposing ample cleavage.

With a wink, she said. "He may be a jihadist, but he's also a man. Bet he never notices me putting this in his drink. By the way, what is he drinking?"

"Looks like beer."

"Even better." She stood and walked toward the table where Nassar sat. Wolfe noticed she was swinging her hips just a bit more than normal. Knowing what would come next, he suppressed a smile as he pulled out his cell phone and dialed three numbers.

Nadia sat down next to Nassar, who stared at her with wide eyes. "Do you mind if I sit with you? This is the only seat left in the room."

The Egyptian quickly looked around and started to protest, but his eyes caught her semi-exposed breasts. As he stared, he stammered, "Okay... Uh... I'm not staying too much longer."

Placing her hand on his, she leaned closer. "Be a dear and see if you can get the attention of a waitress, I need a drink."

On the brightly-lit stage, Vaughn could barely make out what was occurring in the audience but he did catch a glimpse of the beautiful woman sitting down next to the dark-haired man at a table by himself. He filed the info away as he continued his routine.

As Nassar looked around for a waitress, Nadia passed her hand over the man's beer. Drops of liquid could barely be seen spilling into the glass. Bubbles formed but dissipated before Nassar returned his attention her. Once again, his eyes locked on her chest. "I can't find one."

"Oh, that's too, bad. Thanks for trying." She stood and walked away. Nassar visually followed her for a while, then returned his attention to the stage.

The comedian saw this as he started his next joke. "Anybody here ever drink so much you don't know where you are or even how you got home at night?" Some of the younger members of the crowd agreed with whoops and applause. "To me, that's how you can explain some of these alien abductions." He pointed toward the dark-haired man, once again sitting alone at his table.

At that same moment, Nassar was taking a long pull from his glass of beer, getting the courage to leave the bar and go to his car.

"Take, for instance, this guy. He could have been abducted a few moments ago by a beautiful alien. But apparently, he's had too much to drink."

The crowd laughed and applauded. Nassar's eyes widened as the crowd looked at him. This was not in his plans—he needed stealth, not attention, to carry out his mission. As he stood, dizziness swept over him. He grabbed the table with both hands and noticeably swayed. The effects of the drug Nadia slipped into his beer, combined with the fact he seldom drank, intensified his intoxication. Glancing around the room, all he saw were people staring at him. He screamed at the top of his lungs, "*Allah 'akbar.* Death to America."

He then proceeded to fall forward, causing the table to collapse. The beer fell, shattering on the floor and sending shards of glass and beer everywhere.

The comedian, not missing a beat, said, "Guess he won't be getting abducted by aliens tonight."

Wolfe and Nadia slipped out of the club and were sitting in their Jeep as three police cars screeched to a halt in front of the club's entrance. She turned to him. "How did they get here so fast?"

The corner of his mouth twitched. "I called 911 as you were walking over to his table."

She suppressed a smile. "Afraid he would go home with me?"

He shot her a quick glance and a sly grin appeared. "I was afraid you'd give him a heart attack."

They both laughed as more police cars, lights and sirens in full emergency mode, arrived.

It took thirty minutes for the police to discover the hidden weapons in the trunk of Nassar's Toyota Corolla. Once they did, more unmarked cars arrived with men and women wearing FBI windbreakers.

Wolfe, satisfied with their role in the takedown, slowly drove the Jeep out of the parking lot and turned south on Broadway. The two were quiet as he steered the vehicle, lost in their own thoughts. As Wolfe merged off of South 71 onto South 49, he took a quick glance at Nadia. "You okay?"

She smiled, returned the glance and nodded. "Yeah. Just thinking. I would like to spend some time at the property. I miss the solitude."

"Want to go there instead of the condo?"

She nodded.

He did a quick calculation in his head, "It's just past ten We can be there by three in the morning."

"Good."

CHAPTER 11

SOMEWHERE IN SOUTHERN MISSOURI

The clock on the Jeep Grand Cherokee displayed 3:11 in the morning. After navigating the rugged pathway from the highway to his home, Wolfe took a deep breath as he stared at the back of his underground house bathed in the Jeep's headlights. Nadia stirred in the seat next to him, having dozed the last fifty miles of their trip.

Wolfe frowned as the hairs on the back of his neck twitched. He placed his hand on Nadia's arm and said, "You awake?"

"Kind of. Why?"

Extracting his Walther PPK from his ankle holster, Wolfe turned to Nadia. "Something's not right. Do you have your Glock?"

Now fully awake and with a wrinkled brow, she reached for her small purse and removed a slim Glock 43. She held it so he could see it in the dim light of the dashboard.

"Back me up."

"What is wrong, Michael?"

"Maybe nothing, but I just got the same feeling I had when I saw you in the crosshairs of my scope in Barcelona." He flipped the door lights switch to off, eased the driver side door open and slipped out. He cautiously advanced around the earthen berm toward the front of the house.

Nadia waited a few seconds, making sure no one followed him and left the Jeep herself.

It took ten minutes to determine the house was secure before he replaced the Walther in its holster. Nadia descended the stairs and shook her head. "Nothing."

Taking a deep breath, Wolfe looked around. "Notice anything unusual?"

She nodded. "It does not look like anyone has been here for a while. I thought Bobby was to check on the place every other day."

"He normally does..." Wolfe's eyes widened and he swore. "Shit, come on."

Fifteen minutes later, they determined Bobby had not been at his cabin for a while either.

Wolfe pulled out his cell phone and punched in a number.

Howell Country Sheriff Harold Bright weighed in at around two hundred and sixty pounds. A tall, broad-shouldered man, his shaved head and profound paunch added to his ability to intimidate would-be violators of the law. Wolfe felt a grudging respect for the man. The sheriff had spent twenty years as a Marine before being elected to his current position. And, over the course of the last three years, had become a strong advocate for Bobby, helping to raise funds to assist in his recovery from PTSD.

The sheriff's car, emergency lights still rotating, sat parked in front of the cabin. Bright stood in the middle of Bobby's living area and stared at Wolfe, reflections from the beacons illuminating the man's face in sequence. "How long's it been since you spoke to him?"

"At least a month. We've been out of town. What about yourself?"

"Probably six months. Haven't seen him in West Plains for a while, either. What made you suspicious?"

Wolfe blinked several times before answering. "He watches our place when we're gone. When we got back a few hours ago, I could tell he hadn't been there."

Bright nodded. "Doesn't look like he's been here for a while, either. Place's spotless. Okay, I'll have someone stop by tomorrow and see if we can determine how long he's been gone."

Wolfe handed the sheriff a business card. "That's my cell phone. Would you call me if you find out anything?"

The big man just nodded.

Two days later, as the sun peeked above the trees to the east of the underground home, Wolfe stood outside the front door under the overhang, a cup of coffee in his hand. A heavy frost covered the pasture to the south and a cloud formed with each exhaled breath. Steam swirled from the mug as he brought it to his lips. He felt a presence behind him as Nadia, dressed in leggings, sweatshirt and a quilt draped over her shoulder, pressed against his back. She wrapped it around Wolfe.

"You're cold."

"A little." He pointed to a spot sixty degrees above the horizon. "See that?"

She looked in the direction he indicated. "Those are birds, Michael. Lots of them around here."

He shook his head. "Those are not just birds. Those are turkey vultures. They're scavengers with highly developed olfactory senses."

Nadia kept her gaze on the distant birds, which were barely discernible in the glare of the sun. "I thought vultures were only in California."

Wolfe smiled. "They're mistakenly called buzzards in this part of the country. I don't know their scientific name, but their common name is turkey vultures because they look like wild turkeys when on the ground." He paused for a brief moment. "Notice anything particular about their flight pattern?"

"Not from this distance. I can just barely make them out."

Nodding, Wolfe continued, "They're circling. Their olfactory senses allow them to locate dead carcasses underneath a canopy of trees."

She stiffened. "Do you think..."

"Possibly. I need to check it out."

"I'm coming with you."

He turned to look at her. "You don't have to, Nadia. He was my friend."

She gave him a grim smile. "I know, but we are in this together. Besides, we can search more ground faster if I help."

Looking back over his shoulder, he stared at the birds again. "I hope it's a deer or something."

The circling birds appeared larger as they drove

toward the tree line in the Jeep. Dressed in hiking boots, flannel shirts, jeans and Carhartt jackets, Wolfe and Picard trudged into the wooded area as the temperature hovered around freezing. Searching in grids, they quickly covered multiple acres of the timbered landscape, keeping in touch via small hand-held radios.

Three hours into their search, Wolfe heard, "Michael, I found something."

He stiffened. "Where are you?"

"About a hundred paces south of our last check in."

Orienting himself, he set off in the direction she indicated. Five minutes later, he was staring at the remains of a human male sitting on the ground. Its upper torso leaning against a large oak tree, the lower half semi-covered in fallen leaves. "He's been here a while, but it's Bobby."

Nadia looked at Michael. "How can you be sure, Michael? The face is almost gone."

He pointed to the corpse. "That's his favorite coat. He never wore anything else when it got cold."

"Do we call the sheriff now?"

"Yes, but I want to look around first."

She watched Wolfe take pictures with his cell phone. There was no emotion, just a professional detachment as he examined the area around the body. He bent down several times and moved leaves, but did not disturb the scene. Finally, he looked at her and motioned with his head it was time to go.

After he called the sheriff, Wolfe leaned against the Jeep's front quarter panel. Nadia poured coffee for both of them from a Yeti stainless-steel bottle.

He spoke first. "When the Sheriff gets here, don't mention to him what I'm going to tell you."

"Do not worry. I dislike talking to policemen."

He chuckled slightly. "We are supposed to believe

Bobby walked into the woods and committed suicide."

"I did not see a gun."

"There's a Ruger SR22 in his right hand covered in leaves. Above his right ear, covered by his hair, is a bullet hole without an exit wound. Probably a .22 hollow point, low velocity round. I couldn't tell for sure."

"I am sorry, Michael."

"Me too."

"Why did you say we are supposed to believe he killed himself."

"Poorly staged. Whoever did this didn't know Bobby very well."

"How's that?"

"Bobby was left-handed."

"How did you find the body, Michael?" Sherriff Bright watched Wolfe over the top of his reading glasses with suspicion in his eyes as he made notes on a clipboard.

Wolfe pointed to the sky. "Saw turkey vultures circling the area early this morning. We took a chance."

The sheriff, satisfied, nodded. "Looks like a suicide to me. I thought he was doing better."

"We did, too."

"I'll let you know what the autopsy tells us about the cause of death."

"Thank you, Sheriff."

"Did he have any next of kin I need to inform?"

"He has a brother in New York, but I don't think he'll give a shit."

"Why?"

"When I first started working with Bobby, I

contacted the guy. He couldn't be bothered to help his brother. Too busy, he said. Bobby warned me the family had kind of disowned him after he got back from overseas."

"What about parents?"

Wolfe shook his head. "Father is deceased, mother's in a memory care facility in North Carolina. Bobby told me she doesn't remember having kids. Advanced Alzheimer's. That was a year ago—she's probably deceased as well."

The sheriff nodded. "I still need to contact the brother."

"I don't think he'll care, Harold. But I'll get you the number."

Wolfe and Nadia waited until the coroner's office removed the body and the ambulance drove away before returning to their home. Michael was silent the entire trip. Both were cold from being out in mid-thirty temperatures all day, so after a warm shower, they sat at the kitchen table over re-heated bowls of soup made the previous evening.

Nadia broke the silence. "What are you thinking, Michael? You have been quiet a long time."

He shook his head as he took another spoonful of soup. "I can't for the life of me figure out why anyone would want Bobby dead. It doesn't make sense."

"How much do you know about his background?"

Wolfe stopped eating and looked at Nadia. "He was one of my spotters during Desert Storm. Come to think about it, I didn't know much at all. We were both barely out of our teens and caught up in the chaos of the moment. I knew a little about his family, but not much else. Why?"

She shrugged. "That was a long time ago. Things happen to people. They get mixed up in events they cannot control. The way you described him sounds like he may have been hiding from his past. Maybe it caught up with him."

Placing his elbows on the table, Wolfe frowned as he cupped his chin. "What are you getting at?"

"Do you know why his brother would not speak to him?"

"No, we never discussed it."

"Maybe you should ask the brother."

"What makes you think he would tell me anything?"

"Because I know you, Michael Wolfe. I may be the only person in the world who does." She gave him a soft smile. "You are not going to let this go."

He chuckled. "No, I don't suppose I will. You may be right about his past. I know he stayed in the military for a while after I left, but we never talked about it."

"What did he do after the military?"

Wolfe shrugged. "He never said. When I asked, he'd get this faraway look and go silent."

"Does that not sound a little strange?"

"At the time, no. But now..."

"There is something there."

"Yeah, I agree. Where do we start?"

"You..." She paused and smiled. "We should start with the brother."

He returned the smile and reached for her hand.

CHAPTER 12

ALBANY, NY

The Kendrick and Benson law firm occupied half of the second floor in a five-story building near downtown Albany. Wolfe noticed the no-frills décor seemed industrial and inexpensive, not the normal furnishings for a successful law firm. After checking in with the receptionist for their two o'clock appointment, he and Nadia waited in the lobby.

Nadia whispered in his ear, "Seems a bit quiet in here."

He nodded but did not verbally respond.

At 2:13 p.m., a tall, slender man with silver hair appeared from a hallway to their right. He offered his hand to Wolfe. "Kevin Benson, Mr. Lyon. You must be Mrs. Lyon?"

Nadia shook his hand and nodded.

Benson returned his attention to Wolfe. "Is this about my brother?"

"Yes, sir."

"Follow me."

Benson led them to a small conference room halfway down the hallway. When everyone settled around the large table, the lawyer asked, "What kind of trouble is Bobby in now?"

"I beg your pardon?" Wolfe barely hid his surprise at the question.

"I'm merely inquiring about what type of crime Bobby has committed this time."

Wolfe frowned. "Has the sheriff of Howell County, Missouri been in contact with you?"

"I figured it was about Bobby. There's nothing I can do for him, so I chose not to take the call. I'm only seeing you because you're here in Albany. What has he been charged with now?"

"Mr. Benson, your brother is dead."

The attorney blinked rapidly, his expression remaining neutral. He stared at Wolfe. "Dead?"

"Yes."

"How? I thought..."

Leaning forward on the conference table, Wolfe clasped his hands. "Gunshot wound to the head." At this point, the ex-sniper did not care about the lawyer's feelings which seemed uncaring. To Wolfe, who never experienced having a brother, the man's disrespect was unacceptable.

"You're talking about my brother Robert, correct?"

Wolfe nodded.

"What exactly do you wish me to do about this development?"

Nadia placed her hand on Wolfe's arm. She knew he was about to say something less than helpful. "Mr. Benson, Michael and Bobby were friends. They served together in the military. We wanted his next of kin to know."

"And you felt the need to travel all the way from

Missouri to tell me." He paused for a moment. With narrowed eyes, his focus switched from Wolfe to Nadia and back several times. "Where's the body?"

Frowning, Nadia replied, "A funeral home in West Plains, Missouri."

The attorney now looked at a spot on the wall above Wolfe's head. "How much money does he owe you, Mr. Lyon?"

"Mr. Benson, Bobby was debt free." Wolfe's face grew crimson.

"Bobby has owed a lot of money to a lot of people over the course of his life. I stopped paying his way out of debt a long time ago."

"Bobby didn't have any debts. I helped him clean himself up three years ago and he helped take care of my property. He was doing great. He even had a girlfriend."

Benson stared at Wolfe. "Are we talking about the same, Robert Benson?"

Wolfe's nostrils flared and his breathing increased in tempo. Again, Nadia placed her hand on his arm. She felt him relax slightly.

She smiled. "Mr. Benson, Michael and I saw a different side of your brother."

"One you could have seen if you had cared enough to call him or..." Wolfe's voice was low, on the verge of a growl.

"Michael, let Mr. Benson grieve. Our news must be a shock for him."

Benson's reaction startled both of them. "I am not grieving and nothing about my brother shocks me anymore, Mrs. Lyon. In fact, I'm tired of hearing about him. If he owes you money, too bad. Do not get the idea I will be bailing him out." He tapped his fingers on the table. "Our parents always believed in discipline. It was a very structured home. When our father passed away, the structure disappeared and Mother fell apart. Bobby was still at home at the time and I was in college five states away. After the funeral, my mother had a nervous breakdown and spent years in a facility. When Bobby graduated from high school, he immediately joined the Marines." He paused and looked at Wolfe. "Is that where you met him, Mr. Lyon?"

Michael nodded.

"I didn't see him again until the summer of 1995, seven years later. He was different. I was a young attorney by then and just starting my practice at a large firm in Buffalo. We had nothing in common and our visit lasted only a few hours. He left and I haven't seen him since. However, you are not the first to think I will pay his debts."

He paused, but when neither Wolfe or Nadia commented, he continued. "His lack of contributing to the care of our mother placed an unfair burden on my life and my finances."

Nadia could hear Wolfe taking deep breaths. She glanced at him and saw his nostrils flare as he spoke through clenched teeth. "Sorry for your burden, counselor. But that's not the Bobby Benson I knew."

"Then we must be talking about two different individuals." He paused and straightened, seeming to look down at Wolfe and Nadia. "Bobby didn't even attend her funeral."

Wolfe's demeanor changed suddenly. He tilted his head and raised an eyebrow. "When did she pass away?"

"February 2001."

Wolfe blinked several times. "Huh."

"Why are you surprised, Mr. Lyon?"

"Bobby told me his mother was still alive and suffering from Alzheimer's."

Benson shook his head. "No, she never had Alzheimer's."

Nadia frowned. "Mr. Benson, do you have a picture of Bobby?"

"Not here."

Wolfe opened a picture on his cell phone of himself and Bobby standing in front of the newly renovated cabin. He showed it to Benson. "Is that Bobby?"

The attorney frowned and took the phone for a better view. He handed it back to Wolfe. "No."

"Are you sure?"

"I believe I would know what my own brother looks like, Mr. Lyon."

"What was your brother's dominant hand?"

"Why do you ask?"

"Humor me."

"He was right-handed."

"Michael, what is going on?"

Wolfe stared out of the windshield of their rental car on the way back to the airport. "I have no idea. The man I saw working at the lumber store in West Plains was the Bobby Benson who worked with me as a spotter. We remembered the same things."

"Do you think his brother is mistaken?"

He hesitated before answering. "There is a way to find out."

"How?"

"I need to talk to someone."

"Joseph?"

He nodded.

"Will he take your call?"

The side of Wolfe's mouth twitched. "Yes. Even though he is a big shot right now, I still get requests from him."

Nadia smiled.

After returning the rental car and checking into their hotel room near the airport, Wolfe sent a text message with only a question mark to a phone number only he knew. The call came five minutes later.

"Good evening, Michael. Everything okay?" There was a bit of concern in Joseph Kincaid's voice, a tone Wolfe seldom heard from the man.

"Everything is good, Joseph. I have a request."

"Good. I received an excellent report about your last assignment."

"Glad to hear."

"Is there anything wrong?"

"No. Nadia and I have a mystery on our hands. I need information."

"Okay, shoot."

"I need the military records of a Marine Sergeant Robert Benson, discharged 2008."

"Hmmm..."

"Can you get them?"

"Should be able to. It might be tomorrow."

"Not a problem. We're on a six-a.m. flight. Call in the afternoon."

"I'll send it to your secondary email box. I won't ask where you are."

"Probably best."

With the flight time and two-plus hour drive from the Springfield Branson National Airport, Michael and Nadia did not arrive at the Howell County sheltered house until mid-afternoon. An email waited for retrieval when he opened the account. Wolfe read it, downloaded the file attached and then deleted the email.

The military file revealed little Wolfe did not already know about Bobby, except the last year of his enlistment. He'd served various short stints in the brig for disorderly conduct.

Wolfe frowned as he read the last few pages of his friend's military record. His thoughts were interrupted by Nadia appearing next to him.

"Michael, I thought the sheriff was supposed to tell you about the autopsy report."

"He was. I haven't heard anything, yet. Why?"

"I just got a text message from Bobby's girlfriend. She indicated the sheriff told her his death has been ruled a suicide. She wants to talk to you."

The corner of Wolfe's mouth twitched. "He hasn't contacted me. Wonder what that's all about."

CHAPTER 13

RURAL HOWELL COUNTY MISSOURI

J ana Meyers inherited the home, originally built by her grandparents, from her father when he passed away. The structure appeared well maintained but in need of a few modern updates. Two stories with columns across the front portico, it still possessed the wood bench suspended by heavy iron chains on the right side. Jana sat on the porch swing, moving slowly back and forward despite the cold afternoon temperature. As Wolfe and Nadia parked in her gravel driveway, she stood.

Wolfe, having only met the woman once, did not feel he knew her, whereas Nadia thought of her as a friend. When Nadia stepped out of the Jeep, Jana ran to her and sobbed as they embraced. The woman's eyes were red from crying and Wolfe wondered how long she had been on the porch waiting for them.

Not wishing to intrude on the woman's grief, he stayed in the yard as the two friends climbed the three steps leading up to the porch and entered the house.

He had another reason for staying outside. He noticed Bobby's fifteen-year-old Ford F-150 parked next to the detached garage. Curious, he examined the truck bed. Except for a few small twigs and brown dried leaves, it was clean. He checked the cab and found the driver's side unlocked. As he opened it, he immediately noticed the uncluttered interior, a condition Bobby felt unnatural for a working man's pickup. With his curiosity satisfied, he closed the truck door and headed back to the front porch to enter the home.

Jana Meyer sat in a high-back Boston Rocker, each hand gripping the wooden arms hard enough to cause white knuckles. She stared at a blank space on the opposite wall, tears flowing down her round face. Nadia stood next to her with a hand on her shoulder. Neither woman spoke as Wolfe entered the living room.

Looking up at him, Jana asked, "Why?"

"I wish I knew."

More tears flowed. Shorter than Nadia by five inches, Jana Meyer possessed curly blonde hair she wore not quite to her shoulders. A round face, crystal blue eyes and small petite nose completed the package. Today the eyes were red from crying and her hair was disheveled. A year ago, when Nadia had needed her hair trimmed, Bobby recommended his girlfriend, a local beautician. The two had developed, over the course of the year, as much of a friendship as Nadia would allow.

Wolfe leaned against the brick fireplace as he studied the younger woman. He had questions. "Jana, why is Bobby's truck here?"

She looked up at Wolfe, sniffled and said, "Three weeks ago, my car was in the shop. Bobby was letting me use his pickup." She dabbed at her tears with a tissue. "Did you know he was promoted to yard supervisor a month ago?"

Frowning, Wolfe shook his head. "Nadia and I've been out of town. No, we didn't know that."

"Well, he was. He seemed happy and content. We even started talking about getting married." Her voice shook as more tears streaked her face.

Nadia said softly, "Tell Michael what you told me a minute ago."

Wiping her tears again with the tissue, she stared up at him. "When I dropped him off at the lumberyard, he told me I didn't have to pick him up after work. An old marine buddy was in town and they were going to dinner. If he needed a ride, he would call me. He never called and that was the last time I saw him."

Standing straight, Wolfe's expression darkened. "Did he say who the friend was?"

She shook her head. "He might have, but I don't remember the name."

"Did you report him missing?"

She nodded.

"Did you tell the sheriff about this friend?"

Nodding, she wiped her eyes. "They didn't seem to give a shit. One of the deputies I spoke to told me he had disappeared before, sometimes for weeks."

"Did you talk to the lumberyard?"

Looking up, she glared at Wolfe. "They told me they made a mistake in hiring Bobby—he was back to his old habit of not showing up for work. It felt like I was the only person worried about him. Everyone else blew it off as Bobby acting like his old self again."

"You didn't believe that?"

"No. We've been dating for two years. He's not like..." She stopped, her eyes grew wide and the sobbing returned. After a few moments, she calmed and finished her sentence. "He wasn't like that anymore."

Wolfe turned to a window next to the fireplace and gazed over the yard. "Why is Bobby's truck so clean inside?"

"He did that before he let me use it."

Nodding, Wolfe remained quiet for a long time. Nadia busied herself with Jana as the two went to the kitchen to make coffee.

Five minutes later, Nadia walked up behind Wolfe and placed her hand on his back. "Do you want some coffee?"

He shook his head. "I need to have a talk with Sheriff Bright. Somebody is lying to us."

"I'll stay here with Jana while you're gone. She's been by herself since he disappeared."

Wolfe turned. "I won't be gone long."

"When was it ruled a suicide, Sheriff?"

"Yesterday. No evidence of criminal intent, Michael. No signs of a struggle, at the site or at his cabin. Were you ever in the military?"

Wolfe shook his head. Bright knew him only as Michael Lyon, a local businessman who helped Bobby Benson.

"It's hard on some guys. Some never get over the experience. I was a marine, just like Bobby. I guess I was lucky. I've seen more shit as a sheriff than I did as a marine. You know, of course, veterans have a higher percent of suicide than the general population, especially those with PTSD."

Wolfe patience was growing thin. "Did you talk to the girlfriend?"

"Several times. She was unhelpful."

Wolfe did not respond immediately. He stared at Bright for several moments realizing the sheriff was done with the matter. "How long had he been dead?"

"Coroner believes about three weeks. Did you get a hold of the brother?"

Wolfe nodded.

"He won't take my calls."

"I know, he told me."

"What did he say?"

"He basically disowned him."

"Great. Now what do we do with the body?"

Wolfe suddenly realized the sheriff was telling him the subject was closed, no more discussion. "I'll handle the arrangements and pay for the service. Have him taken to one of the local funeral homes."

"Which one?"

"Don't know. Which is the best?"

"Cooper-Mason."

"I'll get in touch with them."

After returning to Jana Meyer's house and picking up Nadia, he drove straight to the funeral home. Wolfe went in and returned five minutes later.

"They agreed to extract DNA from the body for me."

Nadia nodded. "Who's going to do the test? It's not like we have a lot of choices around here."

"I've got a plan. Do you think she's lying to us?'

She shook her head rapidly, her long hair flowing back and forth with the sudden movement. "No, her grief is genuine."

"Kind of what I thought, too. Just wanted your perspective."

"I am still trying to get used to this small-town atmosphere. I do not understand how everybody can be so friendly and then so uncaring if you make one mistake. It is certainly a good thing no one knows our past."

Wolfe chuckled. "Let's keep it that way."

Silence prevailed as they drove back to their underground home in rural Howell County. Ten minutes later, she turned to him. "You are too quiet. What are you thinking?"

"I can't figure out why the sheriff lied to us the night we called him from Bobby's cabin. He already knew he was missing, yet..."

"I did not think of this. He acted like he did not know anything about Bobby."

"Yeah, it appeared to be a big surprise."

"What now?"

"The marines should have a DNA signature they can compare. There is only one person I know who has the ability to get the sample compared to his marine record, no questions asked."

"Joseph?"

"Yeah, one of only two people in this world I trust."

She smiled. "And, just who is the other person, Michael Wolfe?"

He returned her smile and glanced at her. "You."

"That was the correct answer. You are permitted to sleep with me tonight."

They both laughed.

One Week Later

The small bistro in Arlington, Virginia maintained

a reputation as an out-of-the-way gathering spot for authentic Parisian food and an extensive wine list. Joseph Kincaid sat at a corner table in the back, waiting for Wolfe to arrive. A glass of French Bordeaux sat in front of him as he checked the crowd for anyone paying too much attention to his presence. None appeared to care.

Wolfe arrived ten minutes later. After shaking his hand and sitting across from his old CIA controller, he said, "This place looks familiar. Have we met here before?'

"Years ago, Michael. Before you left for Israel. We sat at this exact table."

"I thought so."

"So, why did you want to meet me so far away from the DC crowd."

The corner of Wolfe's mouth twitched. "Let's just say I'm not overly excited about being spotted by certain individuals."

"Fair enough. What's on your mind?"

Both men stopped their conversation as a young college-aged girl took Michael's drink order. When she left, he responded, "I need a DNA sample compared to military records of Sergeant Robert Benson."

"Why the interest?"

"There are too many inconsistencies about his death."

"Such as?'

Wolfe took a sip of the Chardonnay the waitress had just left. He smiled and took another. "He was one of my spotters during Desert Storm."

"I remember now. Who's the other one?"

"Rick Flores."

"He's with the FBI, trains bureau snipers."

"Huh, didn't know that. Rick's a good man. He

doesn't know about me, does he?"

"No. Like the rest of the FBI, he thinks you're dead."

"Good, keep it that way."

A nod was his answer.

"Anyway, I ran into Bobby Benson a little over five years ago in West Plains. He was having issues with PTSD. I helped him get back on his feet and he assisted me with the construction of my home. We fixed up the cabin on the southern edge of my property as a place for him to live. Since then, he found a girlfriend and was promoted where he worked. He was doing good."

"Glad to hear. There's a however in this story, isn't there."

Wolf nodded and sipped his wine. "A big one. He disappeared about four weeks ago. No one seemed to care except his girlfriend. And me."

"What happened?"

"Nadia and I found his body deep inside a wooded section of my land. It appeared he committed suicide."

Joseph was quiet. He studied his Merlot and took a sip. "Appeared?"

"Yeah, he had a Ruger SR22 in his right hand and a small entry wound above his right ear."

The expression on Joseph's face did not change, except his attention was on Michael, not the glass of wine. "What are the inconsistencies?"

"The Bobby I knew was left handed. He could barely wipe his nose with his right."

"Okay, what else?"

"His military record listed a brother—Kevin, in Albany, New York. We paid the man a visit."

Joseph stiffened.

"Don't worry. We introduced ourselves as Mr. and

Mrs. Lyon." Wolfe paused and took a sip of his wine. "He's an attorney in a not-so-successful law-firm. He also could not have cared less about Bobby and tells a completely different story about him."

"Siblings sometimes don't like each other."

"I wouldn't know. He claims Bobby didn't have PTSD and was always right-handed."

"Huh. Maybe he didn't know Bobby had it."

"No, I even showed him a picture. He told me, in no uncertain terms, the man in the picture was not his brother."

A frown was his response.

"Since the brother disowned him, I took care of the funeral and we buried him the day before yesterday. But not before the funeral home extracted a DNA sample." Wolfe reached into the inside pocket of his leather bomber jacket and handed Joseph a tan postcard-sized envelope with a small vial in it. "I need this analyzed and compared to Bobby's military record."

Joseph accepted the packet and immediately placed it in an inside pocket of his navy-blue blazer. "What are your suspicions?"

Wolfe shook his head. "Not sure yet."

"But you have a theory."

This time the answer was a nod.

"And that is?"

"This is pretty farfetched, Joseph."

"That's okay. I like farfetched."

Wolfe smiled. "The man who spotted for me in Desert Storm and the man I helped in West Plains are two different individuals."

CHAPTER 14

WASHINGTON, DC

Deputy Director of Analysis Gerald Reid listened to his morning briefing as the various department heads summarized overnight events. His promotion to Deputy Director four weeks earlier had solidified his goal of being Director within the next few years. He listened intently, trying to decide who among his direct reports were competent and who were not.

At forty-five minutes into the scheduled hour-long meeting, Kendra Burges entered the conference room, walked quickly to his side, handed him a sheet of paper, and bent down to whisper in his ear. As he listened, his eyes widened and a slight smile appeared on his lips. When she finished, she left the room as quickly as she entered. Reid continued to stare at the page handed to him.

He raised his hand and the current speaker stopped. Standing, Reid cleared his throat. "I apologize for the interruption. I need to terminate our meeting early. Please be prepared to stay a few minutes longer tomorrow. Thank you all for your time."

With this statement, he exited the conference room through the door leading to his office.

Kendra stood next to his desk. He looked at her. "When did this come in?"

"It was originally sent to the individual who took your old job. She received it yesterday morning and apparently decided the information wasn't important enough to forward immediately. I just got it a few moments ago."

Reid nodded, his anger at the delay squelched by the sheer implications of the information. "Were there any additional confirmations?"

She shook her head. Reid sat behind his desk, taking his attention away from the memo. "I want to see the actual photo."

She nodded and told him how to retrieve it on the laptop. Two minutes later, he was staring at the image of Michael Wolfe passing through a TSA security gate at Reagan Washington National Airport.

Kendra pointed at the picture. "Security cameras took this snapshot at 6 a.m. yesterday. The facial recognition software flagged it from an alert you posted after Wolfe and Picard disappeared in Barcelona over two years ago. Apparently, the alert was never canceled."

Reid did not comment right away. He stared at the photo and zoomed in on it. "Were there any other hits at the airport?"

"No, that's the only one."

"Have you checked flight manifests for his known aliases?"

"I have someone on it right now. So far, there was a

Patrick Ryan on the passenger list of a United flight to Denver, but the age was wrong."

Reid turned to look at her, his eyes narrowed. "How wrong?"

"The boy was only ten."

He nodded and returned his attention to the laptop. "What was the percent of certainty this person is Wolfe?"

"About eighty-eight percent."

"Hmm... Not exact, but close." He turned from the laptop to stare at his assistant. "If he is, in fact, alive, it means, Picard is as well. How they fooled the Israelis with the DNA will be a matter for a later investigation. For now, we will assume they are both alive. If we get lucky, they'll make another mistake, so we need to be ready."

"What are you classifying him as?"

With a grim smile, Reid looked at Burges. "For now, we will classify our search as a possible foreign threat. Use his German alias and passport photo for identification." He turned and stared at the photo on his laptop again. "We are putting a soft inquiry out for Mr. Hans Lauer, a possible German terrorist."

The notification was short, a one-line mention at the end of the President's detailed morning briefing. Not the one given directly to POTUS by the Deputy Director of the CIA, but the more detailed one provided to the National Security Advisor. Joseph's position as the new president's NSA meant this report landed on his desk. He stared at the name and thumbnail photo, read the notice again, and frowned. The photo was old, at least ten or fifteen years. Michael did not resemble the photo anymore. His concern centered more around Gerald Reid's motivation for putting the inquiry out than him being able to locate the ex-sniper.

As the NSA, Joseph was allowed certain privileges other members of the White House staff were not. A personal Samsung Smart Phone rested in its usual spot in the top right-hand drawer of his desk. He typed a short five-word message. *How soon to secure comm?* He replaced the phone in the drawer and went about his normal routine.

"Wonder what this is all about?" Wolfe showed the text message to Nadia, who frowned. He continued. "We haven't been to the condo for a while. Think we should go?'

She nodded. "Yes, it is too depressing here. I'm ready for a change of scenery."

He smiled. "Have you listened to yourself recently?"

"No, did I say something wrong?"

"Not at all." He chuckled. "You've started using contractions. You just said I'm instead of I am, like you usually do."

She sighed. "I am becoming an American. Pray for my soul, Michael."

Still chuckling, Wolfe typed in a short reply to the text message from Joseph. *Three to four hours.*

He hit the send icon and waited. His reply came two minutes later. *Call this number.* The number was displayed after the message.

Satisfied with the communication, he packed their laptop in a backpack.

After setting all of the security measures in the house and securing the multiple locks, they drove toward their condo near Branson.

Two and a half hours later, Wolfe unlocked the front door to their condo. The air was stale and the temperature cool. While Nadia attended to the thermostat, Wolfe retrieved the laptop and proceeded to make a secure VoIP phone call using procedure learned over the course of their existence as Michael and Nadia Lyon.

When the call was answered, Joseph asked. "What time did your flight leave out of Reagan?"

"Around six a.m. Why?"

"Your image was caught on a TSA security camera."

Wolfe was silent for a few moments. They had received a text message from JR during their drive over alerting them to the incident. Remembering the hacker's request for Joseph to be unaware of this monitoring, he did not mention it. "Who activated the facial recognition search?"

"Don't know. The only reason I know about it is a mention in our daily brief about a soft inquiry and BOLO on your old German *nom de guerre*."

"How many times was my image caught?"

"From the information I have, only once."

"Good."

"How did you fly back?"

"Reagan to Atlanta then to Des Moines. I used my private plane from there."

"The positive is there is no mention of a Michael Lyon in the briefing, only the German name. Which tells me they couldn't trace you after you went through the security gate."

Nadia looked at Wolfe with concern. He glanced at her, smiled and shook his head. With his attention back to the call, he said, "Nadia and I will avoid commercial flights for the foreseeable future. We can use my plane if needed."

"Okay, I'll keep an eye on Reid."

"Thank you." Wolfe paused for a few seconds. "Have you received anything back on the DNA analysis?"

"Yes, about an hour ago. The DNA you gave me matched the records on file with the Marines. The body you found in the woods was the Robert Benson you served with in the Marines."

Wolfe drummed his fingers on the table where the laptop sat. The corner of his mouth twitched as he stared out the window. He returned his attention to the laptop. "What does his Marine file say about his handedness?"

"His military file indicates he was right-handed."

More silence as Wolfe took in the information. "Okay, Joseph, keep me updated about Reid and whatever he thinks he's trying to accomplish."

"Will do."

The call ended and Wolfe turned to Nadia. "Did Bobby ever spend the night at Jana's house?"

Nadia nodded. "She mentioned it several times when I was getting my hair trimmed. Why?"

"I'm not too worried about the airport incident. We'll just be more careful when we fly. Something is very wrong here. We need DNA from the man Jana was seeing."

She tilted her head slightly. "What about his cabin?"

Shaking his head, Wolfe placed the laptop in the backpack. "I already thought of that. Someone did a professional job of sanitizing it. There wasn't a hair left. Bobby wasn't much of a housekeeper so I noticed it the night we got back from KC. The place was way too clean."

"Why did you not say something?"

He was quiet for a few moments. "Until I had the DNA results, it really didn't matter. Now it does." He glanced at his watch. "I need to drive back to Jana's."

Nadia closed her eyes. "There you go again. We are in this together, Michael. We need to drive back to Jana's and then come back here. Right?"

Smiling, he nodded.

CHAPTER 15

NEAR WEST PLAINS, MO

It was nearing four p.m. when they parked in front of the hair salon. Nadia went in under the pretense of getting her hair trimmed. She reappeared at the Jeep in less than five minutes, her eyebrows drawn together. In a measured voice, she said, "Jana did not show up for work today."

Wolfe raised an eyebrow. "She didn't call in?"

Nadia shook her head. "The owner was furious with her. She told me everybody in the shop had to work harder to cover all of her appointments."

After backing the Jeep out of the angled parking slot, he drove the vehicle away from the downtown area. "Did they try to call her?"

Another shake of her head. "No. She also told me this was occurring more and more recently. When I mentioned the death of Bobby, the woman just shrugged and asked me who I wanted to trim my hair." She paused and stared at Wolfe. "She did not care that Jana might be in trouble or something might have happened to her. It was more about her being inconvenienced today. Michael, why do people act that way?"

"I have no answer."

"I hate this place."

"The salon or the town."

"Both."

Realizing anything he said would escalate her aggravation, he remained quiet.

Twenty minutes later, he drove the Jeep slowly by the old farmhouse. The old Ford F-150 remained in the same spot as their last visit, but Jana's car was not parked behind it or visible from the road.

Nadia said, "It does not appear she is home."

Wolfe did not respond. He parked the Jeep fifty feet past the drive. "I saw something we need to check out. Bring your purse."

"What?"

He shook his head, "It might be nothing, but..."

The rural county road where Jana's home resided saw few vehicles transiting its path. What little traffic it did see came from other residents of the remote area.

Extracting the Walther PPK from his ankle holster, Wolfe exited the SUV. He held the gun close to his thigh as he approached the home's front porch. Nadia followed, grasping the Glock 43 hidden inside her purse.

As they stepped onto the porch, he pointed to the slightly ajar front door. Nadia nodded. Neither spoke as they prepared to enter the home. Wolfe opened the screen door and yelled. "Hey, Jana. It's Nadia and Michael. You here?"

Silence answered from the dark interior. He repeated his greeting. More silence. He turned and nodded at Nadia. She withdrew her Glock and held it with both hands pointed down.

Quietly, he opened the inner door and surveyed the living area of the home. Chaos greeted them. Overturned furniture, scattered books, broken picture frames, smashed house plants and torn curtains dominated the scene. He cautiously moved toward the stairs and the upstairs bedrooms. With Nadia close behind, he mounted the steps two at a time. These rooms resembled the lower living area with bed linens flung onto the floor, cut mattresses and torn pillows.

Wolfe turned to Nadia and whispered, "Check the other bedrooms, I'll check the bathroom."

What he feared might be there was not. The room appeared untouched. Carefully, he searched the vanity. He found several objects in the second middle drawer on the right—a man's razor, a can of shaving cream, a Right Guard deodorant stick and a hairbrush. He removed the cap of the Right Guard and found what he hoped for, hairs from the underarm of the user. Next, he checked the brush and saw additional hairs with roots still attached.

When Nadia appeared from the other bedroom, he asked. "Anything?"

"No, but there is a pattern to the destruction."

"I agree." He showed her the hairbrush and deodorant. "Let's check the kitchen. I need a Ziploc bag for these. Maybe we can learn who the man I thought was Bobby really is."

Wolfe called the Sheriff after they returned to the Jeep to report the disappearance of Jana Meyers.

Wolfe leaned against the front quarter panel of his Jeep now parked in front of the house. He watched Howell County deputies scurrying in and out of Jana's home.

Nadia sat in the passenger seat with the door open, looking up at Michael. "How much longer do you think they will need to determine she is not there?"

He chuckled, glanced at her and shook his head.

Both grew quiet as Sheriff Bright walked toward them. With his hands on his hips, he pinned them with a glare. "Why were you two out here?"

"Nadia uses Jana to trim her hair. We stopped by the salon and were told she hadn't shown up for work. We got worried. Seems we had a reason to be."

The sheriff stared hard at Wolfe. Finally, he nodded and wrote something in a small notebook. "Did you go in?"

Wolfe shook his head. "When we got here the front door was ajar, so we looked in. That's when we called you."

Another nod. "She's not here and her car is gone. From what we can tell this happened last night after she got home from work."

"Oh?"

"Where were you and Nadia?"

Smiling, Wolfe tilted his head. "Condo in Branson. We ate at the Olive Garden. Want a receipt?"

Ignoring the comment, the sheriff flipped a few pages back and read from his notes. "Can of soup was on the stove, opened and ready to pour into a pan sitting there. A bowl and silverware were on the counter. The kitchen looks relatively untouched. All the bedrooms and living areas are trashed."

Wolfe closed his eyes and shook his head. "What's going on, Sheriff?"

"I wish I knew, Mr. Lyon. I wish I knew." He turned and walked away.

Wolfe glanced at Nadia when Bright was out of earshot. "We probably need to go back to Branson and get an Olive Garden receipt."

She chuckled and nodded.

Though the return trip to their condo took two-and-a-half hours, neither of them spoke until they were thirty minutes from their condo, Nadia turned to him. "What if the DNA from the hairs you have match the DNA from Bobby's Marines records?"

"It won't."

"But what if it does?"

"Trust me, it won't."

"Do you think he staged his own death?"

Wolfe shook his head.

She stared at him, waiting for an answer.

Finally, he glanced at her. "You mentioned you saw a pattern in how the house was torn up. Care to share what you observed?"

She glanced briefly at him. "Same thing you saw."

"Which was?"

"There was no method to it. The whole scene looked random, like someone just started throwing stuff around."

He nodded. "What else?"

"I didn't see any signs of a struggle or any blood."

"Neither did I. Don't you find that odd?"

Nadia turned to look at him again, "Do you think she staged it?"

"Yes, and I think she had help."

"Send the DNA samples to the following PO Box." Joseph recited the address as Wolfe wrote it down.

"Joseph, I need another favor."

After a moment's hesitation he heard. "Such as?"

"How hard would it be to have airline passenger manifests searched?"

"Depends on the reason. Why?"

"I'm curious about something."

"What might that be, Michael?"

"We didn't see any signs of a struggle at the house. Nadia and I believe it was staged to make whoever investigated her disappearance think it was a kidnapping. It was a diversion designed to limit the search for her and her accomplice."

"What do you mean, limit the search?"

"Keep it local. My guess is they'll find her car in some remote location."

"Okay, how can you be sure?"

"Think about who Nadia and I worked for. We were trained to notice deception."

Joseph chuckled. "You apparently see something more sinister in this than I do."

"That's why I need the DNA analysis as quick as possible, plus the passenger manifests."

"Which airports?"

"I'd check Memphis, Springfield, although that might be too obvious, Little Rock, Tulsa, KC and possibly St. Louis. Memphis is a bigger hub—I'd start there."

"Do you think she's traveling under a false name?"

"Getting authentic-looking fake identification documents you can travel with isn't that easy. Plus, it takes a lot of money, something Jana didn't have. My guess is, if she and her companion flew, it would be under their real names."

There was silence for a few moments. "FedEx won't deliver to a PO Box. Overnight the samples to my home address." He recited the information. "I'll get them to the lab the same day." He paused. "If your suspicions are correct, what are the implications?"

"I wish I knew, Joseph. I wish I knew."

The call ended and Wolfe closed down the laptop.

He looked up at Nadia, who had listened to the entire conversation. "What do you think?"

"I do not know the implications either, Michael. If what you suspect happened, someone posed as Bobby for all these years and then killed the real one to hide it."

Wolfe shook his head. "Something else is going on here. Something we aren't seeing. There are too many questions without answers. I think we need to wait for the DNA results before we start speculating."

She stared at him for a few seconds, then just nodded.

CHAPTER 16

VIRGINIA COUNTRYSIDE, SOUTHEAST OF ALEXANDRIA

Kendra Burges woke early and rolled over, her outstretched arm finding only empty space on the bed. The absence of Gerald Reid brought her to total alertness. She always rose before him. Where was he? She stood after throwing back the covers and rushed toward his office at the opposite end of the hallway.

No Gerald. The room was dark with an inactive computer. Her mind raced as she hurried to the kitchen. There she found him pouring water into the Cuisinart coffeemaker. "Gerald, what are you doing?"

He turned, a faraway look on his face. "Making coffee."

"You never make coffee and you never get up this early."

"Couldn't sleep."

"What's wrong?"

"He's out there alive somewhere. I know it."

She did not respond but watched as he scooped more coffee into the filter. Finally, she said, "That's enough."

He turned. "Beg your pardon?"

"Enough, that's enough coffee grounds."

"Oh..." He stopped. "You sure? Doesn't look like enough."

She stepped over to glance at his preparation. "More than enough." She closed the coffeemaker and pressed the start button. "What's wrong?"

"I know Wolfe's alive. He's mocking me by avoiding detection."

She took a deep breath. "It could have been a false-positive on the facial recognition. It's happened before. You know the software is not always one hundred percent accurate."

He shook his head. "No, he's alive. I never did believe he and Picard were killed in Mexico City. They're too smart."

She stared at him. "Why are you so obsessed with this? It's not like you to fixate on something so—trivial."

His nostrils flared and he screamed. "TRIVIAL! Michael Wolfe may be a lot of things, but he is not trivial."

She narrowed her eyes and crossed her arms. "Then what is it? Why are you so concerned about the possibility he might be alive? It's been over two years. Don't you think if he were alive, we would have heard by now."

Staring at her, his face turned crimson. The room fell silent except for the hiss and sputtering of the last drops of water heating on the coils of the coffee maker. Then, just as quickly, his expression softened. He turned, "Want coffee?"

With the sudden change in his demeanor unnerving, she stared at the back of his head while he poured a cup. He turned and offered it to her. Accepting it, she remained quiet.

As he poured another he said, "Michael Wolfe was one of the best Marine snipers ever trained. He made impossible shots and had the patience of Job." Reid looked over his shoulder, "Rumors flourished about who assassinated an American ex-pat living on the Island of Madagascar in 2014. It was a windy afternoon on the eastern shore of the island near a town called Toamasina. Retired three-star General William Little was entertaining a few guests on the veranda of his 10,000 square foot mansion." He paused and sipped his coffee. "Did I mention that General Little was suspected of pilfering millions of dollars of artifacts from both Kuwait and Iraq during Desert Storm?"

She shook her head but remained quiet.

"We in the CIA knew about it, but before we could touch him, he disappeared and later showed up in Madagascar with millions of dollars from the auctioned-off antiquities. Did you know Madagascar does not have an extradition treaty with the United States?"

"Common knowledge."

"Yes, that's why Little was there. He was safely out of the US government's reach. Anyway, in the middle of the veranda, while talking to his guests, his head suddenly explodes." Reid smiled as he said. "Brain tissue and blood splattered everyone around him."

"Gerald!"

He looked at her. "It's true. I..." He paused for a heartbeat. "read the report. His security guards couldn't figure out where the shot came from until they found a disturbed area on the beach 1600 meters from the veranda. The sniper left the spent shell on top of a sheet of paper with all the names of the men who died under Little's command in Desert Storm." He took another sip of coffee. "Do you know how far 1600 meters is?"

"No."

"It's a mile. The sniper made a headshot from a mile away, on a hot, windy afternoon in Madagascar. Not too many men in the world have the skill to make a shot like that, Kendra. Michael Wolfe does."

"So, what does this have to do with your obsession with Michael Wolfe?"

"I'm getting to that. As a sniper during Operation Desert Shield and Desert Storm, he earned the reputation as one of the deadliest snipers in-theater. No one knows the total of his confirmed kills. I heard estimates it was somewhere between Carlos Hathcock's ninety-three confirmed and Chris Kyle's one hundred sixty."

"Surely the Marines must know."

He shook his head. "Officially his Marine total is only twenty-seven. After leaving the Marines, he graduated from Georgetown University with a degree in International Business Management. The CIA recruited him and he worked for us from 1999 to 2004. He met an Israeli woman, fell in love and moved to Tel-Aviv. There are rumors he still worked for the CIA at this time, but I can't confirm it. He and the woman married and he assisted the Mossad when they needed his skills."

"This isn't the Picard woman, is it?"

"No, the wife was killed by a Palestinian suicide bomber in an outdoor market six months after the wedding."

Kendra nodded.

"From what I was told, by a source within Mossad,

Michael never got over her death." He paused and sipped his coffee. "He possesses an innate ability with languages. He's fluent in French, German, Spanish, Hebrew and last I knew passable in Arabic and Urdu."

"Was that why the Mossad recruited him?"

Reid nodded. "Yes, since he didn't look Jewish, he could slip in and out of most European and Middle Eastern countries without being noticed."

"What did he do for them?"

"My source would not tell me, but I can guess."

"Assassinations?"

"More than likely."

"Why did he leave Israel?'

Shaking his head, Reid refilled his coffee. "That part is vague, but it occurred several years after he started living with Nadia Picard. My source believes it was a disagreement with Asa Gerlis."

"Isn't he dead?"

Reid gave her a sly smile. "Yes."

"So, what about Wolfe. What happened to him?"

"He returned to the states and fell off our radar."

She smirked. "I don't believe that, Gerald."

"It's true. However, during this period a lot of suspected terrorists met with untimely deaths, particularly in Belgium, which was becoming a hotbed for Islamic Fundamentalism in Europe."

"So, you think Wolfe was responsible?"

Reid shrugged. "Officially, the agency will not acknowledge it, but I believe it was him. So, you see, my dear Kendra, Michael Wolfe is not trivial. He is a menace. A menace with the skills of a trained assassin. It is my mission to find this threat and stop him from doing whatever it is he has planned."

Joseph Kincaid's cell phone chirped as he looked at the time. Twenty-two minutes after six in the evening. He smiled at the caller ID and answered. "Sorry, I'm running late tonight, Mary."

Mary Lawson was tall and slender, with shoulder length tightly curled black hair. Her heritage came from Jamaica, France and for attitude, a bit of Louisiana Cajun. After graduating in the top ten from Columbia University Law School, she had spent her entire career at the Justice Department and retired as the deputy director of the Office of Violence Against Women. Having met during the first few years of their careers working for the government, she and Joseph had fallen in love over time and were devoted to each other. Despite their affection, both pursued separate paths, but not other lovers. Now retired and married living in a rural part of Southwest Missouri, she and Joseph had made a deal with the current occupant of the White House. Joseph would serve as the National Security Adviser for the first year of his presidency. He was nine months into the arrangement.

"I kind of thought so. I was out all day as well and thought you might like to meet at our favorite place for dinner."

"I'd love to." He glanced at the time again. "I can be there by seven."

"Great. I'll take Uber and then we can come home together."

By eight-thirty, after sharing an entrée of eggplant three-cheese lasagna, they were only three-quarters of the way through a delicious bottle of Chianti. She reached into her purse and pulled out an envelope addressed to Joseph. "This arrived by FedEx just before I left the house. I had to sign for it."

He accepted the package, glancing at the return address. With a slight smile, he opened it and skimmed the contents. "Interesting."

"Am I allowed to ask what it's about?"

"It's the answer to a mystery a friend of mine discovered."

She sipped her wine and looked over the top of the glass. "In other words, his eyes only."

Joseph nodded.

Wolfe answered the call, noting the time: 9:03 p.m. "Good evening, Joseph. A little late for you, isn't it?"

"Not really. I have news for you on the DNA samples."

One eyebrow rose. "Oh, tell me."

"The DNA collected at the woman's house is not the same person you found on your property."

"Kind of what I guessed. Any idea who he might be?"

"Don't know yet. I will have to run it through several DNA databases. Although I can tell you one thing."

Wolfe remained quiet.

"Without comparing the two men's DNA to a mother or father, the results are unofficial. But similarities between the two samples suggest they share one parent. The two men were half-brothers."

CHAPTER 17

SOUTHWEST MISSOURI

After a restless night, Wolfe stood on the back deck of the condo, his hands on the railing, his gaze on a hawk soaring over the trees on the opposite side of the cove. A noise from behind him did not divert his concentration on the bird.

Nadia closed the sliding glass door, walked over to where he stood and placed her hand on his back. "You spoke to Joseph over twelve hours ago. You have said nothing since."

With a glance over at her, he said, "Still trying to sort it out."

"Tell me. Maybe I can help."

"As you and I suspected, there are two men involved. The real Bobby, who we found in the woods, and the man I helped, who posed as Bobby."

"Joseph confirmed?"

"Yes, he confirmed. The DNA analysis revealed they were half-brothers."

Nadia remained quiet, watching the hawk as well.

Finally, she returned her attention to Wolfe. "That could explain why the older brother did not recognize the picture you showed him."

His response was a nod.

After several moments, she said, "Where was the real Bobby all these years?"

"That my dear, Nadia, is what I have been trying to figure out. So far, I don't even have a hypothesis."

She smiled. "A hypothesis, Michael?"

"Sorry. It's the only word that fits."

"We do have a source for more information, though."

He looked over at her. She still followed the hawk as it caught an updraft and gained height. "What source?"

"The older brother. Surely he would know about a younger half-brother."

Wolfe nodded. "Think he'd take my call?"

She shook her head. "I believe we will have to confront him face to face."

"We're not flying commercial."

"No, but you do have your own plane."

"Let me think about it. Before we go, I need a little more background on Kevin Benson."

The 1979 Beechcraft B55 Baron rested quietly in its own hangar on the western side of the 5101-foot-long runway that comprised the West Plains Regional Airport. It was located ten miles northeast of West Plains, which allowed Wolfe and Nadia to access it without venturing into town, a task they wished to avoid on this particular day. Wolfe leased the building but owned the plane.

He bought the plane, sight unseen, from an estate

sale in Atlanta, after returning to the United States. It was shipped to the hangar in several sections via flatbed trucks. Now fully restored with modern avionics, electronics, engines, and props, the plane flew better than when new.

Leasing a large building at the airport allowed Wolfe to leave his Jeep inside while using the plane. After parking the SUV next to the Baron, he exited, smiled and admired it. While the cost of a functioning used 1979 Baron would have been cheaper, this aircraft possessed all the bells and whistles of a new Beechcraft while retaining the classic lines of the older model. Wolfe expressed a passion for only two things in life—Nadia and this airplane. He was about to spend more than a few hours with both.

He turned to her. "As we discussed, there are a few security cameras between here and the flight office. None are connected to TSA so we should be good, but wear your hat just to make sure."

She nodded and placed a floppy hat on her head while Wolfe retrieved his Stetson Sturgis from the back seat. The couple walked toward the airport's flight service office. Inside they were greeted by an overweight man in his mid-sixties with droopy eyes and yellow teeth. "Mornin' Mr. Lyon." He turned to Nadia. "Ms. Lyon. How can I help you two today?"

Wolfe handed him a completed flight plan form. The older man accepted it, scanned the document and slid a hand into a pant pocket. "Albany, New York, with a refueling stop in Columbus, Ohio." He looked up. "Good plan. The Baron's all fueled up, like you requested. We'll shut the hangar door after you take off. When do you think you'll return?"

"Not sure. We might have to go elsewhere after our meeting in Albany. We just don't know at this point."

"Just let me know. I'll have the door open for you

when you return."

Wolfe smiled and shook the man's hand. "I appreciate it, Danny."

As they were walking back, Nadia chuckled. "Why is he always so glad to see you, Michael?"

"Every time I'm here, I tip him a hundred-dollar bill."

"I didn't see you give it to him."

"It was clipped to the back page of the flight plan." He smiled. "Didn't you see him put his hand in his pocket?"

She chuckled as they entered the hangar.

Albany, NY

As they suspected, Kevin Benson did not return their calls nor did he allow his assistant to schedule an appointment. Wolfe's solution was simple. They parked the rental car several spaces from Benson's ten-year-old Mercedes C180 and quietly waited.

The wait only took an hour.

Benson kept his head down as he approached his car, fumbling with the key fob to unlock the doors. He opened the back door and tossed his briefcase onto the rear passenger seat. As the attorney started to close it, Wolfe approached from his blind side and shoved the man into the car. He scrambled in after him as Nadia got behind the wheel. Wolfe found the fob, now loose on the floor and handed it to her. She started the car and backed out. All of this took less than ten seconds to accomplish. No one outside the vehicle noticed.

Benson, still in a prone position on the back floor

board, regained his dignity and managed to sit across from Wolfe, his back against the opposite door. Now with an ashen face, he blinked rapidly. Finally, he found his voice. "What is the meaning of this?"

"You won't take my calls or make an appointment." Wolfe stared at the attorney.

"I have nothing else to say to you."

"Ah..." Wolfe gave Benson a hard smile. "Nothing to say or nothing you want to say?"

The initial shock of the abduction started to wear off as the lawyer frowned. "I will sue you for kidnapping and bodily harm."

Wolfe gave the man a hard stare. "No, you won't."

"Wait and see."

"I don't have to wait, counselor. I know a lot about you and your so-called legal practice. You're an ambulance chaser. Not a very good one I might add, since you can barely afford the rent on your office and are frequently late paying your assistant. There's never been a Kendrick in the law firm of Kendrick and Benson, just Benson. What do you tell clients on the occasion they ask to see Mr. Kendrick?"

Benson stared at Wolfe, ignoring the question.

"Kind of what I thought." He paused for a heartbeat. "You're divorced with two kids you haven't seen or spoken to for five years. You're constantly late with your child support payments and your ex-wife threatens you with legal action until you pay. The New York State Bar Association has investigated your practice numerous times, but can't quite seem to find enough evidence to disbar you. Need I go on?"

"What do you want?"

"Where has your brother been the last few years?"

The attorney shot a look at Wolfe and then stared at the floor. "I don't know what you're talking about."

"Sure, you do. You knew the moment I showed you

the picture of the man I thought was your brother that it wasn't him. Now, I will ask nicely. Where is he?"

Turning to stare at Wolfe, the man frowned. "This is harassment."

Wolfe sighed and extracted his Walther PPK from his ankle holster. "Answer the question, Kevin."

With wide eyes, the attorney stared at the small pistol. "What are you going to do with that?"

"It was itching my ankle. Where's your brother?"

Still staring at the gun, Benson started to tremble. "Are you going to use it?"

With the Walther in Wolfe's right hand, he pointed it halfway toward the attorney. "Maybe, if I don't start getting answers." He paused to glare at the lawyer. "I will ask nicely only one more time. Where has your brother been?"

The attorney's eyes remained fixed on the weapon. "A federal prison in South Carolina."

Returning the PPK to its original position away from Benson, Wolfe tilted his head and frowned. "Why didn't you say that when I was here last time?"

Benson just shook his head.

"Why is he in prison?"

Finally looking at Wolfe, Benson swallowed hard. "I'm not proud of it."

"I don't give a damn if you're proud of it or not. Why is he in prison?"

"Drug smuggling and manslaughter."

"When was he released?"

"As far as I know, he hasn't been. There's still fifteen years left on his twenty-year sentence. Why?"

This gave Wolfe pause. He stared at the attorney for several moments. "Because when they analyzed the DNA from the body we found, it was your brother. Did you have a half-brother?"

Benson blinked several times and slowly nodded.

"Care to tell me about it?" Wolfe put the PPK back in its holster.

"Another embarrassing episode of my family. My father had an affair while my mother was pregnant with Bobby. They were born several weeks apart. He continued to have affairs with other women while Bobby and I grew up. My father didn't die, Mr. Lyon. Before I started college, he left us and we never saw him again. Likewise, my mother didn't die from a mental breakdown. She died from a broken heart."

Wolfe crossed his arms. "It happens."

Benson took a deep breath and let it out slowly. "Yes, it happens. Though seldom is the scorned woman forced to raise her husband's bastard son."

"What was the half-brother's name?"

"Martin."

"Did you and Bobby get along with Martin?"

"No one got along in our little slice of hell, Mr. Lyon. My mother treated us all the same. She had a hard time being in the same room with us. She told us constantly we reminded her of our father's betrayal."

Not taking his eyes off Benson, Wolfe remained quiet for a dozen seconds. "Head back to the attorney's office."

Nadia nodded and started looking for a place to turn around.

He then returned his attention to the attorney. "I'll need his social security number."

"I don't have it."

"Figure it out, counselor."

"I can't. I don't know it."

Wolfe reached over and grabbed the man, one-handed, by the front of his now sweat-soaked shirt and growled. "I am really tired of your unhelpfulness. My ankle's itching again."

Wide-eyed, Benson recited the number without

hesitation.

"Did you get that, Nadia?"

She nodded as she maneuvered the Mercedes through traffic.

After releasing the attorney, he stared hard at the man. "It would be a wise idea for you to forget this car ride."

The attorney said nothing as he stared straight ahead.

"I'm not a cop, Kevin. I don't play by cop rules. Just keep that in mind if you decide to discuss our little meeting with anyone."

"You don't scare me."

Wolfe placed his hand by his ankle. "You should probably rethink that statement."

"If you're not a cop, who are you?"

"I can and will become your worst nightmare."

He stared wide-eyed at Wolfe for several seconds before he returned his attention to the floor and nodded.

"What are you thinking?" Nadia asked on the drive back to the airport.

"Being raised alongside Bobby and Kevin explains how Martin slipped into the role of Bobby with ease. For some reason, Martin needed to disappear. Since Bobby was in prison, it was the perfect opportunity for him to take on his brother's identity and vanish into the middle of the country. The fact they are similar in appearance didn't hurt either."

"If Bobby was incarcerated, how did he get out and how did he find his half-brother?"

"Don't know. Maybe we should start at the prison."

CHAPTER 18

EDGEFIELD COUNTY, SOUTH CAROLINA

Two Days Later

After establishing their identities as Michael and Nadia Lyon, Michael worked for Joseph over the next six months tracking individuals no one else could find. During this period, Nadia taught French at the local high school in Branson but grew bored with it rather quickly. Now, two years later, they both worked for Joseph using US Marshal *nom de guerres*.

Their US Marshal badges gave them legitimacy when pursuing fugitives or terrorists and opened doors normally closed to everyday citizens. These identifications were not to be used for arrests—they were only to be used for gaining information or access to information. Both Nadia and Wolfe protected these IDs with care and never violated their stated purpose. They considered this visit a search for information.

At 2:46 p.m., they were escorted into the office of

Captain Darwin Rodriguez, the person in charge of Correction Officers at Federal Correction Institute Edgefield. The man stood stiffly as they entered the room.

Wolfe introduced himself and Nadia. "I appreciate you taking the time to meet with us, Captain Rodriguez." They showed their IDs. "I am Patrick Ryan, US Marshal and this is my partner, US Marshal Holly Harper."

Captain Rodriguez stood several inches shorter than Wolfe and fifty pounds heavier. With close-cropped white hair, thinning on top and a permanent scowl, he studied them over half-readers positioned halfway down his nose. The captain displayed all the signs of wanting to be anywhere instead of his office talking to them.

The captain examined the IDs and, without comment, handed them back to Wolfe and Nadia. "What can I do for the US Marshal Service today?" There was a note of suspicion in his voice.

Noting the attitude, Wolfe proceeded. "We are inquiring about the early release of an FCI inmate. His name was Robert Benson, incarcerated at FCI Edgefield on felony drug and manslaughter charges on June 11, 2012, with a sentence of twenty years." Wolfe paused as he tilted his head. "We can't find any court decision permitting an early release."

"You said was, Deputy Ryan. Is this individual deceased?"

Wolfe nodded.

Rodriguez turned to a computer screen and started typing, "How's the last name spelled?"

"B-E-N-S-O-N."

He continued to type and after several moments stopped, studied the screen and returned his attention back to Wolfe. "He was released into the custody of a

Department of Justice attorney named Kendra Burges
on January third of this year."

Nadia spoke next. "You said Kendra Burges?"

The captain nodded.

She looked at Wolfe.

Rodriguez frowned. "What happened to Benson?"

Wolfe answered, "Hunting accident." He paused.
"Captain Rodriguez, can we see the paperwork given
to this institution authorizing his release?"

"I don't see why not." He picked up his desk phone
handset, punched in a few numbers and waited.
"Cheryl, can you bring the file on Benson, Robert to
me?" He listened. "Yes, thank you." He returned the
handset to its cradle. "If he's dead, why is the Marshal
service spending taxpayer's dollars talking to me?"

Wolfe recognized the start of blame deflection from
the captain. In a harsher tone than before, he said,
"There are no records of the DOJ or the Bureau of
Prisons authorizing his early release, Captain. When
his body was identified, alarm bells went off. Thus, the
reason we are here—to find out why he wasn't still in
custody."

Sitting back in his chair, Rodriquez took off the
glasses. He stared at Wolfe as he wiped them with the
end of his tie. "Deputy Ryan, all I can tell you is we
received the proper paperwork to release Benson into
the custody of the attorney for the Department of
Justice."

"Did you confirm her identity?"

"Beg pardon? I'm sure..." He stopped and folded
his arms. "Let's wait for the paperwork." At that
moment, the door to his office opened and a middle-
aged woman entered and handed a file to Rodriquez.
He took it and laid it on his desk. After returning the
glasses to his nose, he opened the file and started
reading. Looking up, he smiled. "Here it is, right on

top." He handed the paper to Wolfe.

Reading the document carefully, Wolfe committed names, times, and reasons, to memory before handing it to Nadia. Returning his attention to Rodriguez, he said, "We'll need a copy of this before we leave."

The captain nodded.

"What kind of inmate was Benson?"

"I personally never dealt with him, but I can let you talk to his case manager."

"That would be helpful, Captain."

Ten minutes later a tall, slender man with stooped shoulders, a hawk nose and wispy thinning hair entered Rodriguez's office. Like the captain, Jarod Cronin displayed no enthusiasm at meeting with two deputies from the US Marshal Service. During introductions, Cronin gave each a limp handshake, frowned, and then folded his arms over his sunken chest.

"Thank you for meeting with us, Mr. Cronin." Wolfe gave the man a smile before moving on to his question. "What kind of inmate was Robert Benson?"

"Complete asshole."

Wolfe fought to contain his surprise. "Could you be a little more precise in your description?"

"Intolerant, combative, easily irritated, unmanageable, and incorrigible. Is that precise enough for you, Deputy?"

Noticing Rodriquez taking a defensive stance, Wolfe replied, "It's a start."

Nadia asked the next question. "How long were you his case manager?"

"Five years."

"Was he always like that?"

The thin man shook his head. "No, only in the last two."

Wolfe tilted his head. "What changed?"

Cronin leaned against the captain's desk. "I don't know and he never said. But I believe it had to do with a visit from his brother."

"His brother is an attorney who lives in Albany, New York."

Rodriquez typed on his keyboard and studied the screen for several moments. "Brother did not identify his residence as Albany, New York. He indicated he lived in West Plains, Missouri. He also did not claim to be an attorney. The form he filled out says he worked at a lumberyard where he lived."

"What name did he use?"

Referring to the screen again, the captain said, "Martin Benson."

"Did he show an ID?"

The captain shook his head. "It doesn't say here. My guess is he would have needed to."

Wolfe nodded and stood. "Gentlemen, you've been helpful. If we can get a copy of the release form from the DOJ, our business here is complete."

Both Rodriguez and Cronin visibly relaxed.

"So, what now, Michael?"

"Not sure yet." Wolfe fell into silence as he maneuvered the rental car out of the prison parking lot. He traveled Northeast until they came to the intersection of Gary Hill and Highway 25. Once they were on 25, Wolfe glanced at Nadia. "We'll find a hotel for the night and head out early in the morning. Daniel Field is only 500 nautical miles from West Plains. We won't need to break the flight up into two legs. Besides, we need to find Jana. My guess would be she's with Martin."

"Where would we start?"

"I believe he's somewhere on my property. He knows it better than I do."

"I would think he would be afraid someone might find him there."

Shaking his head, Wolfe didn't answer right away. Finally, he glanced at her. "Not necessarily. The property is over three hundred and twenty acres, most of which is rugged rolling wooded land. I know of at least three caves on the property and I haven't taken the time to explore all of it. My guess would be Martin has."

Nadia nodded. "I take it you realized who got Bobby out of prison."

"Yeah. Reid's assistant."

"Michael, I do not think Reid believes you are dead."

The side of Wolfe's mouth twitched as he glanced at her. "We'll assume he doesn't believe you are either."

"How would he know about Bobby?"

"Easy. He could be checking anyone who served with me. Bobby was my spotter, as was Rick Flores. I haven't spoken to Rick for almost five years. I don't believe he could tell Reid where I live. He's never been to the property, nor do I believe Rick would be inclined to help the guy. He doesn't like the CIA."

"How would we find out if Reid reached out to him?"

"Joseph."

FBI Special Agent Rick Flores stood a shade over five-foot-seven and weighed in at one hundred and eighty pounds. Broad shouldered with a thin waist, he was still in prime physical shape even though his fiftieth birthday was several years in the rearview mirror.

As a sniper instructor at the FBI Training Facility, Quantico, Virginia, Flores requested the meeting occur at one of the firing ranges of the facility. As he shook the hand of Joseph Kincaid, he said, "Never met a National Security Advisor before."

Joseph shrugged. "Nothing special, just a fancy title."

Flores chuckled. "What can I do for you, Mr. Kincaid?"

"We had a mutual friend."

"Had?"

Nodding, Joseph continued, "Michael Wolfe."

"Yeah, I heard. Hell of a marksman. What about him?"

"Has anyone from the CIA contacted you about him recently?"

With a slight grin, Flores nodded. "I don't hear anything about Michael Wolfe for a decade and then all of a sudden, people start coming out of the woodwork asking questions about him."

"How many people?"

"A few." The sniper trainer cocked his head. "Mr. Kincaid, I was born at night, but it wasn't last night. What's going on?"

"So, someone with the CIA contacted you?"

Flores nodded.

"When?"

"About three months ago."

"What did he want?"

"He was a she. She wanted to know if I had heard from Michael recently. I laughed and told her not since his death."

"Her reaction?"

He chuckled "She got all serious with me, claimed there was evidence he wasn't dead. I laughed again.

CIA spooks bother me—they don't have a sense of humor."

"Some don't. Was her name Kendra Burges?'

Flores stopped smiling and looked at Joseph with narrowed eyes. "How'd you know?"

"She impersonated a DOJ attorney and secured the release of Bobby Benson from FCI Edgefield in May of this year."

"Yeah, I heard Bobby got into trouble. He spotted for Michael..." Flores' eyes grew wide. "Wait a minute. They really do believe Michael's alive, don't they?"

Joseph nodded.

Flores pursed his lips. "So why is the president's National Security Advisor looking into this?"

"I'm not here in that capacity, Agent. Michael was a friend and I don't want his name slandered or blamed for some CIA screw up. He's not in a position to defend himself."

"I guess not." He grew quiet as he contemplated the gravel next to his shoes. He returned his attention to Joseph. "What do you need from me?"

"I need to know exactly what she told you."

CHAPTER 19

SOMEWHERE IN HOWELL COUNTY MISSOURI

The following day, after an uneventful flight from Augusta, Georgia's Daniel Field, Wolfe and Nadia arrived at their Howell County earth sheltered home an hour before sunset. After unpacking, Wolfe used his cell phone as a Wi-Fi hotspot to view Google Earth on his laptop. Using techniques taught to him by Joseph's computer hacker friend, he searched the satellite image of his property.

Nadia watched over his shoulder. "You suspect something, don't you, Michael?"

He looked up and grinned. "You just used a contraction, Nadia."

"Stop it. I did not."

"You're becoming Americanized."

She frowned, straightened, placed her hands on her hips and in a string of French expletives, told him exactly what she thought of his statement.

As he tried hard to keep a straight face, he failed and laughed. Her frown disappeared and she started laughing too. He said, "To answer your question, yes I do." He pointed to a section southeast of the barely discernable structure they currently occupied. "I continue to be amazed at how invisible this place is to satellite images. If I didn't know where to look, I wouldn't be able to find it. But if you travel east of our cleared land, the trees and undergrowth grow denser. Many of the hills and valleys get steep in several sections of this area. There's a freshwater creek just outside my property line, here." He pointed toward a crooked line on the image.

Leaning over, she rested her chin on his shoulder and stared at the laptop. "It does not look like a river." He could feel her warmth against his back.

"It's not. It's fed by an underground stream further to the north. I've only been there a couple of times and that was before I built this house. I've never been back. I think this area"—he made a circling motion over the image—"is where they might be."

"Where would they be staying? There are no houses there."

"No, no houses, but there are numerous caves in the area. I know where a few are, but have never taken the time to explore them."

She put her arms around his neck and raised her chin to the top of his head. "Should we check them out tomorrow?"

"I think we have to—or at least see if we can find any evidence of recent activity around any of them."

She slid a hand down and undid the top two buttons on his shirt. Then the same hand slid under the shirt and rubbed his chest. Wolfe took a deep breath and let it out slowly. "What are you doing?"

"Do I have to tell you?"

"No."

"Good. I am going to our bedroom."

"I'm right behind you."

The time was 9:26 p.m. when his cell phone chirped with an incoming text message. *VoIP call ten minutes.*

Michael acknowledged the message and opened his laptop again. Exactly ten minutes after the text message arrived, he accepted the call.

"Good evening, Joseph."

"How was your trip?"

"Interesting. We confirmed Kendra Burges, identifying herself as a DOJ attorney, presented paperwork to the FCI Edgefield Warden authorizing the early release of Bobby Benson. We obtained a copy of the document."

"Good. Get it to me."

"There's more."

"Oh?"

"When I asked what type of inmate Bobby was, they told me he was uncooperative and violent. I don't remember him that way."

"People change, Michael."

"Yeah, well it gets better. He received a visit from a person identifying himself as a brother two years ago this past May. Their records indicate it was the half-brother, Martin. Up to that time, he was a model prisoner. Afterward, not so much."

"Huh."

Wolfe asked, "What did you find out?"

"As you suspected, Kendra also made contact with Rick Flores several weeks before her visit to FCI Edgefield."

"Did Rick tell her anything?"

"No, I don't believe he did. He seemed to have a healthy distrust of the Agency."

"He always has. What about the social security number we gave you?"

"It does belong to a Martin Benson born in Albany, New York. Plus, I found other interesting information about him."

Wolfe remained quiet, waiting for Joseph to continue.

"While Bobby joined the Marines, Martin joined the Army Engineer Corp. He enlisted when he was eighteen, claiming both parents deceased. He also failed to mention anything on his application about having two brothers."

"That's interesting."

"His career lasted twenty years with two deployments overseas. He missed Desert Storm but spent one tour in Iraq and one in Afghanistan."

"What did he do?"

"Built bunkers."

"Makes sense. He designed my house. I wondered where he got the skills and knowledge. He and I never really talked about..." Michael paused.

"What's the matter?"

"Thinking back about the first time we met, I'm the one who brought up the subject of his spotting for me. He just agreed with me."

"Did he look that much like Bobby?"

"To me he did. But I was taking into consideration how long it had been since I had seen the man. You have to remember—I was just a kid during Desert Storm. Bobby was a couple of years older. While we were working on the house, we never discussed our time in the service. I figured if he wanted to discuss it, he would. He never did. Now I know why he didn't know details." Wolfe paused. "What did his record say about his mental state at the time he mustered out?"

"Clean bill of health, honorable discharge, no PTSD."

"That really doesn't tell us much. Some guys hide it for a while."

"He spent most of his time in Iraq in the Green Zone. The only real combat he saw was in Tora Bora in June of 2007."

Wolfe was quiet for several moments. "You said Tora Bora?"

"Yes."

"Does it say what he did there?"

"Studied the cave complex where they thought Bin Laden was hiding."

Wolfe stared at the call icon displayed on the laptop screen. After several moments of quiet, he said, "We're not asking the right questions, Joseph."

"No, we're not. Was your meeting him random or on purpose?"

"I don't see how it could be on purpose. No one knew who I was when I settled on my grandfather's property."

"How long's the land been in your family?"

"Since 1865, right after the Civil War. The cabin I helped Bobby—uh, Martin—fix up was part of the original homestead. There's over three hundred acres here, Joseph."

"What's the name on the deed filed with the county assessor?"

"An LLC I set up decades ago when my grandfather died. Michael and Nadia Lyon, signed a long-term lease on the property two years ago."

Joseph chuckled. "So, your real name is not associated with the property?"

"Only in an obscure document on file with the

Missouri Secretary of State. Someone would really have to know where to look and what to look for to find it."

"Okay, so we will assume, until we have more evidence, the meeting was random."

"I agree. If Martin is trying to hide from whatever, there are caves all over this part of Missouri. That could be the reason he came here—the caves."

"That would make sense."

"It still doesn't answer why Bobby showed up and ends up in the woods with a bullet in his head."

"Sure, it does. Think about it for a minute. They told you at FCI Edgefield Benson's personality changed after the visit from Martin."

"Yeah."

"During the visit, Martin probably told his half-brother something really upsetting. Life-changing, so to speak."

"Yeah."

"What he told him we can only speculate about. But it was enough to cause Robert to travel to West Plains..." He stopped in mid-sentence.

Wolfe picked up on the train of thought. "There's a chance Reid knows Nadia and I are alive and where we are."

Silence was his answer. "They probably have a strong suspicion now. The conversation with Flores was a dead end. But if Martin told his brother about you two years ago, and my guess would be he did, that could be the reason his behavior changed so much in prison. So, when Kendra Burges asks Bobby about you..."

"He tells her he knows where I am but he'll only tell her if she gets him out of prison first."

"It's the only explanation that fits the facts, Michael."

It was Wolfe's turn to remain quiet for a few moments. "Joseph, why does Gerald Reid have his hair on fire about Nadia and me?"

"An excellent question, one I don't have an answer for."

"Neither do I. I've never met the guy. I only worked for you while I was with the CIA."

"I've never met him either, although I was aware of who he was." He paused briefly. "I think I need to find out a little more about Gerald Reid."

"I agree. What if he was the one who set up Nadia and me in Barcelona?"

"Why, Michael? Why would he do that?"

"Again, I don't know. Unless..."

"Unless what?"

"Can you find out if Reid had a relationship with Geoffrey Canfield or Asa Gerlis?"

"What are you thinking?"

"We know the video of Gerlis was faked. He's alive and hiding somewhere. Who started giving me assignments after Canfield had the heart attack? Reid, Gerlis, or someone else?"

"Keep talking. You're asking the right questions."

"After Gerlis disappeared, who was Nadia's control? And why were we both sent to Barcelona for assassination? My bet is Reid had a relationship with Gerlis and Canfield. If that's true, there is something about the relationship they want to keep hidden."

"Let me see what I can find out."

CHAPTER 20

CARMONA, SPAIN

Gerald Reid sat at a small table situated near the back wall of the busy café. He sipped on a remarkably good rustic Grenache wine as he waited for an individual to join him. Officially in Paris for a conference, Reid had made the trip to Southern Spain on a private chartered jet. He smiled as he watched his man enter the café.

Asa Gerlis scanned the room, saw Reid and walked straight to the table. Without sitting, he glared at the CIA deputy director. "Why are you here?"

Reid smiled and raised his glass of wine. "Enjoying some of this country's wonderful wine. Sit, join me, Asa."

Through clenched teeth, the shorter man said, "My name is not Asa Gerlis."

"Of course, it is. You just aren't using it on a daily basis anymore." Reid frowned. "Now sit down before you draw attention to yourself."

After pulling out a chair across from Reid, he lowered himself and continued to glare. "I am sitting. Why are you here?"

"I like what you did to your face, I barely recognized you when you walked in. But you haven't lost that wonderful scowl you perfected over the years."

"If you are going to insult me, I will leave." He started to rise, but Reid placed a photograph from his jacket pocket on the table. Staring at the photo, Gerlis sat back down. "When was this taken?"

"Do I have your attention, now?"

"Yes, yes, when was this taken?"

"Less than a month ago at Reagan National."

Gerlis picked up the picture and studied it. "It is him. Yes?"

"Yes, it is."

"Where is he?"

"We're not sure, yet. But he is alive and I would venture a guess so is the woman."

Looking over the picture, Gerlis narrowed his eyes. "You guess? You don't know?"

Reid shook his head.

"How did they fool Israel's Mossad? They claim they have DNA proof Wolfe and Picard are dead."

"I know. They shared the analysis with the agency."

The ex-Mossad agent continued to stare at the photograph, but remained quiet.

"What are you calling yourself these days, Asa?"

"My name is Diego Luis. I own a small art gallery."

"Ah, totally legitimate. Right?"

Gerlis stared at Reid, his blue eyes narrow and threatening. "Careful, Reid. I know secrets about you, too."

"Yes, yes. We wouldn't need to be sitting here insulting each other if you had hired a competent marksman in Barcelona two years ago."

Gerlis folded his hands together after placing the picture on the table. He leaned forward. "Then, you should have been the one who hired him."

Reid ignored the comment. "What do you know about the Picard woman?"

"Not much more than what was in her file at Mossad. Why?"

"Any family?"

"Both parents are dead. They immigrated to Israel from Marseille when she was fifteen due to the rising antisemitic attitude in Southern France."

"They could be in France. Wolfe speaks French like a native."

"Possibly, but I doubt it."

"Why?"

"Your country is vast. There are plenty of isolated areas where Wolfe can hide. The woman will be with him. I doubt they have been apart since the botched assassination."

Reid straightened in his chair and narrowed his eyes. "Why do you say that?"

"She was in love with him and he with her. Once he left Israel, she was useless."

Reid kept his attention on the ex-Mossad agent. Finally, he gave the man a nod and sipped his wine.

Gerlis picked up the glass of wine left a few moments before by a waitress. He stared at Reid over the top. "You have still not answered my question. Why are you here?"

"I'm getting to it. I need someone more capable than the man you hired for Barcelona."

Without commenting, Gerlis sipped his wine and then glared at Reid. "I have no resources like that anymore. I am just a simple businessman. You are a powerful man within your country's spy den. Use one of your own."

Shaking his head, Reid said, "Exactly why I need outside talent."

"I cannot help you."

"Can't or won't."

"A bit of both."

"Careful, Asa. I had footage of your so-called execution analyzed."

A slight smile appeared on the older man's lips. "So?"

"Whoever did the computer graphics was good. Very good. But there is a video analyst who works for me who is better. She found a slight problem."

The smile disappeared. "There are no problems with it."

"Sure, there are. There is a barely discernable pixel count discrepancy at the junction of the neck and shoulder of the man executed. It is invisible to the eye and to a cursory examination. But on closer inspection, it's there."

"Do not get cocky, Reid. I know things about you that would end your career."

"Oh, I haven't forgotten. We both know secrets about each other we don't need others knowing." He smiled and took a sip of wine. "It gives us an understanding. That's why it would be in both or our best interests for an independent contractor to search for Wolfe and the woman."

"I thought you didn't know where they are?"

"I don't, but I might have a lead."

"Care to share?"

"Not at this moment."

Gerlis tilted his head. "Who will pay for this individual? They do not come cheap."

"Don't worry about funding—just let me know how much and where to transfer it."

With a nod, Gerlis stood. "Same method as before?"

"Yes. Text me the new password and I'll open up the Gmail account."

Reid sipped his wine as he watched Asa Gerlis exit the small café.

Joseph Kincaid read the report and frowned. He rose from his desk in the West Wing and walked into his deputy's office.

Jerry Griggs looked up from his computer screen. "What's up, boss?"

The National Security Advisor leaned against the doorframe. "I wish you wouldn't call me that."

The younger man smiled. A veteran of the CIA, he and Joseph had worked together several times over the years and had developed a mutual respect. Tall, slender and prematurely bald, Jerry's green eyes sparkled with mischief. Joseph valued him for his tactical and strategic thinking. He also enjoyed the man's dry humor.

"Sorry, boss. What's ya need?"

Closing his eyes and with a slight shake of his head, Joseph said. "Why is Gerald Reid in Paris?"

Griggs shrugged. "No clue. He didn't ask my permission, if that's what you're referring to."

Barely hiding his smile, Joseph shook his head again, this time with emphasis. "No, he didn't ask mine either. Find out why he's there and while you are at it, check into why he disappeared for thirteen hours yesterday."

Raising his eyebrows, Griggs did not take his eyes off Joseph. "Disappeared?"

Joseph nodded.

"Like, he's there one second, then poof, he's gone? Or just wasn't seen for thirteen hours?"

"He was observed leaving in a cab before dawn. He wasn't seen the rest of the day by anyone until a reception that evening."

"Huh..." He stared at his computer screen for over a dozen seconds. "Let me do some checking. I know the Station Chief in Paris."

Joseph nodded and returned to his office.

After driving the twenty-seven kilometers to the airport in Seville, Gerlis, using his Diego Luis passport, boarded a non-stop flight for the hour-long trip to Madrid where he kept an apartment. The following day, he traveled via car to the city of Zaragoza, the capital of the Aragon region of Spain.

By noon he sat in a sidewalk café with a pot of strong tea, waiting for the individual he would be meeting. His wait lasted only several minutes.

The younger man appeared suddenly and sat across from Gerlis. "Why did you want to meet?"

"I need you to finish the job you started two years ago in Barcelona."

"I see. I thought they were killed in Mexico."

Gerlis shook his head as he poured tea for his guest. "I learned otherwise yesterday."

The other man raised his eyebrows as he sipped the strong tea. "And what did you learn, Asa?"

With a grimace at the use of his name, Gerlis replied, "Your targets are still alive."

Silence was his response. The sniper stared at Gerlis for more than a quarter of a minute before putting down his glass and folding his hands in front of him. "I see. So, the information the Israelis' are spewing is nothing more than lies?"

"No. They believe Wolfe and Picard to be dead. How they were deceived is unknown. The Americans have a picture of Wolfe taken at an airport recently. Until the picture was found, the Americans believed them dead, also."

"Did you see this picture?"

Gerlis nodded and sipped his tea.

"Was it Wolfe?"

Again, the older man nodded.

"Hmmm..."

"Their location is unknown at this time. The Americans believe they are in France."

"But you do not."

"No."

"Where do you believe them to be?"

"Somewhere in the western United States. There are vast amounts of undeveloped land where a man as resourceful as Michael Wolfe can hide."

"My dear Asa. I will not be traveling to the United States to look around this vast amount of undeveloped land you mentioned."

Gerlis shook his head. "Not what I have in mind."

"Then what do you suggest?"

"I plan to have the Americans find him and then you can finish your assignment."

After a thoughtful sip of tea, the younger man stared hard at the man across from him. "If I have to go to the United States, my price just went up."

"To be expected. The American CIA will pay for your troubles."

A frown appeared on the sniper's face as he leaned forward. "I have no desire to work for the American CIA."

Gerlis leaned back and raised both palms. "Not what I meant. They are willing to pay me whatever it takes to have this accomplished. You will merely be the instrument for finishing the job."

After another sip of tea, the sniper asked, "When will you know his location?"

"Soon, my friend. Soon."

CHAPTER 21

HOWELL COUNTY, MO

With the temperature hovering in the mid-thirties and a steady wind out of the northwest, it felt like a typical late fall day in Southern Missouri. Wispy clouds raced across the sky as a cold front moved in from across the upper plains. A blanket of leaves littered the ground, having abandoned their hosts several weeks prior. Without foliage, the densely-treed land provided little shade from the sun as it warmed the two hikers trudging alongside the small creek next to Wolfe's property.

Hiking boots, insulated pants and multiple layers kept them comfortable as they searched for caves.

"If I remember correctly, there's one not far from here."

"You said that thirty minutes ago, Michael."

"I know, but..." He paused as he spotted a dark slit in the landscape twenty yards up the rise to his right. He pointed. "There's one." He climbed the hill until he came to the horizontal opening in the side of the land. Nadia followed, holding the shotgun she carried pointed at the ground. Unclipping the Maglite from his belt, he bent down and pointed the light beam into the crevasse. "This one's not very tall and I don't see evidence of someone crawling in and out."

Nadia glanced at a hiker's GPS unit she carried. "Do you want me to mark this location?"

"Yes, let's keep track of every one we find today."

They continued their search.

With the sun at its zenith, the two hikers had located only four caves. None of these appeared capable of providing an opportunity for Martin to construct a place to hide. They stopped for a few minutes and sat on a fallen log to nibble on energy bars and drink water.

Wolfe asked, "Where are we in relationship to the house?"

She consulted the GPS unit and pointed. "House is about three miles north. The cabin is also north. We aren't on your property anymore."

He smiled but chose not to tell her she had just used a contraction. "This is state land. If we don't find anything in the next hour, we'll head back to the house and rethink our search."

She nodded. "Good. It is starting to get a little chilly."

Wolfe watched the sky as cumulus clouds played hide and seek with the sun. "Clouds are thickening, which means the temperature will start dropping soon. Want to head back now?"

She shook her head. "Not if you don't."

He stood. "Not yet. The stream is getting wider and I've never followed it this far south before. To be honest, I don't know what's around here."

They found the cave ten minutes later.

The vertical entrance stood a shade over five feet tall with a three-foot-wide opening at the base. Toward the top, it narrowed to a little over fourteen inches. Wolfe pointed to the ground in front of the cave. "Note the crushed leaves."

Nadia nodded. She held the shotgun with both hands, aimed at the ground.

He unclipped the Maglite and pointed it inside the opening. "It must go back a way. I can't see a back wall." Turning to look at her, he unholstered his H&K HP40 handgun. "I'm going to look around inside. Make sure no one surprises me."

She nodded.

Ducking to avoid hitting his head, Wolfe straightened once he entered the cavern. Holding the Maglite in his left hand, away from his body, he kept the H&K at ready. The initial room he entered sloped downward at a ten-degree angle for ten feet before opening into a larger cavity. He stood still as he swept the light around the expansive space. The light fell across two sleeping bags, a Coleman lantern, a small propane cook stove and a large Yeti cooler.

Keeping the light away from his body, Wolfe yelled, "Martin, it's Michael. We need to talk." He waited for a response. When none came, he repeated the announcement. The only sounds he heard were his voice echoing within the cavern and the trickle of running water. As he swept the flashlight around the room, he saw a dark opening on his right. After moving toward the gap, he trained the Maglite at the floor. The path tilted steeply downward and he could see water flowing over the rocky ground, but the light could not penetrate the gloom ahead.

He retraced his steps and bent to look at the floor. It was smooth—not a natural state for a small Missouri cave. Someone had been working inside the cavern to make it more habitable. As he stood, he heard Nadia say in a quiet voice, "Someone is approaching from the south, Michael."

He hurried to the cave entrance. She had stepped inside to keep from being seen. He smiled at her. "Let's greet them."

Wolfe emerged from the cave entrance, his H&K still in his right hand. Nadia followed with the shotgun at ready.

Martin Benson and Jana Meyer looked up from navigating the leaf-covered ground to stare at Wolfe and Nadia just outside the cave opening.

The ex-sniper spoke first. "Hello, Martin. Want to tell us what's going on here?"

"When did you figure it out?"

A Coleman lantern illuminated the front cavern, casting an eerie glow on each of their faces. Nadia still held the shotgun in both hands, but not in a threatening manner. Wolfe, having holstered his H&K and crossed his arms said. "For the moment, I'll ask the questions. Did you kill Bobby?"

Martin remained quiet while Jana frowned. She started to say something, but Martin stopped her with a hand on her arm.

Wolfe glanced at Nadia, who raised the shotgun slightly.

Martin smiled at Jana. "It's okay, I'll answer." He turned his attention to Wolfe. "He was looking for you."

"I know."

"You know? I don't understand."

"We've been to Albany and FCI Edgefield."

"Ah…" Benson took a deep breath. "Is Kevin still an asshole?"

Wolfe did not respond.

"I guess I need to explain."

"That would be nice."

"It started the month you two were gone. I was spending more time at Jana's than at the cabin. My half-brother Robert contacted me at the lumberyard. I didn't want him to know where Jana lived until I knew why he was in West Plains. So—I told her I was meeting someone and would call her later. One of my buddies from work dropped me off at JT's Steak House. When I sat down across from him, he was already drunk. I don't know how long he had been there or how many beers he had. That's when the argument started."

"About what?"

"He's always blamed me for screwing up his family. This argument was no different than any of the others. It covered the same old tired ground."

"Did he explain how he got out of prison fifteen years early?"

Benson shook his head. "No, I asked him. He never told me. When he wasn't telling me how I screwed up the family, he was demanding to know where you were."

"Why?"

"All he would say is finding you would get him a pardon."

"Did you tell him where you lived when you visited him in prison two years ago?"

Benson stared at Michael for ten seconds. His eyes narrowed. "How did you find out about my visit to the prison?"

"Warden at FCI Edgefield. Go on with your story."

Taking a deep breath, Martin tilted his head. "You know more than you're letting on, don't you?"

Wolfe narrowed his eyes as his glare intensified. "Yes, so make sure you remember that."

The man stiffened and stared at Wolfe for several moments. Finally, he relaxed, gave Wolfe a half smile and nodded.

"Go on with the story, Martin."

"At one time, Bobby and I were close. We had to be—Kevin was gone, his mother was crazy and we only had each other to rely on. When we graduated from high school, he told me one night he wanted to make it on his own, so he joined the Marines. I felt lost. Since he didn't want me around anymore, I also joined the military, only a different branch. My visit two years ago was a futile effort to reconnect with him."

"That doesn't explain why you've been using his name?"

Benson nodded and stared at the floor while he held Jana's hand. "I'm getting to that. Our visit was going okay until I mentioned you."

"Why did you talk about me?"

"I didn't think anything about it. I was proud of the work we did on your house and the cabin. It was something I wanted to share with him. He listened uninterested until I told you were the sniper he spotted for in Kuwait."

Wolfe did not respond.

"That's when he went psycho on me. Why did he do that, Michael?"

"A good question. The last time I saw him was Desert Storm in the early 90s."

"Then what he said later doesn't make sense."

The ex-sniper stiffened. "What did he tell you?"

"He told me he was in prison because of you."

"Really? Did he explain?"

"Kind of. He told me if he could tell the Department of Justice where you were, they'd let him out."

"And this was two years ago when you visited him?"

"Yeah. He said he'd made a deal with the DOJ. If he ever learned where you were, he could tell them and get a pardon."

"So, he made the deal two years ago. Is that correct?"

"He made it before my visit."

Wolfe pursed his lips. "Huh."

"I thought he was crazy. That's why I never mentioned it to you."

"I'm guessing here, but you didn't tell him where you lived, did you?"

"I had planned to, but his anger at you was so intense, I decided not to."

"So how did he know where to find you?"

A shrug was his answer.

"Martin..."

"I sent him a letter telling him Jana and I were getting married."

"So, he knew from the return address."

"I didn't put a return address on it."

Nadia said, "The letter would have had a postmark from West Plains."

The impostor frowned. "I didn't think of that."

"So how did he end up dead on my property?"

"I'm getting to that. When he got loud at JT's, I took him outside to his rental car. That's when he took a swing at me."

"There was a fight?" This came from Nadia.

Benson gave her a sad smile. "He was so drunk it wasn't much of one. He missed, fell flat on his face and knocked himself out. I stuffed him into his vehicle and took him to the cabin to sober up."

"Did you stay?"

Shaking his head, Martin remained silent.

"Don't start lying to me."

"I've had to deal with his crazy family as long as I can remember." He paused and looked into the darkness above them. "As I drove him out here, I realized getting back in contact with him had been a huge mistake."

"I get that."

"When we got to the cabin, he had sobered up enough he started threatening me. He told me if I didn't tell him where you were, he'd find Jana and hurt her."

Wolfe focused his attention on his friend. The pieces of the puzzle started falling into place. "Where'd the gun come from, Martin?"

Benson remained quiet.

"I expect you to be truthful, Martin." Wolfe crossed his arms. "Did your brother commit suicide?"

Martin shrugged.

"Again, where did the gun come from?"

More silence.

"Martin, I can't help you if you don't tell the truth."

"I found it in a cave at Tora Bora. I never declared it and smuggled it back to the States."

"Was it already at the cabin?"

Benson nodded again. "I kept it in a kitchen drawer with a box of twenty-two caliber hollow points."

"Why didn't you contact Jana after you left the cabin?"

"I had my reasons."

"I think it would be a good idea to tell me."

The impostor shuffled his feet without answering.

Wolfe placed his hand on the H&K in its holster. "I

don't have time for these theatrics, Martin. Spill it."

"I drove to Tennessee."

"Why?"

More shuffling of feet.

"Your evasiveness is starting to tell me you're making this up as you, go. Want to try again?" Wolfe withdrew the H&K and held it by his side.

Benson stared at the gun and then looked at Jana. He sighed and closed his eyes. "Bobby got involved with some bad people. Real bad people, Michael. I didn't want them to find me. I figured if they knew Bobby was out of prison, they'd follow him here and then..."

"Find you and Jana."

He nodded. "That's why I've been posing as Bobby. I figured if they were looking for Martin Benson and knew Bobby was in prison, well, they'd leave anyone named Bobby Benson alone."

"I'm not sure your logic was sound, but apparently it worked. How'd you get the ID?"

"It was the week before he went to prison. I stole his driver's license one night while he was drunk. Since we look similar..." His voice trailed off without finishing his sentence.

"Who are *they*?"

"He was arrested in Miami for drugs and manslaughter. What do you think?"

Wolfe paused. "Was Bobby mixed up with a drug cartel?"

A nod was his only answer.

Nadia stepped further into the light of the lantern. "Jana, why did you tear up your house?"

Jana gave Benson a quick glance. He nodded. She returned her attention to Nadia. "We wanted to leave a message for you and Michael."

With a frown, Nadia shook her head. "I don't

understand. Why didn't you just call me?"

"Martin thought if someone besides you and Michael were looking for us, they would think I was kidnapped."

Rolling his eyes, Wolfe snorted. "You two didn't think this through very well." He turned to Martin. "Did you kill your half-brother?"

Benson stared hard into the eyes of Wolfe but still did not answer.

"I'll take that as a yes. Do you have somewhere you can go out of state?"

With a nod, Martin said. "That's why I drove to Tennessee—to make arrangements."

"How long can you stay?"

"Indefinitely."

"Then why are you two still here in a cave hiding?" Jana said. "I didn't want to leave until we could explain things to you and Nadia."

Wolfe shook his head. "Then I think you two should leave for Tennessee right now and forget about West Plains. Permanently."

Both Martin and Jana nodded.

CHAPTER 22

WASHINGTON, DC

Two Days Later

Jerry Griggs rapped a knuckle on the doorframe of Joseph's office. Kincaid looked up and waved him inside. After shutting the door, the assistant sat down across from his boss and smiled. "I have news from Paris."

Joseph grinned. "Good or bad?"

"Depends on your perspective."

"Tell me."

"Reid failed to tell anyone where he was going the day he disappeared."

"To be expected."

"Yes, but the station chief has a history with Reid and doesn't trust the guy. So, he checked up on him. Apparently, Reid was spotted boarding a private jet at Paris-Le Bourget Airport—that's an airport exclusively dedicated to business aviation. It's located about seven kilometers from Paris."

"I'm familiar with it. Where did he go?"

"A flight plan for the plane was filed for Seville, Spain with a return the same day."

"Any word about what he did there?"

Griggs shook his head. "Nothing that can be confirmed."

"Anything that can't be confirmed?"

"One of the station chief's assistants had, uh..." Griggs paused. "An informal interview with one of the pilots. I'm told she is very pretty."

With a slight grin, Joseph nodded. "I'm sure she is."

"The pilot told her Reid rented a car and was gone for about six hours. When he returned, they immediately flew back to Paris in time for the reception that evening. My friend was now very curious, so he had someone check with the rental car service and found out the driver only put fifty-four kilometers on the vehicle while it was out."

Joseph grinned again. "I will assume you know the answer to the next question. What is exactly twenty-seven kilometers from the airport, Jerry?"

"Glad you asked. The town of Carmona."

Standing, Joseph walked over to a window and stared out over the back lawn of the White House. "Who would Reid be meeting in Carmona, Spain on a clandestine trip?"

"I have pictures."

Joseph turned to stare at Griggs. "Pictures?"

The young assistant placed a photograph on Joseph's desk. "AESA security cameras took this. Facial recognition software gives it a seventy-eight percent chance of being Asa Gerlis."

Picking the picture up, the ex-CIA man stared at it for a minute. "It's him."

"You sure?"

"He's had surgery and grown a beard, but it's him."
Joseph placed the photo back on his desk.

The younger man returned the picture to a file.
"Thought he was dead."

"Lots of ways to fake a video. A body was never found."

Griggs frowned. "So, what's going on, Joseph?"

"Not sure, but I believe it is time to have a private chat with the Director."

With a smile, Griggs stood. "I bet you know someone who could arrange that."

His response was a nod.

The Next Day

"Thank you for doing this today, Marvin."

"My pleasure, Mr. President."

Marvin Young, having been appointed to the position of Director of Central Intelligence just before the previous president, President Richard Bryant, died of a massive aortic aneurism, smiled. He was the last hold-out from the previous administration. The current president, Roy Griffin, still had doubts about the man.

Griffin handed the president's daily brief binder back to Young. "Would you mind joining Joseph and me in my private office?"

"Certainly, Mr. President."

Griffin led the two men out of the Oval Office down a short hall and gestured for them to enter his private office just across from the President's private lavatory. The room contained a small desk and two comfortable wing-back chairs for guests.

Now in his mid-fifties, Roy Griffin stood a bit over

six-feet-tall. Male-model handsome, he wore his blond hair longer than current fashion, causing certain pundits to proclaim him the next John F. Kennedy. Even by his home state of California standards, he was wealthy. He was keenly aware his looks and money were the main reason he was elected to Congress. And, by a quirk of fate and the death of the previous president, he now held the highest office in the land.

Because of this turn of events, he constantly reminded himself to make a difference and bring calm to a dysfunctional Washington, DC. Originally elected by his image-conscious Northern California district as a member of the House of Representatives, he'd been drafted by his party to unseat the previous junior senator from California. After being a Senator for four years, he'd been asked by the previous occupant of the Oval Office to become his Vice President. Now he was the Leader of the Free World.

"What can I do for you, sir?" The DCI sat with a slightly concerned look on his face.

Griffin started the conversation. "How well do you know Assistant Director Gerald Reid?"

Young shrugged and cleared his throat. "Uh, how well does anyone know Gerald Reid?"

Griffin remained quiet, forcing the DCI to say more.

"The man works twelve to fourteen hours a day. When he's not at the agency, he's at his place in Virginia, working. Why?"

Joseph asked the next question. "What was the purpose of the meeting he attended in Paris recently?"

"A conference with his European counterparts. It was designed to begin the process of developing enhanced communication strategies between agencies on suspected terrorists." Young looked at Joseph and then the president. "Why do you ask?"

Griffin handed Young a sheet of paper outlining Reid's trip to Spain. "I am asking, Marvin, to find out why Gerald Reid disappeared from the conference for thirteen hours to have a meeting with a former Mossad agent, who by the way, was thought to be dead."

Young stared at the sheet and scanned the contents rapidly. When finished, he looked up, his mouth slightly agape and his eyes blinking rapidly. "I was unaware of this, Mr. President. I'm sure there is a perfectly sound explanation."

"I'm sure there is, Director Young." The sudden formal address caused the DCI pause. He realized this was a serious meeting not a casual conversation.

The President didn't smile. "I believe you have a larger problem than Reid just slipping away for a few hours. It might be a good idea to find out why an Assistant Director of the CIA is clandestinely meeting with a dead man."

Now on the defensive, Young straightened in his seat and sat at the edge. "How do we know it was Asa Gerlis? There's a video of his death. Surely there's been a mistake in the identity of the individual Reid met with."

Joseph handed Young two pictures, one from the Seville airport and the other, an older photograph. "Picture on the left was obtained from a friend of mine with the Mossad. The one on the right was taken at the Seville airport three days ago."

Silence filled the room as the DCI studied the photos. The more he stared, the more his nostrils flared. His attention turned to Joseph. "You were with the agency. What do you think, Joseph?"

"It's been a while. I could only speculate."

"I'd be interested in your speculation."

"I've never met Gerald Reid. All I have to go on is his record and what others say about him."

The DCI glanced at the pictures and then back to Joseph. "Which tells you what?"

"He has his own agenda."

Griffin said, "Marvin, I think you would agree with me that having an Assistant Director with interest other than the good of the country is not what we need right now."

There was a slow nod of the DCI's head as he studied the pictures again. Then, more to himself than the others in the room, he said, "I think I need to have a video analyzed." He looked up. "Mr. President, I don't have any answers for you at the moment. Give me a day or two."

Griffin nodded and Young left the room. Once he was gone, Joseph said, "Do you trust him?"

"Don't know. Depends on how he handles this."

The National Security Advisor nodded.

"Joseph, what's your interest in Reid?"

"When I took this job, Mr. President, I told you I would be truthful and never lie to you."

Griffin nodded.

"I've never lied, but there are pieces of information I've not told you."

"That's understandable. Go on."

"Just over two years ago, after Gerlis faked his own death, an individual who did contract work for the agency was targeted by an assassin. There were actually two individuals targeted—the other was a Mossad agent. Both escaped. At one time, this individual was a highly successful overseas operative for the CIA. Because he was very good at what he did, the agency released him and allowed him to do contract work."

The president frowned. "What did he do, Joseph?"

"His specialty was tracking down known terrorists across Europe and the Middle East and—uh—stopping them from being terrorists anymore."

The President gave Joseph a sly grin. "Okay."

"After the incident in Barcelona, his cover was blown and he returned to the States. He now works undercover for the US Marshal service." Joseph felt bad about the stretching of the truth, but continued, "He's been instrumental in identifying and stopping numerous individuals planning mass shootings. His effectiveness has prevented a number of these incidents, thus saving hundreds of lives."

Griffin smiled. "I see. And you felt it necessary to keep this information from me?"

"Yes, sir."

"Is he still active?"

"No, sir."

"Why?"

"Three men—Reid, the supposedly dead Asa Gerlis and an MI6 agent named Geoffrey Canfield. Gerlis was the control for the Mossad agent and Canfield was our agent's contact while operating in Europe."

"Who was the Mossad agent?'

"A woman."

Griffin raised his eyebrows and displayed a slight grin. "Interesting."

Joseph nodded.

"I assume names at this point are not important."

"Not really. For their own protection, neither are currently using their real names."

"I see." He paused and tilted his head. "Why is this preventing him from doing his work at the US Marshall Service?"

"Canfield died very suddenly with a heart attack. I knew the man—very healthy, didn't drink to excess, nor did he smoke. Not long after that, Gerlis stages his own death. As I said, Canfield was our man's contact and Gerlis was the Mossad agent's. Then all of a sudden, an attack is made on both of these individuals at the same time. My next question is, why?"

"Sorry, Joseph, I don't read spy novels."

"Neither do I, but I believe there's a connection."

"Gerald Reid?"

Joseph nodded slowly.

Griffin chuckled. "Since I have a few other things to concentrate on, besides this little spy drama, I'll let you handle it."

"Thank you, sir."

Standing, the president signaled the meeting was over. "Joseph, in the future, don't forget to tell me about operations like this."

"I won't, sir."

"Good." The president gave Joseph a sly smile. "I'm glad you're on my team." He paused for half of a heartbeat. "One more thing. If you find that Gerald Reid is endangering this country for any reason, I want to be advised immediately."

"You'll be the first to know, Mr. President."

CHAPTER 23

TABLE ROCK LAKE AREA, SOUTHWEST MISSOURI

Michael Wolfe's phone vibrated with an incoming text message. After glancing at it, he hurried to the bedroom they used as an office to get the laptop ready for an incoming VoIP call.

Joseph's voice emanated from the speaker. "Good morning, Michael."

"Morning, Joseph."

"I have an update for you."

Nadia appeared in the doorframe of the room at their lakeside condo. Raising an eyebrow, she listened to the conversation.

Joseph continued, "We have confirmation Asa Gerlis is alive."

Wolfe glanced at Nadia as she moved closer to the computer. "How?"

"Reid met with him in Carmona, Spain three days ago."

"So, he's in Spain?"

"It would appear so. He's grown a beard, his hair is gray and he's had surgery to change his appearance. Not much, but with a cursory glance, you wouldn't recognize him. I'll send you a current picture after we finish talking."

"Why was he meeting with Reid?"

"I was hoping you and Nadia might be able to answer that."

Turning his attention away from the computer, he glanced at Nadia. She gave Wolfe a concerned stare. He returned to the computer. "Interesting. We also learned something recently, which is probably related."

"Tell me."

"Someone interviewed Bobby Benson in prison two years ago and made him a deal. If he could tell them where I was, his sentence would be commuted. He didn't have this information until recently. We believe he told Kendra Burges and was released from prison to find me."

"So, you think Reid never believed you and Nadia were dead?"

"No, I don't think he ever did."

"Then it makes perfect sense why he was meeting with Gerlis. He was relaying the information to him."

"I believe that's a good assumption. My next assumption would be Gerlis is the one who coordinated the attack on Nadia and me."

"I would agree."

"I'm sure Reid is involved with it as well."

"Makes sense." Joseph paused briefly. "Where does Canfield fall into this mess?"

"I'm not sure. Did Reid ever deal with Geoffrey?"

"A good question—one I don't have an answer for. But I plan to find out."

"If so, it might be the crossing we're looking for."

"What do you mean, Michael? What crossing?"

"Thinking back, it all started with Canfield's untimely death, which I now suspect was a murder. Then, not long afterward, Gerlis fakes his own and the ambush on Nadia and me occurs."

Joseph remained silent.

"Now we learn Reid's been contacting my old spotters trying to find me. Why?"

"I would only be able to speculate."

Wolfe let him think.

After several quiet moments, Joseph said, "I believe you need to stay away from your sheltered home for a while. At least until we can determine how much Reid knows."

Wolfe thought about the preparations he and Nadia had taken before closing the house down and preparing it for what he feared would be a lengthy absence. "Nadia and I have already taken that precaution."

"Good. I believe I need to delve into Gerald Reid's history a little more."

"Be careful, Joseph."

"Not my first rodeo, Michael."

After the call ended, Wolfe looked at Nadia. She seemed to be hugging herself, her arms grasping her shoulders.

"Don't worry, Nadia."

She shook her head. "I am not worried about us. I am worried someone will find the house and destroy it."

One side of his mouth twitched. "That could happen, but it can be rebuilt. If someone locates the path leading to the back, the house is indistinguishable from the surrounding terrain. If you approach from the south, the only feature identifying it as a structure is the front entrance. We placed the netting there. You have to be within fifty yards to determine its artificial. From a distance, you can't."

She nodded.

"If and when someone approaches from either the north or south"—he held up his cell phone— "I'll be notified with this."

Another nod.

"Even if they gain access to the inside, we didn't leave anything behind identifying the owners."

"I know, but it is our home. The only one I have ever really felt comfortable in. I do not want to lose it."

He stood and placed his arms around her. She returned the embrace.

Taking in the fragrance of her hair, he was silent for a long time. Finally, he said, "Like I told you earlier, don't worry. Once we get this little issue settled, we can go back."

"How long will that be?"

"As long as it takes."

Two Days Later
Tel Aviv, Israel

Uri Ben-David shook the hand of his old friend Joseph Kincaid. "I haven't seen you in a long time, Joseph. You are looking well."

"As do you, Uri."

Located in an isolated section of Jaffa, the safe house resembled a home occupied by a newly divorced male. Threadbare furnishings and spartan décor offered few creature comforts. It was a perfect setting for their meeting.

"I never congratulated you on your new lofty position." Ben-David crossed his arms and smiled. "National Security Advisor to the President of the United States. Very impressive."

Joseph snorted. "It's not that lofty. But the perks are pretty good. I don't have to fly commercial anymore."

With the niceties of their meeting over, the Israeli narrowed his eyes. "Now, what is so important that you travel halfway around the world to visit my country, Joseph?"

"A little fact-finding for my boss."

"You could have called."

"It's a little more sensitive than a phone call."

Ben-David raised an eyebrow and gave Joseph a small grin. "How sensitive?"

"Your counterpart in the US is Gerald Reid, correct?"

The Mossad agent nodded.

"When was the last time you had contact with him?"

Ben-David stayed quiet for several moments. "Why do you ask?"

The ex-CIA man leaned forward. "We have a few concerns."

"I see." Ben-David paused. "Reid and I haven't actually spoken to each other for two years. Our assistants do most of the day-to-day communications. Personally, if I did not have to speak to the man again it would be fine with me."

"Care to tell me why?"

"The man is distasteful. He is too pompous and has too high an opinion of himself."

"I've heard that."

"In this business, that can lead to mistakes."

Joseph nodded.

"The last time we spoke was just before you sent us the DNA on Wolfe and Picard."

"What did he want?"

"He was looking for Wolfe."

"Did he say why?"

The Israeli shook his head, stood and walked to the kitchen of the small apartment. He busied himself making a pot of coffee. "There is something I believe I need to tell you about Asa Gerlis."

Joseph did not respond.

"We were investigating Gerlis just before he faked his own death."

"You knew about it?"

Ben-David measured coffee into the machine and pressed the start button. "No, not until Reid brought it to our attention."

"Interesting."

"I would not use that word exactly. Catastrophic might fit better."

"What were you investigating?"

"Uh..." With a grim smile, Ben-David said, "He was a mole, Joseph. Planted in our country under the guise of a Polish immigrant."

Trying not to show his surprise, Joseph sat back in the straight-back wooden chair he occupied. "You're sure? He was with Mossad for, what, twenty years?"

With a nod, the Israeli reached for two coffee mugs in a cabinet above the coffeemaker. "When we saw the video, we too thought he was dead. The investigation was shelved and everyone involved gave a collective sigh of relief. After Reid's visit, we also had the video analyzed. It was indeed a very well-made fake."

"Who knows?"

"Myself, the director and the two analysts."

While Ben-David poured two cups of coffee, Joseph stared at a spot on the wall. As the coffee mug was placed in front of him, he looked at his host. "Did Gerlis ever have contact with an MI6 agent named Geoffrey Canfield?"

"More than likely, Canfield was Gerlis' counterpart at MI6, just like..."

Joseph finished the sentence. "Reid was at CIA."

The coffee mug was halfway to Ben-David's lips when it stopped.

Continuing with his thoughts, Joseph said, "Canfield was Michael's control during a time when he did contract work for us and a few other agencies in Europe. We don't think Geoffrey's death was due to natural causes."

"Do you think Gerlis was involved?"

"Possibly. Reid may be involved also. We just don't know."

After a sip of coffee, the Mossad agent asked, "Why would they target Canfield?"

"Again, we have lots of questions, but no answers."

Ben-David grinned. "You sound like you still work for the agency."

"I only have my country's best interest at heart."

His response was a chuckle.

Taking a sip of coffee, Joseph peered over the cup. "Reid met with Gerlis in Carmona, Spain four days ago."

Ben-David almost spat out coffee as his eyes widened. "What?"

Joseph nodded and gave him the details.

After he finished, Ben-David tapped his finger on the table. "Do you think he is hiding in Spain?"

"We don't know. It would make sense—the attack on Wolfe and Picard occurred in Barcelona, and now his meeting with Reid."

"What kind of assets do you have available?"

"I don't have assets, I'm just a consultant to the

president." He paused as he gave Ben-David a mischievous grin. "The CIA has assets available and they are looking for him as we speak."

"Joseph, we are dancing around the real reason you are here, are we not?"

"Yes."

"If Gerlis was a mole, then there is the possibility Reid is as well?"

After taking a sip of coffee, Joseph nodded. "Anything is possible."

"We think Gerlis was originally from Kazakhstan."

"Muslim or Russian?"

"An interesting point. We originally thought Muslim, but since you mentioned it, he could have been a Russian."

After a few moments of quiet, Joseph asked. "Or is this about something entirely different?"

"Such as?"

"Think about it. All three men can't be moles—they could, but I doubt they would know about the other. Uri, what can create a bond between men more compelling than love of country?"

He paused and a smile appeared. "Money. It is always about money."

"Well said, my friend. If Gerlis was a Muslim mole, I would think he would return to a country where the Mossad could not touch him. Why would he hide in Spain?"

"We could touch him in a Muslim country, Joseph."

"I realize that. It was a figure of speech. Why Spain?"

"It is a large country with lots of political factions. Plus, wait a minute—"

"Exactly, it has one of the lowest costs of living in Europe. A man with money could live a very comfortable life there." Joseph sipped his coffee again. "I've heard Reid lives on a very palatial estate in Virginia. He works for the CIA. Where did he get the money?"

"It might be a good idea for you to find out, my friend."

CHAPTER 24

MISSOURI

D roopy eyes studied the small stack of hundred-dollar bills laying on the counter. "I'm sorry to hear you'll be away for a while, Mr. Lyon. What about your lease on the hangar?'

"Would you have an opportunity to sublease it, Danny?"

"Maybe." The short middle-aged man continued to stare at the money. "So, you're gonna keep it?"

"At this stage, yes. My lease is paid up through the end of the year. If we find we will be gone longer, I'll make a decision then. But for now, business as usual."

He looked up and grinned, his nicotine-stained teeth in full display. "I would hate to lose such a good tenant."

Michael tapped the money. "This is a small thank you for all your help these past years."

Danny started to push the money back but hesitated. "You don't have to do that."

"I know, but I want to."

The money disappeared into a side pant pocket before Wolfe could take another breath. "Danny, I do have a favor to ask."

"Sure, anything, Mr. Lyon."

"If anyone inquires—and I don't believe anyone will, but in case they do—tell them the plane is based out of a different airport, now."

"Which one?"

"I don't know yet. Depends on the new location for my business."

The shorter man nodded. "What if I don't remember anything about you?"

Michael extracted several more hundred-dollar bills from his wallet and placed them on the counter. "I believe that would be a better response."

"Gonna miss you, Mr. Lyon."

"We'll be back, I just don't know when."

Back in the hangar, Nadia leaned against the Jeep and watched Wolfe return. "What did he say?"

"I believe he'll deny knowing anything about us until someone flashes money—or a gun."

Nadia chuckled. "Will we be back?"

With a grim smile, Wolfe said. "I don't know. I hope so, but..."

"I know. I'll pick you up at the Branson West Airport."

Wolfe drew her into an embrace and they kissed. "Hopefully, by the time you get there, I will have all the paperwork taken care of."

She put her hand on his cheek and locked her focus on his eyes. "Be careful, Michael."

"Always."

◆

"Lyon Enterprises, LLC is the corporate entity responsible for any charges here, Ms. Davenport."

"I see." Beverly Davenport, Airport Manager, looked up from the signed contract with a big smile. In her mid-forties, she was trim and athletic, still attractive, but to cover the signs of age, wore more make-up than needed. Plus, her hair appeared unnaturally black. "Twelve-month contract, just like you asked. Mr. Lyon."

"I will assume I can extend our stay, if needed."

"Of course. Just give us a month's notice."

"Excellent."

"What does Lyon Enterprises, LLC do, Mr. Lyon?"

With a smile, Wolfe replied. "Consulting."

Nadia walked into the office and stepped up behind Wolfe, placing a hand on his back. "All done?"

Davenport surveyed the newcomer with distaste as her smile disappeared.

Wolfe looked at Nadia and kissed her cheek. "Yes, my darling, we're all done here."

After they were back in the Jeep, Nadia chuckled. "You never call me 'my darling'."

He shrugged.

"And the kiss on the cheek—what was that all about?"

"Beverly Davenport was becoming too friendly and inquisitive. Our little display of affection stopped her taking it to the next level." He smiled. "What's wrong with a little peck on the cheek?"

Nadia guided the Jeep out of the airport parking lot. She glanced at Wolfe and, with a mischievous grin, said, "I'm French, Michael. A kiss on the cheek makes me feel like I'm your sister."

He reached over and patted her thigh. "Trust me, I will never treat you like a sister." He hesitated, but said it anyway, "You just used two contractions."

"I know. Disgusting, isn't it?"

They both laughed.

⬥

"I need a favor, Joseph."

Joseph, having returned to Washington earlier in the afternoon, sat in the spare bedroom of his apartment. "Is the plane safe, Michael?"

"That's one of my favors."

"Okay, what can I do?"

"I need a flight plan deleted from the FFA database."

Silence was his answer.

"I need the one I filed for Branson West to disappear."

"Why?"

"In case someone gets too inquisitive."

"Reid?"

"Or someone he's hired. After our discussion with Martin Benson, I think there is a better than fifty percent chance they know where my house is. Or, at least have an idea of the general vicinity."

"Okay, I get it. I have a resource who can take care of it."

"JR?"

"Maybe."

"Sorry I asked."

"Michael, just know I will handle it. You don't need to know details."

"Got it." After a slight pause, Wolfe continued, "What happened to Canfield's body?"

"If I remember correctly, it was cremated. Why?"

"Was there an autopsy?"

"I'm sure there was, but I don't remember any details. I can find out. Why?"

"Just trying to make sense of something that doesn't make sense."

"Okay. Don't worry about the flight plan. Consider it gone."

"Thanks, Joseph."

Wolfe ended the call, closed the laptop and stood. He wandered through the condo looking for Nadia and found her on a sofa reading.

She looked up. "Will he take care of the flight plan?"

Wolfe nodded. "I need some air. I'll be on the back deck."

She smiled and returned to her reading.

Cool, crisp air greeted Wolfe as he emerged onto the suspended platform off their kitchen. This high above the cove, Michael could see across the lake numerous points of lights marking the presence of other residences. He looked up at the night sky ablaze with the Milky Way ribbon. A muted silence hovered over the water. Only the sound of wind whistling through tree limbs and waves hitting the shore below could be heard.

As he gazed skyward, a question without an answer lodged in his thoughts. He ran the frequent conversations held with Geoffrey Canfield over in his mind and the same question kept popping up. How was Canfield mixed up with Reid and Gerlis? The answer eluded him.

He lost track of time until he heard the sliding glass door open and then felt Nadia's arms around his waist as she pressed herself against his back. "You must be getting cold. Come in, Michael."

"I can't figure it out."

"What?"

"Why or how Canfield became involved with Reid and Gerlis."

"You may never know. Canfield is dead."

Wolfe twisted around in her embrace to face her and wrapped his arms around her. "Is he?"

She did not respond, her attention on his eyes.

"Gerlis faked his own death. Maybe Canfield did as well."

"Michael, you are making no sense. How can you fake a heart attack?"

"Easy. There are drugs that mimic the symptoms. I'm sure Geoffrey knew more than one physician who could be bribed to sign the death certificate and then have a body cremated in his place. London is full of homeless, nameless souls who die on the streets every day. Once a body is cremated, it destroys all the DNA for comparison." He paused. "It just takes money."

"Did he have money?"

"Not that I knew about. But he always told me to put money away for a rainy day. Which I did. I've been out here thinking back on some of the numerous conversations we had while sipping Scotch in his library. I recall him mentioning a lifelong dream."

"Which was?"

"Retiring to a warm island in the Caribbean."

Her eyes narrowed. "Do you believe he is alive?"

"The more I think about it..." He nodded.

"A lot of possibilities there, Michael. It would be like, as you Americans say, looking for a needle in a hayloft."

"Haystack."

"Whatever. Where would you start looking?"

"Geoffrey is an unapologetic anglophile and he hates being cold. He'll be in a warm part of the world still under the jurisdiction and sovereignty of the United Kingdom."

"Does England still have colonies?"

"Not like a hundred years ago. They're more

protectorates than colonies."

"So where would that be?"

"The Cayman Islands."

"Why there?"

"A few minutes ago, I remembered a conversation he and I had one evening. His consumption of Glenfiddich that night was profound. He was quite drunk, actually. During one of his inebriated soliloquies, he waxed poetically about the state of British affairs. It was during this particular monologue he mentioned something he had never spoken of before."

She snuggled closer to ward off the cold breeze swirling around the deck.

"He told me about making a bid on a small cottage in West Bay. He never mentioned it again, so I don't know if he bought the place or not."

"How would you find out?'

"The only way I can think of would be to go."

She smiled. "I could work on my tan."

"Yes. You do look sexy with tan lines."

She hesitated. "Michael, how do we get to the Cayman's without flying?"

He smiled and hugged her tighter. "Several years ago, I heard about an old friend who operated a charter boat service out of Key West."

"Won't that be expensive?"

"Probably, but I bet I can make a deal with him."

She buried her head against his chest. "I am cold."

"Let's go in."

CHAPTER 25

Michael Fuckin' Wolfe, how the hell are ya, son?"

Wolfe extended a hand to Chief of the Boat Rufus Carroll. "I'm good, Chief. How about yourself?"

Chief Carroll, to everyone who knew him, hated his first name and seldom used it except on official documents. Standing just under five-foot-ten and in his late fifties, he still had broad shoulders and a trim waist. He was dressed in grease-smeared overalls, a sleeveless T-shirt displaying deeply tanned biceps and forearms with a lifetime of tattoos collected from different locales around the world. His longish gray hair, swept back and tied in a ponytail, plus his sea and sun weathered face gave him the appearance of a man ten years older.

"I couldn't be better unless there were two of me." He turned his gaze to Nadia. "And who is this lovely young lass?"

Nadia smiled and offered her hand. Wolfe introduced her. "Chief, this is my wife, Nadia."

Carroll shot a quick glance at Michael and then returned his attention to Nadia. "I can see Michael got the better end of that deal."

"Nice to meet you, Chief. Michael has told me a lot about you."

"I doubt he told you everything, otherwise you wouldn't be here. But then I can tell you tales about him that'd curl your hair." He paused and looked at Michael. "You didn't come all the way to Key West to chit-chat. What's on your mind?"

"That's what I like about you, Chief. You don't care much for social niceties."

The older man shook his head. "Don't have time for them. What's up?"

"Do you still do charter work?"

"Never stopped."

"How much to take us to Grand Cayman?"

"How long you want to stay?"

"Couple of weeks, maybe less."

Carroll crossed his arm and looked at Nadia and then back to Wolfe. "Cheaper to fly."

"Don't want to."

The Chief stared at Wolfe for a long time, his brow furrowed and arms still crossed. Finally, he relaxed and smiled. "If it was anybody but you, I'd say, hell no. But I owe you. Let's say five thousand for the two weeks."

"Four."

"Forty-five"

"Done."

Two Days Later

"I like the name of your boat, Chief."

"So, do I. *Escape* seemed like the right metaphor." He glanced at Wolfe, who was standing next to him on the bridge. "Why am I taking you to Grand Cayman?"

The side of Wolfe's mouth twitched. "Someone I know is hiding there. I need to talk to him and find out why."

Carroll chuckled and looked ahead. "That was a bullshit answer. Want to try again?"

"Not at the moment."

"Very well."

Silence fell between the two men as *Escape* made its way toward the western side of Cuba. Carroll nodded at Nadia sunbathing on the bow. "She's a beautiful woman, Michael. Think she'll take her top off?" He smiled mischievously as he said it.

The twitch returned. "Yes, she is and no she won't." He turned to his friend. "You're becoming a dirty old man, Chief."

"Becoming?"

They both chuckled.

"I noted a slight French accent."

Wolfe smiled, "Her father was a diplomat. She grew up in France."

Carroll's eyes lit up and he laughed out loud. "You are so full of bullshit. You never were good at lying."

Wolfe stared out over the open sea. "She is from France, but I met her in Israel. Someone tried to kill us in Barcelona a few years ago and now I'm trying to find out why."

"Enough said. I'll do what I can to help."

"Thank you, Chief."

Grand Cayman Island – Twelve Days Later

"If he is alive, Michael, maybe he is somewhere else on the island."

Wolfe and Nadia sat at a table outside a small cafe watching tourists meander in and out of shops, bars, and restaurants. Nadia sipped tea and Wolfe drank strong bitter coffee.

Wolfe shook his head. "If he's alive, he'll be here."

"You've checked property records with no luck."

With a grin, he looked at her. "Are you forgetting we have different names now?"

Chuckling, she lifted the tea to her lips. "Oh, that. Forgot." She glanced around and then turned back to Wolfe. "We are scheduled to leave tomorrow. What are we going to do then?"

He remained quiet, concentrating on something across the street only he could see. Standing, he reached into his jean's pocket and threw a ten-dollar bill on the table. "Let's go."

She followed him as he hurried across the busy avenue and fell into a purposeful stride on the sidewalk. "What is it?"

His only response was to quicken his pace. When they arrived at a dingy bar, he stopped before going in. Turning, he smiled. "Wait three minutes. If I haven't come out, head inside and find me."

"What is it?"

"I think I saw him. I just have to make sure."

"Three minutes?"

He nodded and disappeared inside.

While his eyes adjusted to the gloom, he heard numerous conversations in distinct British accents. With a slight smile, he realized the establishment catered to expats from the United Kingdom. He spotted Geoffrey Canfield sitting at a table in the back looking straight at him. A wide grin was displayed on his ex-controller's face as he raised a high-ball glass and motioned for Wolfe to join him.

As Wolfe approached, Canfield stood and offered his hand. "'Bout bloody time you figured it out, Michael. I was starting to worry."

Nadia stood outside the bar, sweeping the area to make sure no one paid too much attention to her. When her mental clock told her three minutes elapsed, she entered the bar and stood still. After the bright Caribbean sunlight, the darkness and loud conversations assaulted her senses. As her eyes adjusted, she saw Wolfe hunched over a small table at the back of the crowded room, conversing with an older man. She made her way toward the table, gathering looks and stares from the inhabitants, all of whom stopped their conversations as she passed.

As she approached, Wolfe noticed and motioned for her to join them. Both men stood and Canfield offered his hand. "You must be, Nadia."

"And you must be Geoffrey Canfield."

"But alas, I am."

They all sat and Wolfe said, "Geoffrey goes by Greyson Collins here on the island."

Nadia smiled. "At least you can still use your monogrammed shirts."

Canfield's eyes sparkled and he chuckled. "Yes, we have to maintain a bit of decorum even when away from civilization, don't we?"

She returned the smile and nodded.

Wolfe picked up the conversation. "You were about to tell me why the big charade."

After the older man sipped his drink, he took a deep breath. "Yes, I was." He paused. "Where are my manners? You don't have a refreshment, Nadia."

"No, thank you."

Pressing his lips together in a grimace, Canfield studied his glass as he turned it clockwise. "Rather embarrassing, I must say."

"Geoffrey, you're stalling. Who threatened you?"

"That bastard Gerald Reid. It wasn't a threat—the bugger actually had someone try to kill me. I got lucky, Michael."

"Why did he want you dead?"

"Because I know too much about him and his Israeli pal, Asa Gerlis."

"Did you know Gerlis staged his own death?"

Without a change in expression, Canfield shook his head. "Not surprising. How?"

"Photoshopped his own image onto the body of some poor soul being beheaded."

The older man grimaced. "Dear God."

Nadia spoke next. "There is speculation he was a Russian mole within the Mossad and staged his own death to go back to Russia."

Canfield gave a slight nod. "He was a bloody Russian. But he wasn't a mole. He's a greedy bastard with a deep hatred of the communists." He paused. "He was executing his escape plan. I'm surprised Reid hasn't done it yet." Canfield noticed his drink was empty and searched the room for the barmaid. He saw her and waggled his glass. She smiled and went to order him another. He turned back to Wolfe and Nadia. "Reid is such a bastard."

"Geoffrey, you're dancing around something. What are you trying to say?"

"Not proud of it."

Wolfe rolled his eyes. "What is it, Geoffrey?"

"A long time ago, Reid, Gerlis and I made a deal with the devil."

CHAPTER 26

SOMEWHERE IN HOWELL COUNTY, MISSOURI

Gregg Simpson wasn't a developer, nor was he even a real estate broker—he was a newly recruited member of Gerald Reid's anti-terrorist group. His record search at the Howell County Court House had one objective in mind—find a specific piece of property. With information provided by Robert Benson to Kendra Burges during interviews at FCI Edgefield and then Benson's subsequent death after being released, Reid dispatched Simpson to Howell County to search for the location of the property. These events were the first clues as to the possible whereabouts of Michael Wolfe.

Simpson looked up from the computer screen and smiled. Turning to the young woman with bored eyes attending the reception counter, he said, "How do I make a hard copy of a file?"

She did not return the smile. "Just press the print

screen button at the top."

"Thank you."

Twenty minutes later, he walked out of the courthouse with locations of five pieces of property matching his search parameters, all neatly printed at the expense of the Howell County Courthouse.

After five years as an Army Ranger, Simpson had decided he needed one more adventure and made an application to the CIA. After interviews with several lower-level agency functionaries and finally Gerald Reid, he had been offered a position. Slender and athletic, with dark brown hair and a perpetual two-day beard, he was, at best, nondescript—another reason for his hiring.

With a vague description of the property supplied by Benson, the first two properties he searched were quickly dismissed due to a lack of an old cabin on the land. The third location contained an updated cabin which appeared to be built in the late 1800s. This piece of property he scrutinized closer. After driving the Jeep north thirteen hundred yards, he topped a small rise in an open field and saw a sight which piqued his curiosity. Nine hundred yards down the sloped pasture, he saw what appeared to be camouflage netting. With a slight smile, he accelerated the Jeep toward the spot. As he grew nearer, the area morphed into a door on the side of the hill.

The second he stopped the vehicle in front of the camouflaged entrance, a pair of motion-detector security cameras started recording his arrival at Michael and Nadia's underground home. The images were downloaded to a server within the house which immediately backed them up on a cloud-based file system. The software controlling the cloud-based system sent an automated text message to a preprogrammed number.

The owner of the earth-sheltered home received an electronic notification before Simpson could even step out of the Jeep.

Grand Cayman Island

Michael Wolfe glanced at his cell phone after feeling the vibration of an incoming text message. He smiled and returned the phone to his cargo pant pocket, his attention again focused on Geoffrey Canfield. "Sorry for the interruption. What do you mean a deal with the devil?"

"Ever hear of a retired United States general named William Little?"

Wolfe's ability to hide his emotions with a practiced neutral expression failed him. His body stiffened and he narrowed his eyes.

Canfield nodded. "I take it you have."

After glancing at Nadia for a split second, Wolfe cocked his head to the side as he said to Canfield. "What about him?"

"How much do you know?"

"I'd rather hear what you have to say."

Canfield nodded. "Little began his career in the army after graduating from West Point. His rise to command level was more meteoric than most careers, not because of ability, but because your country's military felt it needed more diversity. He proceeded to have a lackluster and, many would say, unchallenged career, until Operations Desert Shield and Desert Storm."

Nadia asked. "What happened?"

"General Little's true personality made itself known."

Without taking his eyes off Canfield, Wolfe said through clenched teeth, "I was there."

"Yes, I know. You also may have been involved with some of his disastrous operations without knowing it."

"I was."

"Then you know most of the ones he initiated resulted in high casualties with little strategic gains."

Wolfe could only nod.

"I was with MI6 at the time attached to an SAS squad as their intelligence officer. Some of the lads were coming to me complaining about Little. So, I started a quiet inquiry."

"What'd you find?"

"The man was corrupt and self-serving. He surrounded himself with junior officers who were just as ethically challenged as he. They all profited from the war."

Wolfe knew all of this, but remained quiet.

"After we liberated Kuwait and pushed Saddam Hussein's forces back into Iraq, General Little quietly went back to the states for a brief tour at the Pentagon. The brass quickly discovered how inept the man was. He left the military and moved abroad to the island of Madagascar. He claimed his early retirement was due to the passing of a rich aunt. He explained, to those who would listen, she left him forty million dollars. No one could determine if the aunt ever existed. With an inheritance that large, he also inherited a large tax bill. He never paid the IRS. Since Madagascar does not have an extradition treaty with the US, he spent the next twenty-two years becoming quite the influential person in the small country."

With Wolfe remaining quiet, Nadia asked another

question. "Did something happen to him?'

Canfield almost smiled but hid it with his hand. "He was assassinated by a sniper in May of 2014."

No comment came from Wolfe.

Canfield continued, "He was standing on his veranda when his head suddenly disappeared in a pink mist of blood and brain tissue. His security detail could not find the sniper hide until they extended their search out beyond 800 meters. At a distance of 1600 meters down the beach, they found it. I'm told it was an extraordinary shot. Not too many men have the skill set or ability to do that, Michael."

With a neutral expression, the ex-Marine nodded. "I agree, that's a difficult shot, especially on a windy beach."

"Exactly. You wouldn't know anything about it, would you?"

"I was at a conference in Dubai at the time." Wolfe paused. "So, what does this have to do with making a deal with the devil?"

"I'm getting to it. Because of my initial investigation during Desert Shield and Storm, the CIA and Mossad took it upon themselves to offer assistance. It just so happened the CIA assigned a young recruit named Gerald Reid to the task. It was also Asa Gerlis' first overseas assignment for the Mossad. There I was, a ten-year veteran for Her Majesties Foreign Service, basically training two rookies." Canfield took a sip of his gin and tonic. "You haven't asked what we were investigating."

"I don't have to. I know."

"Figured you did."

"General Little, with the help of his junior officers, was looting antiquities from Kuwait and parts of Iraq."

Canfield nodded. "Do you know what happened to

those objects?"

"No, I just knew what he was doing." Wolfe felt a small pang of guilt about lying to the older man, but he did not need Canfield asking too many questions. "There was a secret auction held in Geneva. Conservative estimates on the dollar value of that sale reached one hundred million dollars. Remember, I said conservative."

"Why didn't Interpol shut it down?"

"Because the auctions were not public and all the pieces went to private collectors. It was over before anyone knew what was going on. By then the evidence had disappeared, the men behind it hid their money and General Little was untouchable in Madagascar."

"Apparently not too untouchable."

"Figure of speech, my boy."

Wolfe stared at Canfield for several awkward moments until a small smile creased his face. "Let me guess. You, Reid and Gerlis discovered all of this and made a deal with Little to keep quiet."

Canfield nodded his head. "Not proud of it, but we did."

"How much, Geoffrey?"

"I don't know what Reid or Gerlis got, but my share paid for my retirement."

"Wasn't it equal?"

"No. I wanted nothing to do with it at first. But once they told me what would happen if I didn't, well..." He paused. "Let's just say they convinced me it was time to retire. So, here I am, enjoying my Senior years in a warm climate with a female companion who takes care of me."

"You mentioned earlier you think Reid tried to have you killed."

"Almost succeeded."

"Why do you think he did that?"

"Because they have continued to dabble in stolen art and felt I was a liability."

Wolfe remained quiet for several seconds. "So, who faked the heart attack and autopsy?"

"Doctor friend of mine."

"Aren't you afraid he'll give you up?"

"Who do you think my female companion is, Michael? She wanted out of London as bad as I did."

Wolfe laughed. "Good for you, Geoffrey. There's one problem though."

"What's that?"

"Reid and Gerlis must think I know something about all of this."

"Why would he think that?"

"Because they both knew I worked with you. They set Nadia and me up. We were targets of a sniper in Barcelona. Now they have people looking for us."

Canfield stared at Wolfe for a few moments, took a sip of his drink and smiled. "Michael, you, of all people, are more than capable of taking care of a problem like that. Plus, you have the help of Ms. Picard. If memory serves me, she is just as capable."

Wolfe shot a quick glance at Nadia, who shrugged. Returning his attention to Canfield, he stood and said, "I appreciate you telling me all of this, Geoffrey. I wish you happiness and a long life. If you ever need anything, let me know." He handed his ex-controller a folded sheet of paper. "As far as I'm concerned, you died of a heart attack in London."

Opening the note, Canfield read it, smiled, refolded it, and placed it in his shirt pocket. "Thank you. One more thing."

"Yes."

"Gerald Reid and Asa Gerlis were on the veranda in Madagascar when William Little met with his accident."

Wolfe's mouth twitched as he stared at Canfield. Without saying another word, he and Nadia left the darkness of the bar for the bright Caribbean sunlight.

Escape slid through the calm waters north of Grand Cayman on its journey back to Key West. Wolfe and Nadia stood on the bow, watching the water pass by the ship. In an unspoken agreement, they did not discuss the meeting with Geoffrey Canfield until far out at sea, away from curious ears and electronic eavesdropping.

"Do you believe Geoffrey, Michael?"

"Until I know different, yes."

"He could still be involved with Reid and Gerlis."

"He could. But..."

"You know him better than I do."

"He's very capable of deception, It's in his DNA. But this time..." Wolfe shook his head. "I don't think so."

"Now what?"

"Remember the text message I received after you arrived at the table?"

She nodded.

"Someone triggered the security cameras on the sheltered house."

Nadia remained quiet as she glanced at Wolfe then back at the water. After several moments, she said. "Did you see who it was?"

"Haven't looked at the video yet. We'll have to wait until we get to Key West before I can get a cell phone signal."

"You don't seem upset about it."

He shrugged.

She turned to look at him. "You knew they would

find it, didn't you?"

"You just used contractions in two consecutive sentences."

After closing her eyes, she shook her head slowly. "You are avoiding the question."

"Yes, I am."

She glared at him in silence.

He glanced at her as the corner of his mouth twitched. "It was inevitable. Reid was not going to give up. He would have kept looking for us and it might have been at a time when we weren't prepared. Now that he thinks he's found us, he'll be more predictable."

Nodding, she returned her gaze to the open ocean in front of them. "I get that. What do we do now?"

"Canfield said something at the table I didn't quite understand. He said you were as capable as I was, then you just shrugged. What did he mean?"

"He was merely pointing out I was trained by the Mossad, just like you were trained by the CIA."

"No, he wasn't. He was referring to my training as a sniper."

She shrugged.

"There you go again."

With a slight smile, she glanced at him. "So was I."

"Really."

She nodded.

"How good are you?"

"Not as good as you, but I am better than most."

"You've never mentioned it."

Another shrug.

"Nadia?"

"Most of the targets I would encounter would never suspect a woman sniper. It would allow more freedom to observe them and determine the best way to complete my assignment. For all practical purposes, I would be invisible to them. My training went well, but I was never operational."

"Why?"

"You."

He frowned and looked at her as she stared off into the horizon. "Me? How would I have kept you from going operational?"

With a slight smile, she turned her attention back to him. "You were not an Israeli. With your language skills, you could pose as French, German, or a Canadian. To our enemies, you were more invisible than a woman."

"I never thought of it that way."

As she stepped closer to him, she wrapped her arms around his waist. "I am glad I never had to see if I could do it."

"Do what?"

"Pull the trigger with another human being in my sights."

He did not comment.

"It is just as well, Michael. We have other concerns to deal with right now."

He returned the embrace. "Yes. Yes, we do."

They stood silently as the *Escape* cut through the calm ocean water, remaining in each other's arms and their own thoughts. Five minutes later, Wolfe said, "What if we are looking at this all wrong?"

She broke from the embrace. "What do you mean?"

He continued to study the horizon. "I have never been able to get my head around why we were targeted in Barcelona, or why Reid didn't believe our ruse in Mexico City."

A slight smile came to her lips as she listened.

Wolfe continued, "After listening to Geoffrey, I was convinced Reid believed we knew about their arrangement with William Little." He paused. "I don't think that's the case at all."

"Gerlis was the one who suggested I train as a sniper."

"Really?"

"Yes."

With a nod, he returned his attention to the horizon. "I wondered why Geoffrey thought it necessary to tell me Reid and Gerlis were in Madagascar."

He heard Nadia gasp. She said, "They know you were the one who made the shot."

A slight grin crossed his lips. "They aren't worried we know about the money. They couldn't care less. We couldn't prove anything anyway." He paused, turned and focused on her eyes. "They're scared to death of us."

CHAPTER 27

Joseph Kincaid looked up from his computer to see Griggs standing at his office door displaying a broad smile.

"Please tell me you've decided to quit and this is your last day."

"No, it's my sworn duty to make your life miserable."

Pressing the palms of his hands against his weary eyes, Joseph said, "Why the smile?"

"It's Friday and it's five o'clock."

"Not buying it, Jerry. What's going on?"

The smile disappeared as he walked over to the desk and laid a file in front of Joseph. "Gerald Reid is in full freak-out mode. The identity of the man in the security video you gave me is a CIA employee named Gregg Simpson. He's an ex-army Ranger. He just started with the agency working directly for Reid." Griggs tilted his head. "Didn't know deputy directors had their own private operations officers."

After opening the file, Joseph skimmed the pages and looked up. "They generally don't. Does the FBI know about this?"

Griggs shook his head. "At this point in time, it isn't on their radar. By the way, where did you get the video?"

Joseph shrugged as he picked up his desk phone's handset and punched in a number he knew by heart. As he waited, he looked at his assistant. "Maybe I can help them find it." When the call was answered, he said, "Paul, we need to talk." He listened, then replied. "Yes, I know where it is." He glanced at his wristwatch, "I can be there in an hour. I have a few things to finish here." More silence. "Good, see you there."

The smile returned to Griggs' face. "Was that the FBI Director?"

Joseph nodded. "I am sure he'll be interested in what you found." He paused. "Nice work on this, Jerry."

FBI Director Paul Stumpf carefully read the pages handed to him by National Security Advisor Joseph Kincaid. Now in his early sixties, Stumpf, at one time a dedicated marathon runner, still maintained a lean body. But after having both knees replaced, he was starting to add a few pounds to his five-eleven frame. His perfectly styled dark brown hair displayed the first hints of gray appearing around his temples. His rimless glasses allowed his arctic blue eyes to focus on Joseph, a slight smile on his face.

"When did you find this out?"

"It was brought to my attention this afternoon.

That's why I called."

Stumpf removed his glasses and pinched his nose. "Gerald Reid has been a serious pain in my ass for years. He continues to run domestic ops without telling us. When we confront him about it, he shrugs and tells us to do a better job."

Joseph remained quiet.

"You know for certain this Michael Wolfe person is dead?"

"DNA analysis by Israel's Mossad confirmed it." Joseph felt a momentary pang of guilt for lying to his friend, but it quickly passed.

Staring at the file, Stumpf put his glasses back on. "Okay, I'll have a chat with the DCI. I really don't want to involve your boss over something like this—yet."

"That's why I brought it to your attention."

"Want to be at the meeting?"

"Wouldn't miss it."

The Next Morning

Gerald Reid fumed. He was far too busy this morning to have a status meeting with the DCI. Meetings with this particular DCI were dreadfully long, unproductive and always on short notice. His anger grew as he walked toward the conference room. An important project would be delayed because of this nonsense.

As he entered the conference room, he realized this was not a normal status meeting. Director of Central Intelligence Dwight King pointed to a chair across from the men at the table. "Sit down, Reid."

Reid did not sit immediately. He stared at the Director and then at the president's National Security

Advisor, Joseph Kincaid. He noted FBI Director Paul Stumpf and Attorney General Noel Taylor were at the table as well. He returned his attention to King. "What is this about, Director?"

"Shut up and sit down. We'll ask the questions."

Hesitantly, Reid sat and folded his hands on the table. His practiced expression of sheer boredom appeared on his face. He was anything but bored.

King started the inquisition. "Why do you have operatives working inside the United States?"

"I beg your pardon, Director?"

"You heard me."

"I have no idea what you are talking about."

"Careful, Mr. Reid." Attorney General Taylor gave him a slight smile. "You are currently on very thin ice, legally speaking. Don't add lying to federal authorities to the charges."

Reid stared at the AG and then at Director King. "I have men all over the world collecting data for analysis. You will have to be more specific."

"Why did you have an operative in Southern Missouri searching for a dead man?"

"If you are referring to our search for Michael Wolfe, he has been declared an enemy combatant and known terrorist. And we know he is alive."

Taylor chuckled. "Declared by whom?"

"My department."

Stumpf frowned. "Since when did the CIA take over for the FBI declaring someone an enemy combatant inside the United States?"

"When the FBI doesn't do it's job, Director Stumpf."

King slammed the table with his palm. "Reid, you will refrain from pointing a finger at another department when the finger is being pointed at you."

Reid's eyes widened. "Yes, Director."

"What is your proof Wolfe is alive, Reid?" The question came from Stumpf.

"A TSA security camera photograph of him at the Newark Airport, confirmed by facial recognition software."

King extracted a piece of paper from a file in front of him and showed it to Reid. "This is the official report from Israel declaring that DNA analysis on the body of a deceased individual in Mexico City was confirmed to be ex-CIA Operative Michael Wolfe. Now you are saying a grainy photograph disproves a DNA test? Is that what you are basing your actions on, Mr. Reid?"

Realizing the absurdity of his argument, Reid remained quiet.

"I hope not, because if you are, you are in serious legal jeopardy."

Joseph handed a file to Stumpf. The FBI Director opened it and extracted a sheet. After studying it, he looked up at Reid. "Is this the photograph you claim to be Michael Wolfe?"

Stumpf handed it to the Deputy Director. Reid studied it, smiled and handed it back. "Yes, facial recognition gave it an eighty-eight percent probability of being Wolfe."

After handing the photograph to King, Stumpf returned his attention to Reid. "The photograph is of a man named Marcus Hunter. He's a mid-level manager for a food manufacturer based in Alabama. FBI confirmed his identity and interviewed him. He was in New Jersey on business that day." Stumpf stared at Reid for several uncomfortable moments. "Care to comment?"

Reid's eyes grew wider as he moistened his lips. "But the facial recog—"

King interrupted. "Is not foolproof, Mr. Reid. You

have violated several internal regulations and exposed this agency to a Congressional investigation. Something we don't need at the moment."

Steeling himself in his conviction, Reid's expression hardened. "This is a typical Michael Wolfe ploy. He is smart, dangerous and cunning. He's planning a terrorist attack inside the United States. I can feel it. Are you all willing to take that chance, gentlemen?"

Shaking his head slowly, DCI King replaced all the papers back in their respective folders. He took a deep breath and let it out slowly. He looked at Stumpf and then Taylor. Both men nodded slightly.

"Mr. Reid, it has come to the attention of our human resource department and this office that you are over-worked and stressed. Your sixteen-hour days have caught up with you. You have twenty-five years with the agency, which allows you to retire with a full pension. I expect your letter of retirement on my desk within the hour."

"I don't want to retire. I have too much to do."

"Not anymore. You have two choices: retire, like I suggested, or face an inquiry by the DOJ and FBI. If that inquiry discovers wrongdoing, and I mean any wrongdoing, you will be subject to arrest and forfeiture of your pension." King's eyes narrowed. "Is that how you want to play this, Gerald?"

Reid's eyes narrowed and his ego took over. "Go ahead and investigate me, Director. My record is spotless."

Joseph handed the DCI another sheet of paper. King looked at it and smiled. He turned his attention back to Reid as he slid the sheet across the table. "Does the information on this page look familiar, Mr. Reid?"

Staring at the piece of paper in front of him, Reid's face turned white and bile reached the back of his throat. The page displayed a printout of his bank balance. Not the bank account his salary went to, but the one in Switzerland. It showed withdrawals and deposits for the past ten years.

"My letter will be on your desk within the hour, Director."

"Kind of what I thought. We have several gentlemen waiting outside to escort you to your office and keep you company until the letter is completed. Good day, sir." King looked toward the door and said in a loud voice, "We're ready in here."

The conference room door opened and two men entered. Both wore the uniform and badge of the CIA Security Protective Service.

King said, "Gentlemen, will you escort Mr. Reid to his office? He knows what needs to be done. Once he has completed his task, please escort him to his personal vehicle and bid him a good day."

Both men nodded but remained quiet.

Reid stood and walked out of the room, followed by the two officers.

Once the door was shut, King chuckled and handed the bank statement back to Joseph. "How in the world did you find this information?"

Placing it in a file folder, Joseph gave the DCI a slight smile. "Let's just put it this way—I have a very enterprising associate who is excellent at following money trails."

The Attorney General frowned. "Dwight, do you want to prosecute him for the secret account?"

King closed his eyes and shook his head. "I thought about it when all of this information was brought to my attention. No, we've handled this in the quietest way possible. If Reid starts making noise, then yes. We will prosecute."

Everyone in the room nodded and stood to leave.

CHAPTER 28

The driver of the rented white Ford Fusion waited patiently in the parking lot of a Catholic parish. He glanced occasionally at a digital clock embedded in the car's information display. As a man with great patience, his current hour and a half vigil paled in comparison to other operations conducted long ago and in faraway countries.

An hour later, a black Range Rover passed the church. The corner of his mouth twitched as he casually put the car into gear. Knowing the destination of the SUV allowed the driver to follow at an unhurried pace. Keeping a safe distance behind, the driver watched for an opportunity to execute the next phase of his plan.

At an intersection halfway to the black SUV's ultimate destination, a traffic light changed causing the vehicle to stop at the head of the line. An opening in the turn lane next to it presented a perfect location for the driver to complete the next step. He slowed and stopped next to the black vehicle. Now in the turn lane, Michael Wolfe stared at Gerald Reid from the driver side of the Ford. Reid glanced at Wolfe and returned his attention back to the traffic light.

Sudden recognition made his head snap back in Wolfe's direction just as the traffic signal turned green. Without changing his expression, Wolfe stared at the now ex-CIA Deputy Director and turned the Fusion right. He accelerated away from the brief encounter.

The unmoving Range Rover garnered indignant horn blasts from cars behind it as other vehicles appeared in the turn lane, blocking any opportunity to chase after the apparition. Wide-eyed, he finally reacted to the blaring horns behind him.

Frustration and panic caused Reid to press hard on the accelerator and squeal the tires as he drove toward the next intersection. After maneuvering through various side streets, he returned to the one where he last saw the Fusion. Unfortunately, the Ford was nowhere to be seen.

Wolfe glanced in his rearview mirror with a slight smile. The ambush could not have been executed better. Reid was stuck in traffic unable to do anything but move forward. He accelerated the Ford toward a stoplight displaying green. There he made a left turn and disappeared into the mid-day Alexandria, Virginia traffic.

Thirty minutes later, Wolfe walked into the hotel room he and Nadia shared. She sat at the room's desk studying a laptop. Turning, she smiled. "How did it go?"

"Perfect. He looked like he'd just seen a ghost."

"He did, Michael. You are supposed to be dead." She pointed to the muted TV. "CNN is reporting his retirement from the CIA."

Wolfe nodded. "Joseph sent a text message about it fifteen minutes ago."

She folded her arms. "What's next?"

He smiled. Nadia's use of contractions seemed to increase each day. "Were you able to Photoshop the picture?"

She gave him a glare. "I am not the amateur you think I am." She pointed at the computer screen. "I am becoming very good at this. What do you think?"

Suppressing a chuckle, he studied the image. "I think it's perfect. Let's get it printed and overnighted to his house."

At exactly 10:16 a.m. on his first full day of retirement, Gerald Reid used the stylus handed to him, to sign the LED screen confirming receipt of the FedEx package. Reid shut the door and studied the return address on the shipping label. He did not recognize the sender or the address. With only the slightest of hesitation, he opened the flat white shipping package. After extracting the single sheet, he stared at it in horror.

Printed on the picture was a telephoto image of him standing next to his Range Rover parked in his front circle drive, his head in the crosshair of a high-powered rifle scope.

Kendra Burges answered the call after checking the caller ID. "What do you want, Gerald?" Her tone indignant.

"I saw him yesterday."

"Saw who?"

"Wolfe."

She took a deep breath and let it out slowly. "He's dead. Your obsession with the man got you fired."

"I was not fired. I retired."

"Whatever."

"Where are you?"

"At work. I've been reassigned."

Not comprehending, Reid paused for a second. "What do you mean?"

"I've been reassigned and demoted because of you. Thank you."

"Demoted—how? Where?"

"I've been assigned to the embassy in New Zealand."

Reid remained silent.

"I haven't decided to take it yet. I may just resign."

"New Zealand? I don't know what to say."

"Of course, you don't. It doesn't affect you, so why would you give a shit?"

"That's not fair, Kendra. Remember, I was forced to retire."

"Yes, but they didn't send you to the middle of the South Pacific Ocean."

"Don't go. I have plenty of money. We can sell my place and settle somewhere like Portugal or Spain."

"Are you sure you still have money? I bet they know about your Swiss bank accounts. They're the CIA. I bet they've frozen the account and you're as broke as I am."

His eyes widened as he realized his mistake of not checking his bank accounts. He ended the call without another word and rushed to his laptop. Five minutes later, he stared in horror at the balance of each of his Swiss accounts. His balance in both totaled 2 cents each.

The call to Kendra forgotten, he accessed another account he kept in Dubai. With it still intact, he spent the next several hours transferring those funds to a safe location in Hong Kong.

His next task was to book a flight for Barcelona.

Staring at the now-silent phone, Kendra shook her head. With her suspicions about Gerald Reid confirmed, a new task presented itself. How to salvage her career with the CIA without the protection of a deputy director. Taking the position in New Zealand, while distasteful, might present new opportunities. She took a deep breath. As she exhaled, her feelings of anxiety eased. With a grim smile, she dialed the number of her new supervisor to accept the posting in New Zealand.

Nadia sat cross-legged on the hotel bed, her only attire a white terrycloth bathrobe, courtesy of the Marriott. A new text message from an unidentified sender appeared on her cell phone. The message contained a string of seven numbers. She committed the numbers to memory before deleting the message. Her next task was to open her laptop and access a bank account recently opened for their operating funds. Using the numbers she just memorized as the new password for the account, she gained access and smiled.

Wolfe stepped out of the bathroom with a white towel wrapped around his waist. He dried his hair with another. "Why the smile?"

She glanced up. "Gerald Reid is probably very upset right now."

With a chuckle, Wolfe walked closer to the bed, leaned over and studied the computer screen. After a few seconds, he said. "I'm sure he has more." Straightening, he continued. "That should be more than enough to fund the next stage of our plan. My guess is Reid will reach out to Gerlis for another meeting." He paused. "I have a quick errand to run early in the morning. Then we can start surveillance."

"Not too early." With a smile, she reached for the towel around his waist. As it fell to the floor, he opened her robe.

CHAPTER 29

The black Range Rover exited the estate's driveway and turned toward the Potomac River on its way to Dulles International Airport. A gray Chevy Malibu fell in behind the SUV at a discreet distance. With a nondescript car and wearing her hair in a French bun with blocky sunglasses, Nadia blended well into the mid-afternoon traffic surrounding Alexandria, Virginia.

Keeping several cars between her and the SUV, it only took thirty minutes to surmise the Range Rover's final destination. She used the car's hands-free connection to call Wolfe.

"We called this one correct. He is headed for Dulles."

Wolfe replied, "Stay with him and see if you can determine what airline he's using. It might help us determine where he's going."

"Be careful. No telling what type of security he has at the house."

"I will. You do the same."

The call ended and she concentrated on following the SUV.

Forty-five minutes after leaving his property, Gerald Reid parked in a long-term parking lot at Dulles International Airport. By the time he arrived on the departure level, Nadia sat in a waiting area near the ticketing counters watching for him. Dressed in a woman's long navy trench coat, black leggings, and a beige peasant blouse, she blended into the background of anonymous travelers. She positioned herself in the middle of the ticketing area and saw him emerge from the escalators. Following, she kept her distance to observe which airline he chose.

Reid entered the queue for Air France's first-class ticket holders. Nadia faded back and watched as he checked in. On the departure board, she saw the only flight for Air France, this late in the day, went to Paris. She noted a departure time of six-thirty and did the math. Reid would be in the air overnight, not landing in Paris until two a.m. local time.

As soon as he disappeared through the TSA security gate, she returned to her car and called Wolfe.

"He is leaving on Air France at six-thirty for Paris. It does not arrive until two in the morning our time. You will have plenty of time."

"Good. Call me when you get back."

From his vantage point on the northern edge of Reid's property, Wolfe surveyed the back side of the mansion. Using his Nikon Action Extreme 12x50

binoculars to scan the landscape surrounding the structure, he found the object of his search. It resembled a small coffin, beige in color and located on the northwest corner. Wolfe guessed the generator produced 7500 watts considering the size of the home and the remoteness of the property.

He checked his wrist watch and noted it would be dark in less than an hour. With Reid flying to Paris, he could start his operation at some point after ten. He had one additional location to find.

Wolfe arrived back at the north side of the property at ten and parked on a gravel access road near the white PVC fence surrounding Reid's estate. He was now dressed in black cargo pants, black long sleeve T-shirt under a black utility vest, black socks, black Reebok's, thin black leather gloves and a black lightweight balaclava rolled up to his forehead.

Lying prone behind the night vision rifle scope attached to his Barrett XM500 .50 caliber rifle, Wolfe placed the crosshairs on the center of the generator's cover. Keeping his aim squared on a large unmoving target allowed him to check his watch to make sure he timed the rifle shot exactly.

Wispy clouds obscured the stars on this moonless night as he waited. At precisely 10:37 p.m., he heard an explosion off in the distance. At the same moment, the surrounding area in this part of the Virginia countryside, plunged into total darkness. His sabotage of the local transformer had worked perfectly. During the chaos of additional explosions at the transformer site, Wolfe fired twice at the generator. As two .50 caliber slugs tore through the internal workings of the generator, its automatic engagement switch, designed to turn on during a power outage, failed.

As complete darkness descended over the countryside, Wolfe stood and returned to the opened back hatch of his rented Chevy Equinox. He retrieved a small black sling bag with two cylindrical objects inside and placed it over his shoulder. After he lowered the balaclava over his face, he retrieved a black riot helmet from the cargo area and placed it on his head. After securing the chin straps, he secured an Armasight Night Vision Goggle to the helmet. Once he lowered the optic unit, the world was plunged into a green hue. With this accomplished, he disassembled the Barrett and secured it in a foam lined case. The next object he retrieved from the Equinox's cargo hold resembled an exotic looking pistol.

After extracting a burner cell phone from a side pocket of his cargo pants, he turned it on and sent a three-word message. This accomplished, he viewed the distant mansion through the NVG's, placed his hands on the fence and vaulted over. With a quick glance at his wristwatch, he jogged toward the pitch-black structure.

In a strip mall parking lot five miles from Wolfe's location, Nadia heard a rumble in the distance. She then watched as street and interior lights blinked out in the surrounding area. The time on her car clock showed 10:37 p.m. With a pleased expression, she waited. Two minutes later, a three-word text message appeared on a cell phone purchased at a local convenience store that afternoon.

On my way.

She rolled down the window on the gray Malibu and waited to hear sirens.

Wolfe knew the property would have battery or solar powered surveillance devices placed strategically around the exterior of the house. As he approached the multi-layer back deck of the structure, he searched the eves and doorframes for cameras. It took several minutes before he located two. With their locations determined, he raised the exotic hand gun, took aim and fired a red paint pellet at the camera on the right. Without hesitating, he aimed at the one on the left and expertly placed another pellet directly on the lens.

Satisfied both surveillance devices were now blind, he approached the large veranda to determine how best to gain entry. Wolfe laid the now-unneeded paintball gun on a metal bistro table next to the rear entrance. Here he found two ornate French doors, each composed of steel framing and glass panels, standing guard over the home's interior.

Using a small glass cutting tool from a pocket on his utility vest, he scribed a semicircle in the glass next to one of the door handles. Thirty seconds later, he reached in and unlocked the door from the inside.

As he entered, the only sound to be heard came from a large refrigerator in the open gourmet kitchen where he stood. He glanced at his watch and notated the time, 11:01. He would allow himself only one hour to search. If he received a message from Nadia, before the hour was up, he would abandon his task. Satisfied with the plan, he headed into the home's interior.

Wolfe located the library midway down a long hall on the first floor of the 9000 square-foot structure. On entering, he found floor-to-ceiling bookshelves filled with a variety of books on different topics. With closer examination, he surmised the majority of volumes had been purchased in bulk at either a used bookstore or estate sale. He smiled to himself with the realization Reid was a pretend intellectual.

With the need to expedite the search, he started flinging books to the floor from the two eye-level shelves. Within a minute, he found the hidden wall-safe protected by a keypad.

Out of a utility vest pocket, he extracted a small camelhair brush with a rubber bulb on one end. The bulb contained powder sensitive to fingerprints. As he gently blew powder on the keypad, four keys attracted the powder and revealed themselves in the green hue of his NVG. After studying the four, Wolfe mentally reviewed the dossier he read on Reid. The numbers did not match his birthdate, but there was something familiar about them. With a slight smile, he realized the numbers corresponded with Reid's anniversary date with the agency. He tried the month and year. No luck. Month and day. The safe did not open. Day and year did not work either. Finally, he tried month and year backward and the safe popped open.

Inside the wall safe, he found ten bundles of one hundred dollars bills, which he placed on the large oak desk sitting in front of the bookshelves. The next bundle to be removed contained four passports issued by different countries. Wolfe removed the rubber band holding them together and flipped through the pages. All contained Reid's portrait, but none contained the name Gerald Reid. He placed these on top of the cash.

Additional objects remained inside the safe. He extracted all and lay them on the desk next to the cash. Five flash drives and ten CDs in jewel cases comprised the rest of the safe's contents. Each would be examined later. With the safe empty, Wolfe slipped the sling bag carefully over his helmet and removed the two beer-can-sized objects from inside. Into the bag went the cash, the passports, flash drives and the CDs. He closed the safe and resituated the bag back over his shoulder.

He placed one of the cans in his pant pocket and took the other in his left hand. Leaving the library, he approached the staircase leading to the upstairs portion of the residence.

Wolfe felt a vibration in his right pant pocket. After retrieving the phone, he started to read the message when he sensed the distinct muffled sound of a distant helicopter flying low.

Without hesitation, he ran toward the front entrance of the house and pulled the pin on the can-shaped object in his hand. Once within sight of the massive front door, he tossed the object forward, turned and ran back toward the rear of the house. He was almost to the library when the first incendiary grenade detonated.

Not stopping to admire his handiwork, Wolfe reached into his pocket for the second grenade and pulled the pin. As he ran past the library, he tossed it toward the desk and then rushed for the back door.

By the time he emerged onto the large patio, he could hear the helicopter approaching from the south. Glancing at his watch, the digital numbers showed 11:34. With a solid cloud layer obscuring the stars and his black attire, he would be invisible during his trek back to the SUV. Wolfe broke into a sprint and arrived at the Equinox a minute later. Flipping the NVGs up, he turned to see the front of the house engulfed in flames as a Bell Model 429 helicopter hovered low while circling the structure before landing in the front yard.

After slipping the backpack off his shoulder, he opened the driver side door and tossed the bag onto the front passenger seat. The worse thing he could do at this point would be to expose his position with car lights. His solution was to take the Equinox out of gear, flip the night vision goggles back down and push the SUV toward a downward incline. With the vehicle now moving on its own, he jumped into the driver seat and steered the vehicle, without power steering, until the house was out of sight.

Once clear of being seen by anyone in the helicopter, he made sure the vehicles lights were off as he started the engine. Still utilizing his night vision device to steer the SUV, he drove deeper into the dark rural Virginia countryside.

CHAPTER 30

Gerald Reid sat in the Charles De Gaulle International Airport departure gate awaiting his connecting flight to Barcelona, his cell phone pressed to his ear. He stared numbly at the floor by his shoes while the caller described the events at his house. When the caller finished, all Reid could think to say was, "I see. Can they tell what started the fire?"

More listening and more staring.

"I see." He paused, as his mind raced. "No, I just landed in Paris on my way to Barcelona. There is nothing I can do about it from here. Please keep me informed when they discover what caused the fire. My return depends on events in Spain and I will get back to you when I know the date." More silence. "Yes, that will be fine."

Reid studied the now silent phone. After hesitating several minutes, he dialed a number committed to memory. The call was answered on the fourth ring.

"Are you in Barcelona?" Asa Gerlis sounded tense.

"No, my flight is delayed an hour."

"Then why are you calling?"

"Wolfe burned down my house."

Silence was his reply. Finally, he heard. "Are you sure?"

"Who else could it be?"

"Lots of factors—"

"No, it was him, Asa."

"No names."

"Whatever." Reid took a deep breath and let it out slowly. "He's out there. I saw him three days ago."

Gerlis did not comment.

"He's taunting us. I received a picture via Fed Ex. A picture of me in my driveway with the crosshairs of a rifle scope centered on my forehead."

"What did they say about the fire?"

"There was a power outage in the area, which kept the local firefighters from arriving for two hours. There is nothing left of the house and it's too hot to investigate. It will be sometime later today before anyone can start looking for the cause."

Gerlis did not respond right away. When he did, it was short. "Send me a text when you land."

The call ended.

Reid stared at the silent phone and tried not to scream.

At the same time Reid spoke to Gerlis, Wolfe and Nadia were transferring luggage and equipment from the rental cars to the Beechcraft B55 parked at the Shenandoah Valley Regional Airport near Harrisonburg, Virginia.

Nadia turned to Wolfe. "You haven't said a word since we got here."

"Thinking."

"About?"

"How I screwed up."

"I am not sure how you were supposed to know he had agency assets watching the house."

Michael stopped before placing the Barrett's case in the plane's luggage compartment. He faced Nadia and shook his head. "Those guys weren't agency. When the agency cuts you off, they completely cut you off. My guess is a private security contractor."

She crossed her arms and tilted her head before she replied. "So how is that screwing up?"

"The short length of time it took for a response to my intrusion means there were other monitoring systems I didn't plan for."

"Do you think they can tie it back to us?"

"Not officially." He smiled grimly. "We're dead, remember?"

She remained silent as she stared at him. "But Reid knows we are not."

"If he doesn't, he's not as smart as I give him credit."

"I am not following you. What are you worried about?"

"I'm not really worried. I'm mad at myself for not doing more research on his security setup. Most home security companies have retired cops driving around in leased cars. These guys weren't rent-a-cops. When I glanced at the burning house, I could see a helicopter circling the house before it landed. It was a Bell Model 429 and those aren't cheap. Over the course of his CIA career, Reid probably dealt with his fair share of private security contractors started by ex-military types." He paused and finished placing the last suitcase onto the plane. "I saw the identification numbers on the tail boom. I can use those to find out who was watching his house."

"But you already suspect something, don't you?"

He smiled to himself. She'd used another contraction. Choosing not to mention it, he nodded. "Yes, I do. If it's who I think it is, they'll have resources we don't."

She smiled as she walked to her rental car and looked back at him. "Then we will just have to be smarter."

The smoldering remains of what used to be Gerald Reid's lavish home remained too hot for the fire marshal to start his investigation. Travis Fox, owner of Regis Worldwide, walked cautiously around the once-grand structure. As an ex-Army Ranger, Fox started Regis to get in on the United States' increasing dependence on private military contractors. With Gerald Reid supplying his first overseas contract, Fox felt loyalty to the man, to a point. The sizeable sum Reid paid each year for Regis Worldwide to keep his property safe helped Fox overlook the negatives of dealing with the man.

Fox wore a frown as he walked the perimeter. He saw two areas he suspected were the ignition points. The front door and a room in the middle of the house on the west side.

Once the fire marshal arrived to start their investigation, he would be able to confirm his suspicions.

Now in his mid-forties, Fox remained a compact man with broad shoulders, thin waist and sandy brown hair worn short. Mirrored Oakley sunglasses shaded his eyes from the early morning sun now climbing higher in the sky. As he surveyed the scene, his helicopter pilot, Sam Harris, approached with a Samsung tablet in his hand.

"We have the surveillance videos downloaded from the cloud, Travis." The pilot touched the screen and handed the device to Fox. "We think he was parked just outside the fence line on the north side of the property."

Fox nodded as he studied the video. A black-clad figure appeared at the outer range of the infrared camera, moving toward it. When the figure was within thirty feet, he pointed an object at the camera and the screen went dark. Travis looked at Harris. "What the hell?"

"Paintball gun. We found it on the back deck with red pellets."

"Can we trace who bought it? Maybe get some fingerprints."

The pilot shook his head. "Heat from the fire partially melted the gun and all of the pellets left in it. I checked the brand—it's one of those cheap ones you can buy at Walmart. If you close in on the guy just before he shoots, you can see he has gloves on. This guy was a pro, knew what he was doing."

"What makes you say that?"

"Follow me."

As they walked toward the rear of the house, Harris said, "The countywide power failure was deliberate. Someone sabotaged the main transformer for this area around 10:30 last night." When they arrived at the northwest corner of the destroyed home, he pointed at a partially melted beige object. "Notice the two holes in the side?"

Fox knelt down and studied the side of the generator. He looked up. "He disabled the emergency backup power. What do those look like, 50s?"

The pilot nodded. "That would be my guess. Like I said, the guy knew what he was doing."

Standing, Fox brushed his hands on his jeans. "Interesting. Whoever did this possessed a few exotic toys, 50 caliber weapons and, I suspect, incendiary grenades. Okay, let's get a security detail out here and then you can take me back to the hangar. I've got work to do."

As they approached the helicopter, the pilot said in a low voice to Fox, "There's a rumor going around Reid's no longer with the agency."

Stopping, the ex-Ranger stared at his pilot. "Where'd you hear that?"

"I called Barry in IT to get the security camera video. He told me it's all over CNN."

Frowning, Fox stared at the pilot. "Shit." He returned his attention to the smoldering remains. "This may not have been just a well-executed burglary."

"Kind of what I was thinking."

Fox looked back at his pilot. "Apparently, Reid finally pissed off the wrong guy."

Regis Worldwide headquartered on the northern edge of Dulles International Airport. The hangar it occupied was wide enough to accommodate the company's two Bell Model 429 helicopters and its first jet, a recently purchased Embraer Phenom 100EV. Travis Fox retreated to his office in the back corner. Compared to the trappings of other private military contractors, he preferred to spend the company's money on equipment and hiring the best personnel. He sat behind his military surplus gray metal desk and opened his laptop. The first order of business was to see what had happened to Gerald Reid.

On the CNN website, he found several reports. After skimming through several, he concluded Reid had indeed retired from the agency. Rumors and innuendos were rampant, but no solid explanation as to why he retired suddenly were stated. His next task was to make sure his other contacts within the agency and the Pentagon were secure.

By late afternoon, Fox felt his status as a go-to company within the private military contractor sector remained solid. With the last call completed, he looked up to see Sam Harris appear at his office door.

Fox noticed a look of amusement. "Why the grin, Sam?"

"Just heard from the fire marshal."

"And?"

"You were correct—the fire started in two separate locations. Burn patterns indicated two very hot sources, one at the front door and another in the library. While they don't have the chemical analysis back yet, he suspects white phosphorus."

Fox remained silent as he absorbed the news. After a long pause, he nodded. "Last time I spoke to Reid, he was waiting for a flight to Barcelona. Guess I need to call him again and let him know." He pointed to a metal chair in front of his desk. "You might as well sit down and listen."

Fox put the phone on speaker and made the call. Reid answered immediately. "What did you find out?"

"Who'd you pissed off bad enough they'd burn your house down, Reid?"

The ex-CIA official did not reply immediately. After several awkward moments of silence, he said. "Not sure what you're talking about."

"Let's put it this way. Someone sabotaged a local

transformer and they disabled your generator. They then broke into your house and set it on fire. To me, that sounds like someone very upset with you. Care to comment?"

"If there wasn't any electricity how did you know the house was broken into?"

"If your house loses electricity, we know. We were there in thirty minutes after the power was cut."

"I have a safe. They may have been after it?"

"What was in the safe?"

"Money and other things."

Fox rolled his eyes. "What other things?"

"Documents and files."

"Who knew about the money?"

Reid did not respond right away.

"Gerald, I can't help you if you're going to keep information from me."

Although Fox and Harris could not see it, Reid closed his eyes and placed his hand over them. In a voice barely above a whisper, they heard. "Kendra Burges knew about it. She also knew the combination."

"We've spoken on occasion. I'll start with her. Do you think she might be responsible?"

"I don't know. Last time I spoke to her, she seemed upset."

"Should we investigate her?"

"No, I would start with another individual."

"Who?"

"Michael Wolfe."

"Who's he?"

"A very dangerous man."

Fox chuckled. "How dangerous?"

"Let's just say he makes his living with a rifle."

"How do I find him?"

"Talk to Gregg Simpson. Here's his number." Reid

recited the cell phone number. "He'll be able to tell you where Wolfe lives."

After the call ended, Fox looked over at Harris. "What do you think?"

The pilot shrugged. "I'd say this Wolfe person would be a starting place. Reid said he made his living with a rifle."

"Yes, he did say that." Fox tapped a pencil on his desk. "What are you thinking, Travis?"

"While I was checking with my contacts at the Pentagon and the Agency making sure Regis Worldwide was still on the A-list, a couple of individuals I spoke to made comments about why Reid was forced to retire."

"What'd they say?"

"He had become obsessed with a man who died two years ago."

Harris chuckled. "Let me guess. Wolfe."

Fox nodded. "Now Reid claims this dead person burned his house down."

"Huh."

"They also said no one at the Agency was sorry to see him leave. Apparently, he trampled on a lot of careers over the years and left a whole lot of folks in the dust during his rise within management."

"In other words, there are more than a few individuals that know how to use a rifle pissed at him."

Another nod from Fox. "Yeah, more than a few. The Agency is a tight-knit community, Sam. People talk. I didn't consider this fact when we took Reid on as a client. Now he's radioactive and no one wants anything to do with him."

"You're going somewhere with this, aren't you?"

Fox stood. "Yeah, I'm going to get something to eat

and then I'm going to our attorney's office and see how fast we can get out of our contract with Reid."

CHAPTER 31

SOMEWHERE ON THE EAST COAST

W hat are you going to do with the money, Michael?"

Wolfe checked his altimeter and airspeed before answering. "We are going to use it to stay off the grid and figure out how to get our names back."

Faking a pout, she said, "You do not want to be married to me anymore?"

He shot her a quick glance and saw the pout change to a mischievous grin. "I'm tired of hiding and the charade. I don't want to be Mr. and Mrs. Lyon. I want us to be Mr. and Mrs. Wolfe."

"They are both predators, Michael."

He chuckled. "True."

"So, you are telling me you want to get married for real."

"That's what I said."

"You are not going to ask me, just tell me?"

Another quick glance. "Not what I meant."

"I see." She tried to hide her smile. "What did you mean, Michael Wolfe? You assume I want to marry you. Is that what you are saying?"

He took a deep breath. "Nadia, why are you making this difficult? You know how I feel about you. I just want it to be legitimate—not this pretend marriage because we're hiding from our past."

She grinned and watched the North Carolina countryside pass beneath the Beechcraft. Several moments of silence passed before she turned again to look at him. "How do we free ourselves of Gerald Reid and Asa and get our names back?"

"We find them and make sure they never bother us again."

"How?"

"We need to locate them first." He glanced at her. "Probably in Spain."

"Where in Spain? It is a big country."

"Same way they found us over two years ago."

She raised an eyebrow. "How do you mean?"

He smiled. "We draw them into a trap, just like they did us."

"That trap did not work very well."

"No, it didn't. We'll just have to make sure ours is a better trap."

They fell into a comfortable silence. After five minutes of watching rural Virginia pass beneath the plane, she turned to him. "Michael."

"Yes."

"I want to be married to you, too."

The side of Wolfe's mouth twitched.

In a private alcove within the Wilson Air Center FBO at Charlotte Douglas International Airport,

Wolfe sat with Nadia, waiting for a response from a recently sent text message. The Beechcraft, now parked in a closed hangar, was fueled, serviced and ready for them to make a decision on their next move.

The call came thirty minutes and two cups of coffee later.

"Thanks for calling, Joseph."

"No problem. There are more than a few people celebrating Gerald Reid's departure from the agency."

"Not why I needed to talk to you."

Joseph's tone became more serious. "Okay, so talk."

"I need a helicopter serial number traced and I need the name of a discreet jet charter service."

"Where are you?"

"Charlotte Douglas FBO."

"Finding a discreet charter service won't be a problem. Give me the tail number and I'll call you back when I know more. Expect a call from the pilot within the hour. And, Michael?"

"Yes."

"Do you know anything about a house burning to the ground in rural Virginia last night?"

"How would I know anything about that, Joseph? Nadia and I are in Charlotte, North Carolina."

"I didn't think you would." Joseph chuckled. "But thought I would ask." He paused. "If you're interested, they don't have a clue as to who did it. Prevailing theory is professional robbers torched the place to hide a break-in."

"I'm sure the owner is not pleased."

"He was spotted today in Barcelona by some former colleagues of Nadia's."

Wolfe raised an eyebrow. "Really. What was he doing?"

"Checking into a hotel near the Las Ramblas area."

"Know the name?"

Joseph told him. "He's booked for a week."

"Handy information. Thanks, Joseph."

"Glad to have it available. I'll call soon."

Joseph remained good to his word. A text message contained a photo of a man, an FAA Pilot's License number and the number three. Wolfe checked the time and found it was approaching three p.m. When he looked up, he saw the man from the photo walking toward their location in the FBO.

When he arrived at their table, Wolfe stood and shook the offered hand.

"Are you Michael Lyon?"

"Yes."

"I'm Stewart Barnett. A mutual friend told me you and your wife need to charter a jet."

"Yes, we have a meeting in Barcelona."

The pilot nodded. "I have to be in Rome the day after tomorrow. I can drop you two off on my way." He turned his attention to Nadia. "You must be Mrs. Lyon."

Nadia nodded once.

Wolfe studied the young pilot. His slender build and cocky attitude radiated self-confidence. Faded blue jeans, scuffed brown loafers, an untucked white oxford shirt with rolled-up sleeves reminded Wolfe of several Navy fighter pilots he used to know. "What'd you fly?"

"F-18's."

"Iraq or Afghanistan?"

The pilot nodded. "Both."

"Marine expeditionary unit, Desert Storm." Wolfe offered his hand again. "Nice to meet you."

Barnett smiled, nodded and shook Wolfe's hand once again. "Joseph said you were one of the best snipers in theater."

Wolfe shrugged and said. "He tends to exaggerate at times."

The pilot, wearing a Nike ball cap covering close-cropped dark brown hair and a three-day-old beard showing no signs of gray, tilted his head and gave Wolfe a knowing smile. "Right—good to meet you, too."

"How do you know Joseph?"

Barnett flashed a grin. "I used to work with him, before his current job."

Nodding, Wolfe returned the grin. "So did I."

"That's what he told me. He also asked me to give you a message."

"Oh?"

"He said the number you gave him belongs to a private security firm."

Wolfe blinked several times. "Was that all of the message?"

"No, the rest of it didn't make sense. I guess you have to know the context."

"Okay."

"He said they canceled their contract this afternoon. Does that make sense to you?"

"Actually, it does. Thank you."

"No problem. Joseph also told me you're a pilot."

"Two engine rating, props only. Never flown a jet."

"We'll have to remedy that on the way over."

Barcelona, Spain

Originally built and opened in 1859, the Hotel Espana kept up with the times by remodeling on a regular basis to maintain its four-star rating. The hotel offered the perfect spot for Gerald Reid to use as his temporary residence during his stay in Barcelona. It offered two amenities, close vicinity to the Las Ramblas area and next door to the Gran Theater del Liceu. Reid almost forgot he was in Barcelona on business when he discovered which opera was currently in production at the theater. He bought tickets and decided to spend one night engrossing himself in Puccini's La Boheme in a foreign theater.

The opera, scheduled for the evening, did not distract from the business he needed to conclude while here. After arriving at the hotel, he set out along the narrow streets of ancient Barcelona, checking and double checking to make sure no one followed him. Satisfied his arrival at an obscure tapas bar near a parking garage in the center of town went unnoticed, Reid found a table in the back and waited.

The man Gerald Reid traveled four thousand miles to meet appeared unhappy as he approached Reid's table.

Asa Gerlis asked. "Why are you here?"

"Did you not agree to meet me?"

Gerlis took a deep breath, blew it out sharply and sat down. "You are here. What do you want?"

"We need to finish what we started two years ago."

Shaking his head, Gerlis stared at Reid but remained quiet as a waitress set two cups of espresso on the small table. When she was gone, he took a sip. "They are dead, Reid."

"No—they are not."

"Just because you think you saw Wolfe for a brief moment in a car next to you does not prove anything."

"What about the photograph?"

"Someone at the agency getting back at you for all the hell you gave them over the years."

"They are alive. They are alive and they know everything."

"Now you are being paranoid. No one but you and I know. Canfield is dead and took the information with him to the other side."

"Still..."

"Let it go."

"No. What will it cost to have your associate finish the job?"

"If you want to waste your money, go ahead. I will not participate in this nonsense."

"How much?"

"Half a million Euros. Do you want to spend that much on a myth?"

Reid nodded. "If you want no part of it, I'll meet with him."

Gerlis sipped his coffee as he studied the ex-CIA bureaucrat. "I will tell him you wish to speak with him. If he agrees, he will get in touch. If you do not hear anything within two days, it means he is not interested. Then go home."

"I'll find someone else if he's not interested."

"You have not been in the field for a decade or more, Gerald. Times are different. You do not have the contacts you once had and your ambitions have made you lazy. Your tradecraft is sloppy. A blind beggar could have followed you here today."

Reid stared wide-eyed at Gerlis.

The ex-Mossad agent stood, leaned over slightly and said in a low whisper, "If my associate decides to take your money, he will contact you. In the meantime, try not to get yourself killed on the streets of Barcelona."

Gerlis walked out of the small café.

Reid took a sip of his coffee and stared at the empty seat across from him.

CHAPTER 32

BARCELONA, SPAIN

Nadia Picard watched as Asa Gerlis exited the small café. The narrow streets, crowded with tourists, helped disguise her interest in the man. She took her cell phone and sent a three-word text to Michael. He would pick up Gerlis' trail—her objective was to keep an eye on Reid.

Following the man bordered on comical to Nadia. While he tried several diversions to ward off anyone on his tail, she saw through them immediately. Eventually, he arrived at his hotel and sequestered himself in his room. With the help of a young concierge who could not take his eyes off her cleavage, Nadia was told Reid had tickets for the opera that evening. Satisfied with her discovery, she returned to their hotel room several blocks from the Hotel Espana and right across from a famous theater.

Three hours later, Wolfe entered the room. "Found it."

Nadia smiled. "Where?"

"He has a small villa in a secluded area north of Manresa near the foothills of the Montserrat range. Pretty country. What about Reid?"

"He purchased tickets to *La Boheme* tonight. Is he an opera fan?"

Wolfe shrugged. "Wouldn't know." He retrieved his cell phone from his back pocket and started typing as he walked toward the bathroom. Before closing the door, he said, "Just asked Joseph. Hopefully, we'll hear soon."

When Wolfe returned to the bedroom, he was staring at his answer. "Apparently a huge one." He sat on the bed next to Nadia. "That means we have an opportunity to get into his room tonight. Do you know what floor?"

She nodded. "I know the floor, the room number, and already have a passkey."

"I won't ask where you got it."

"Let's just say someone was staring at my tits when he should have kept his eyes on his passkey."

Wolfe laughed. "Third button?"

She nodded again as she undid all of the buttons on her blouse.

Wolfe slipped off his sweatshirt and said as he embraced her. "Yeah, I can see where that would distract a guy."

Wolfe surveyed the crowd filing into the opera house through the open balcony door of their hotel room. He stood back inside the room and used binoculars to study the faces of the patrons as they passed through the theater's front entrance. Without taking his eyes off the crowd, he said, "There he is, tux and everything. Wonder where he got that."

Nadia walked up behind Wolfe and wrapped her arms around his waist. "The Concierge. His hotel has an agreement with a rental place for tourists to rent formal wear."

"Is this guy going to recognize you when we go in?"

"Doubt it. He's probably off duty by now."

Looking at her, he grinned. "How do you know that?"

She pursed her lips. "Well, I might have made a date with him."

Now laughing, Wolfe shook his head. "Where?"

"Opposite end of Las Ramblas. I told him I was staying at the Hotel Barcelona."

"You're mean."

"He was horny."

Chuckling, Wolfe put down the binoculars and glanced at his watch. "Performance starts in twenty minutes. We'll wait and then go to his room. You have the flash drive?"

She nodded.

The halls of the hotel were unusually quiet as Wolfe and Nadia approached Gerald Reid's room. Since most of the hotel guests were attending the opera, the chances of meeting someone were slight. Wolfe moved the passkey over the electronic lock sensor. When he heard a click, he opened the door. After they entered the dark room, he extracted a small Maglite from his jean pocket to illuminate the interior. The object of their search could be seen on a small table against the wall next to the bathroom. Nadia slipped on a pair of latex gloves and walked toward the closed laptop plugged into a power strip on the desktop.

While Wolfe held the light, she sat and proceeded to open the computer.

While it booted up, she inserted the flash drive into a USB slot on the side and waited. An internal light on the drive flashed five times, stopped and then flashed ten times. Satisfied, she detached the device, closed the lid and looked at Wolfe. She placed the small unit in her jean pocket and whispered. "Done."

He nodded and swept the Maglite around the room. He too, slipped on a pair of latex gloves and walked over to the nightstand. After handing the flashlight to Nadia, he opened the top drawer. Nothing. He checked the small closet and found only one suitcase. This he placed on the luggage stand next to the desk.

Wolfe ran his hands along the sides and flat surfaces feeling for anything unusual. He found it on the left side. As he pulled on the fabric, they heard the distinct sound of Velcro separating. He extracted one of the objects and held it next to the light. It appeared to be two passports bundled together with a rubber band. After removing the band, he held it closer to the light and flipped through each. He glanced at Nadia and smiled. He returned his hand to the opening and pulled out the second object he had felt earlier. He held a bundle of 200 Euro notes. Wolfe whispered, "Looks like we found his stash."

He slipped the bundle into his back-jean pocket along with the passports. After returning the suitcase to the closet, he nodded his head toward the door. They were outside the room and walking toward the stairs five seconds later.

As they entered the lobby, Nadia did a quick look to see if the young man she spoke to during the afternoon had returned. Not seeing him, they walked nonchalantly across the room and through the front exit. She dropped the passkey and the gloves into a trash receptacle before they returned to their hotel.

Back in their room, Wolfe checked the opera and noticed patrons mingling just inside the entrance. "Must be intermission." He turned and saw Nadia counting the Euro notes. "How much?"

"One-hundred-twenty Euro notes."

Wolfe frowned. "I wonder how much I missed?"

She looked at him. "Does it matter? You got the passports"

He nodded. "It should be enough to make him panic."

Grinning, she said, "It is not like he can go to the police and tell them he had two fake passports stolen."

"No, he won't go to the police. He'll probably email Gerlis or message him somehow. Will you be able to read his emails?"

"If the program we got from the hacker works." She paused and looked up at him. "Michael?"

"Yes."

"If he accesses one of his bank accounts, we will get his username and password. Is that why you took the money?"

He nodded. "I want Gerald Reid to be broke and without access to more money. Then he will really start to panic."

Reid exited the Gran Theater del Liceu in the company of two females and another male. Wolfe watched through binoculars as they conversed on the street outside. One of the women hugged Reid's right arm and laughed as he gestured with his left. He pointed toward his hotel and then in the direction of Las Ramblas.

"This is funny, Nadia."

"What is?"

"Reid either met someone at the opera or he hired an escort."

"The concierge told me I could make a lot of money escorting single men to the opera."

Wolfe smiled and shot her a quick glance. "How much?"

"He said it would depend on my involvement with the men and their financial status." She shook her head. "I felt like I was talking to a pimp."

Wolfe returned to watching Reid. "We're in Spain, Nadia. You're thinking like someone from a small town in the United States."

"It felt creepy." She paused. "Am I becoming Americanized, Michael?"

He grinned. "A little." He lowered the binoculars and turned to her. "Looks like the group is heading toward La Rambla. Let's go."

Reid and his party were already walking toward Las Ramblas when Wolfe and Nadia walked out of the hotel. They entered the narrow street crowded with tourists and late-night partiers moving toward the area.

Nadia asked. "Can you see them, Michael?"

"Yes, about twenty meters in front of us. They're about to turn right."

Nadia thumbed something into her cell phone and stared at the results. "There are several tapas bars in that direction."

"Let's give him an opportunity to have a few drinks. Then we can have a little fun."

Michael and Nadia observed Reid and his three companions enter a place called Via 70 Wine Bar. They took up station across from the bar at an outside table area of a small coffee shop. Both ordered espressos and settled in to watch Reid and his companions begin the night's revelry.

As he sipped his coffee, Michael turned to Nadia. "I'm having a hard time figuring out what in the hell he's doing. He's in a career crisis, he knows we're alive, and yet here he is, four thousand miles from home, partying with people he doesn't know."

Nadia tilted her head and glanced at Michael. "He had a meeting with Gerlis today. What if he is waiting for Gerlis to do something?"

"Or arrange something." Wolfe smiled. "Like a meeting?"

She returned the smile. "Yes, like a meeting."

"If it is a meeting, who would it be with?"

"Someone who could help him with his problems?" She looked at him over her espresso cup.

"I wonder." He sipped his coffee. "Do you think it might be the man they hired to kill us?"

"Maybe, if he's still active or even alive. Individuals in that line of work sometimes have short careers."

Wolfe stared across the street at the tapas bar. "Should we rethink letting him know we're in Barcelona?"

Nadia did not respond as he continued to study the four individuals across the street. Reid and his companions sat at a table with numerous glasses of wine and several trays of tapas. They were laughing and ignoring their surroundings. Wolfe set the cup down after a final sip of his expresso. He gave Nadia a slight smile. "It would have been fun, but we can probably learn more by monitoring his emails. He's let his guard down tonight—let's not give him an excuse to raise it."

She nodded and they both stood as Wolfe took a last look across the street inside the wine bar. His eyes narrowed as Reid glance in his direction. With a slight smile, he surmised Reid could not see out of the bright interior of the restaurant into the dimly lit sidewalk across La Rambla. As they walked back toward their hotel, a plan started to form in Wolfe's mind. His smile widened as he followed Nadia.

Gerald Reid anticipated an evening of learning more about the young lady sitting next to him. She was on her third glass of sangria and laughing harder with each glass. After taking another sip, he glanced out the front window of the bar. He could see scores of individuals looking for the right place to party and enjoying the warm evening. Out of the corner of his eye, he thought he saw a familiar face. Putting his sangria down he squinted at a figure he thought he recognized across the street. He frowned as the apparition disappeared into the surrounding crowd.

He stood and moved closer to the window, but the phantom had disappeared. Taking a deep breath, he attributed the sighting to his consumption of Spanish sangria. Returning to the table, he once again focused his attention on the young woman sitting next to him.

She grinned, her eyes droopy and voice slurred. "What did you see?"

"Thought I saw an old acquaintance. I was wrong."

"Good, we don't need any interruptions tonight."

He smiled and forgot about the image he thought he saw across La Rambla.

CHAPTER 33

BARCELONA, SPAIN

Back in their hotel room, Wolfe glanced at the clock on his cell phone and did the math. Washington was six hours behind Barcelona. It was approaching midnight in Spain, so Joseph would be either finishing his day or at his apartment with Mary. He sent a simple text message and waited for the call.

Fifteen minutes later, his phone vibrated. He answered it immediately. "Hope I didn't catch you at a bad time."

"Nonsense. How's your trip?"

"Interesting."

"How so?"

"Our prospect met with his principal partner today."

"We figured that. Any major announcements?"

"No. He seems to be waiting for a response. We need to know what our competition is talking about.

You have his number. Any ideas?"

"A few. Let me see what I can do and get back to you."

"Thank you."

The call ended. No names, no locations, no key words were used to flag NSA interest in an international call, yet both callers understood the real meaning of their conversation.

Wolfe smiled as he watched Nadia undress and slip naked under the bed covers. He stripped off his shirt, jeans, and socks before getting in beside her. "Tomorrow will be interesting."

She snuggled against him, enjoying his warmth. "Shhh..." She reached for him and drew his lips toward hers. "We are in Barcelona, one of my favorite cities. No more talk of Gerald Reid."

Joseph Kincaid ended the call and sipped the single malt scotch from a crystal highball glass. Mary would not arrive for another hour, having spent the day meeting with various members of Congress along with the first lady. The time difference between Washington and Tel Aviv meant it was just after one a.m. there. After determining what needed to be done, he went to his personal laptop and opened an app. Using the VoIP program, he dialed a number only he and a few other individuals on the planet knew.

The call was answered after five rings with a cautious, "*Shalom.*"

"Uri, it's Joseph. Did I call too late?"

"Ah, my friend. Unfortunately, my day is not quite over yet. To what do I owe the pleasure of this call?"

"I'm on a secure line. Are you?"

"Always. Why?"

"Are you still looking for Asa Gerlis?"

A lengthy silence ensued. Finally, he heard, "Maybe. Do you have news?"

"I have a phone number I want you to monitor."

"Why us? Why not use your NSA?"

"Because, my friend, you can do it without as much red tape as it would cause me."

"Ahh... True. Do you know where he is?"

"My conversation was with someone on an open line. We did not discuss particulars, but there is a chance the phone number I can give you will receive a call from Gerlis in the near future."

"I see."

"I think both of us would benefit by your listening to any calls this phone number might receive."

"Whose number is it?"

"Gerald Reid's."

"Interesting. Where is he?"

"Barcelona, Spain."

"It gave me great pleasure to hear of his departure from the agency. Did you have anything to do with it?"

"Uri, I'm shocked you would think such a thing."

"Joseph, you are not, as you American's say, a boy scout. Do not act like one."

"Let's put it this way—Mr. Reid was caught dabbling in domestic affairs. Plus, he had a foreign bank account with a sizeable sum he conveniently forgot to declare. My boss was not happy and neither were the directors of the CIA and FBI."

"Tsk, tsk. Not too smart on Reid's account."

"No."

The call went silent for a dozen seconds. "Give me the number. I will have it monitored."

"Thank you. I owe you."

The vibration of a cell phone brought Joseph out of a light sleep. He quickly put on his glasses and checked the number. An international call with Israel's prefix. When he accepted the call, he heard, "We need to talk."

"I will call you right back."

Mary rolled over and groaned. "What time is it, Joseph?"

"A little after four. Go back to sleep."

She did not respond as he heard her breathing change to a gentle rhythmic cycle. With a smile, he headed toward his office.

Five minutes later, Uri Ben-David announced through Joseph's computer speakers, "We intercepted a call to the number you gave me."

"When?"

"About two hours ago."

"And?"

"Voice recognition software confirms it was Gerlis."

"Where is he?"

"Also, Spain. But the call was too short for our technicians to pinpoint exactly where. It was somewhere in the Barcelona area."

"What did you learn?"

"He told Reid to expect a call in the next day or so."

"I take it Gerlis did not identify the person who would contact Reid."

"No."

"Where does that leave you, Uri?"

"Freidman has called an emergency meeting to discuss this turn of events. I have a feeling we will be sending a team to Spain in the morning. Plus, our technical staff will be working overtime searching our archives for any calls from the number Gerlis used."

"Interesting."

"Joseph, are you keeping secrets from me? You never explained how you knew Gerlis would call Reid."

"No, you're correct. I didn't."

"Care to explain?"

"Not particularly."

Ben-David chuckled. "Very well. Secrets among friends, yes?"

"Something like that. Will you keep me informed if your people intercept another call?"

"Yes."

"Thank you."

The call ended and Joseph frowned. If the Mossad was sending agents to Spain, he would need to let Michael and Nadia know. He made the call.

Wolfe answered immediately. "Yes."

"Do you have alternate means of communicating?"

"Yes."

"Use it and call back."

After retrieving one of the pre-paid cell phones purchased at a small electronics store, Wolfe dialed the number he knew went directly to Joseph's VoIP application.

He was answered immediately.

"Michael, we might have a small problem."

"Such as?"

"Former friends of Nadia are sending someone to find Gerlis."

There was no reply from Wolfe.

Joseph continued, "The good news is you were correct—Gerlis told Reid to expect contact from someone in the next day or so."

"I take it there were no details."

"None."

Wolfe glanced over at Nadia, who sat at hotel room desk working on the laptop. "Nadia is able to monitor his emails and internet activity."

"Anything of interest?"

"A little. Nothing earth-shattering."

"I won't ask for details."

"Probably best."

"Michael, it goes without saying. Be careful. We don't need the Mossad knowing you and Nadia are alive. No telling what they would do."

"I agree."

The call ended and Michael stared at the now-silent cell phone.

Nadia raised her eyebrows. "What was that about?"

"Mossad is sending a team to find Gerlis."

"When?"

"Soon. Probably tomorrow."

The following morning Nadia worked on the laptop while Wolfe went for coffee and pastries. He returned to the room and found her grinning.

"Reid just got an email telling him to be at a café on La Rambla at 3:30 this afternoon."

With a smile, Wolfe placed one of the coffees next to her and sipped on his. "Which one?"

"The same one we were at two years ago."

"Huh."

"I do not believe he has discovered his cash and passports are missing."

"How can you tell?"

"He has not accessed his bank accounts yet."

"At some point he'll have to."

She nodded. "What about his meeting?"

"We need to find a camera store and spend some of Reid's 20,000 Euros."

By 2:40 p.m. Wolfe and Nadia were in a position to observe any meeting taking place at the Ristorante Ideal, the same tapas bar where Nadia had waited over two years ago. She was across the street in a second-floor hotel room with a Nikon D750 Digital SLR Camera attached to a NIKKOR 70-300mm zoom lens, her view of the sidewalk café unobscured.

Wolfe watched from a vacant apartment two buildings to the southeast equipped with binoculars. They maintained communication using a set of hand-held radios purchased at the same time as the camera.

Time crawled as they waited for the meeting to take place.

At 3:25 p.m., Gerald Reid entered the café and spoke to a waiter as he pointed to a table near the front of the designated sidewalk dining area. When the waiter nodded, Reid sat and observed the tourist milling around. Nadia snapped digital images of the entire process while Wolfe surveyed the crowd surrounding the café.

Every few seconds, for the next fifteen minutes, Reid continued to refer to his cell phone. With a frown on his face, he suddenly stood and withdrew money from his pocket. A man stepped up behind him on the sidewalk and grabbed Reid on the right arm. At the same time, the newcomer removed the cell phone from Reid's left hand.

Wolfe recognized the move. "Nadia, make sure you get clear pictures of the man behind Reid."

The radio crackled as he heard, "His back is to me. I have the camera on automatic. When he turns, we should get one."

Wolfe concentrated on the encounter occurring in front of the café with his binoculars. Reid grimaced in pain as he brought his now empty left hand over to hold the spot touched by the assailant. Because of the angle of his observation post, Wolfe only saw half of the attacker's face. He lowered the binoculars as he hissed. "Shit." He then watched as Reid's attacker melted into the mid-afternoon crowd on La Rambla and disappeared.

He brought the binoculars back up and saw Reid stagger slightly. A mask of horror appeared on the man's face as he fell forward, collapsing the table with his weight.

"Did you get a picture of the man?"

No response came over the radio.

"Nadia, did you get a picture?"

Still no response. He trained the binoculars on the hotel entrance. He did not see her. As his stomach muscles tightened and his face grew ashen, he vacated the room and ran down the stairs to the sidewalk exit.

With the Nikon on automatic, the camera recorded six images every second, yet the attacker failed to turn her way. Seeing her opportunity about to vanish, Nadia rushed out of the hotel room, leaving the radio behind.

She exited the hotel into the crowded street and ran in the direction the attacker had taken. The crowd seemed unaware of the drama taking place in a café across the street. Nadia used this as a cover and ran, staying close to the shops and restaurants on her side of the busy thoroughfare. She saw a break in traffic and darted across to the crowded center pedestrian lane, dodging street performers and artist kiosks. She made her way toward a man moving rapidly away from the café with his back to her.

He looked behind himself to check oncoming traffic. She realized an opportunity to get a picture was about to present itself. She stopped and started the Nikon on automatic exposure as she pointed it at him. As he crossed the street, he took a final glance behind him and disappeared down an alley.

Nadia breathed hard as she retraced her steps back to the hotel, stopping only once to see if she had a clear picture of the man. One frame showed his face— it was only three-quarters of a view, but it was a clear picture. With a smile, she sprinted back toward the hotel room and the radio.

Wolfe found the hotel room empty. As he rushed to the window, he noticed the hand-held radio sitting on the nightstand next to the bed. His eyes blinked rapidly as he froze, his mind refusing to contemplate the unthinkable thought of losing Nadia. He used the binoculars to survey the street below and saw nothing of her. A noise heard at the room's door caused him to turn. Without a weapon, he prepared to charge the door.

Relief spread through his body as Nadia stepped into the room. Her smile immediately disappeared when she saw his distressed look. "What's the matter, Michael?"

He swept her into his arms and embraced her tightly.

She pushed against him and looked up. "What is it? Michael, you're scaring me."

"Nothing." He managed to say as he buried his face

in her hair and breathed the familiar scent of her shampoo. "You just used two contractions in three sentences."

They watched from the hotel window as paramedics tried to revive Gerald Reid. She turned to Wolfe. "Think he will survive?"

"He was dead before his body crashed into the table."

"How do you know?"

His mouth twitched.

She looked back at the scene across the street. "Gerlis?"

"That would be my guess."

"Now what?"

"Joseph indicated Mossad would be sending someone or several someone's to look for Gerlis. I don't want them to find us instead, nor does Joseph."

"Airport?"

He nodded. "Yes. We can be back in the States by morning."

"What about Reid?"

"What about him?"

She paused, realizing the finality of what they witnessed. "Never mind. Let's get to the airport."

PART THREE
El Sombra

CHAPTER 34

One Week Later

H e was assumed killed in a drone strike in 2010 just inside the Pakistani border. At least he was supposed to be in the Toyota Land Cruiser destroyed by the drone. Since it was Pakistan, no one was able to confirm his presence in the vehicle."

Joseph Kincaid removed his glasses and subconsciously chewed on a temple tip as he listened to Uri Ben-David's voice over the secure line.

"Whose drone?"

"CIA."

"Why was the Mossad so interested in him?"

Ben-David took a deep breath and let it out slowly. "He was on our radar because we knew him to be a highly trained sniper in Saddam Hussein's Republican Guard. He disappeared right after Hussein's execution and is suspected of being responsible for the assassination of several Mossad assets in Iran and Syria from 2007 through 2009."

"Did the picture confirm his identity?"

"Yes. While it was only three-quarters of a view, the facial recognition software gave it a ninety percent match."

"So, he's been hiding for a little over a decade?"

"It would appear so. You never told me how you obtained the picture."

"We had an asset keeping tabs on Reid during his stay in Spain."

"You did, or the agency?"

"What do you think, Uri?"

"What I think is you have never really retired from the agency."

"Urban legend." Joseph paused for a moment. "What's this man's background?"

"You completely avoided my question." Ben-David chuckled. "His father was an Iraqi diplomat who married a Spanish woman. As a child, he attended primary school in England and college in the United States. I'm told his English is perfect with a slight Boston twang."

"Harvard?"

"That is what I am told."

"So, he could slip into the United States with ease."

"Yes. When he shaves his beard, he looks Western European."

There was silence for several moments. Joseph broke it. "Have your teams had any luck finding Gerlis?"

"Vanished. When we arrived at the address you gave us, it appeared to have been abandoned recently. We spoke to the owner. They are on an extended holiday in Australia and were unaware someone was occupying the property. It is isolated with few neighbors. The ones we did talk to did not notice anything unusual."

"So, he could be anywhere?"

"Yes."

"You realize, Uri, he poses a threat to Israel and the United States?"

"I am aware of this. What do you propose we do?"

"I don't know what to propose to my president, let alone to Israel."

"Thought that was in your job description."

Joseph smiled despite the pointed criticism. "It is. I'll think of something before I tell him."

"I feel your pain. I have to speak to my Prime Minister in an hour. I too, do not know what to recommend."

After a sigh, Joseph said, "Can you give me twenty-four hours before you speak to your prime minister?"

"It is not a good career decision to miss an appointment with him."

Chuckling, Joseph replied. "Blame it on me."

"Now that, he would believe." There was a five-second pause. "Okay, you've got twenty-four hours."

"Thanks, Uri."

"Make sure I am not going to regret this, Joseph."

"You won't."

Ending the call, Joseph closed his eyes and rubbed his temples. Under his breath, he murmured, "I'm getting too old for this shit." Realizing he had just summarized his feelings with a cliché, he smiled slightly and dialed another number.

"Michael, have you ever heard the name Omar Said?"

"There's a slight familiarity to it, Joseph. Why?"

"It's the name of the man in the photograph."

"Huh."

"He's also known as El Sombra."

"The Shadow, yeah, I've heard that name."

"In what context?"

"During my time in Israel. He was rumored to be the person responsible for several Mossad agents going missing."

"I was told that as well."

"Did Ben-David tell you anything about his background?"

"I didn't say I spoke to Uri."

"Whatever. What's the man's background?"

Joseph told him. Michael did not respond right away. "That's not much to go on."

"No, but it's more than we had before Nadia took the photo."

Both men were quiet as each gathered their thoughts. Finally, Joseph said. "Have you been to the house?"

"I flew over it on the way back from the east coast."

"And?"

"It looked intact. I'd have to survey it from ground level before I can make a better assessment."

"Do you want me to send a neutral party to check it out?"

"Probably not. I know the area and can tell if anything is amiss. What happened to the man Reid sent there?"

"Not sure, I'll find out."

More silence.

"Joseph?"

"Yes, Michael?"

"Asa Gerlis is not someone who is going to leave loose ends lying around. I'm sure Reid tried to convince him that Nadia and I are alive. If Gerlis has any doubt whatsoever we aren't dead, he'll send El Sombra to find us."

"Why do you think that?"

"Because if the situation was reversed, I would."

"But we know about Omar."

"Gerlis doesn't know we know. Let's keep it that way."

Wolfe ended the call. He sat at his desk, looking out the window of the condo bedroom he had converted into an office. He scratched the five-day-old stubble on his chin as he watched a hawk soar over the trees across the cove.

He did not hear Nadia lean against the doorframe until she spoke. "What did Joseph say?"

"They identified the man in the picture."

"Am I to guess his name, Michael?"

Smiling, Wolfe glanced at her and then returned his attention to the hawk. "Omar Said, the offspring of an Iraqi father and a Spanish mother."

"The name is unfamiliar to me."

"What about the name El Sombra."

She straightened and raised her eyebrows. "Are they sure?"

He nodded.

She walked over and placed her hands on his shoulders. "Uh, oh."

"I would agree. Uh, oh."

"What do we do now?"

The hawk flew out of Michael's line of sight as he stood and faced her. "As long as Gerlis is alive, we will never be able to stop looking over our shoulder. As I've told you before, I'm personally tired of running from the past. It's time to make a stand."

"Where? Spain? We would be at a disadvantage."

He shook his head. "No, on our land."

She crossed her arms and glared at Wolfe, tapping

her foot. "We could be waiting a long time. How do we know Gerlis will know where we are?"

"We tell him."

Her stern look dissipated as she chuckled. "How do you propose we do that? Call his cell phone and invite him for tea?"

Wolfe's mouth twitched. "I hadn't thought about doing it that way, but it's a pretty damn good idea." He turned, picked up his cell phone and redialed Joseph's number.

Using the VoIP program installed on Nadia's laptop two years ago by JR, they waited until 1 a.m. to call the number provided by Joseph. Nadia set it up and, before pressing the connect icon, she looked up at Michael. "How do they know this is Gerlis' number."

"Joseph said our Israeli friends discovered it when they were monitoring Gerald Reid's phone calls."

"He could have thrown the phone away by now."

"He could have, but I doubt it. There's no reason for him to suspect the Israelis are listening to his conversations. Until we call him."

She smiled. "Yes, Asa Gerlis is an overconfident prick." She paused. "Will not Uri Ben-David be upset we are about to burn this number for them?"

Wolfe shook his head. "They would have expected him to anyway. I'm sure they are monitoring all calls from Spain right now for a voice match."

"Are you ready?" She stood and he sat in front of the computer.

He nodded. "What do I do?"

"Use the mouse to click on that icon." She pointed to a red symbol of an old fashion phone handset.

He did. It took several seconds before they heard

the distinct sound of a phone ringing. After five rings, Wolfe looked up at Nadia. She smiled and put her finger to her lips. "Just wait."

On the eighth ring, they heard a cautious voice say, "*Hola.*"

Wolfe glanced at Nadia who smiled, nodded and said in a whisper, "It is him."

"*Buenos dias,* Senor Gerlis. This is Michael Wolfe."

The response was a long silence, then, "You must have the wrong number." The voice spoke English with a slight Israeli accent.

Smiling, Wolfe realized Gerlis had not disconnected the call, which meant he was curious. "No, I am sure I am talking to the supposedly dead Asa Gerlis."

"You too, are supposed to be dead."

"Yes, I suppose I am. I guess that makes us ghosts."

"Is Nadia with you?"

Wolfe answered with a growl, "No, thanks to you, she is not. God rest her soul. That's why I called. You owe me a life, Gerlis. I plan on making it yours."

"You will never find me."

"Think about it. I found your cell phone number." Wolfe ended the call with a smile. He turned to Nadia. "Wonder how long it will take him to freak out and get in contact with the sniper."

"I would say he is destroying the phone right now and trying to figure out how you found him."

Wolfe frowned. "He can't trace the phone call, can he?"

"No. If he has the means, and I doubt he does, it will appear to have been made from a small pastry café in Paris."

"Good. Then the only way to find us will be to send El Sombra to talk to Reid's man, Simpson or Kendra Burges."

Nadia frowned. "You sure this is a good idea?"

"No, it's a horrible idea, but I don't know any other way."

She put her arm around him. "Mossad will now know you are alive."

"Yeah. I know."

"They will assume I am too."

"Probably."

She hugged him and he returned the embrace.

CHAPTER 35

SPAIN

A sa Gerlis stared wide eyed at the now silent cell phone in his hand. The only sound he heard came from his pounding heart. With a bit of panic and practiced efficiency, he removed the phone's back cover, disconnected the battery and extracted the SIM card. He then placed the small phone on the floor and smashed it with the heel of his shoe. After gathering the pieces of the now destroyed phone, he placed them in a small sack retrieved from the wastebasket in the bathroom.

He tossed the sack onto the bed next to the open suitcase and began packing. The sound of separating Velcro echoed in the quiet room as he separated the lining on the left side of the suitcase. He extracted a well-used passport and placed it on the bed next to the sack with the smashed phone.

He walked to the nightstand, retrieved a different passport and placed it in the now-empty space. After pressing the long strip of Velcro together, he checked to make sure the seam was once again unnoticeable.

Gerlis gathered his few remaining clothing items and threw them into the open suitcase. With a quick look around the room, he determined everything was packed. Placing the passport in his back pocket, he lifted the luggage off the bed and grabbed the sack. Once he settled the hotel bill, he practically ran toward his car in the hotel parking lot, stopping only long enough to deposit the sack containing the shattered phone in a sidewalk trash receptacle.

Two hours later, Gerlis sat in front of a branch vice president of Deutsche Bank in Zaragoza, Spain.

"It is nice to make your acquaintance, Senor Reid. How may I help you today?"

With a smile, Gerlis handed the man his passport and a folded piece of paper. "I need to open a new account and consolidate the funds from the accounts listed on that page. Those accounts are currently in one of your banks in Zurich. I wish for them to be transferred to the new account here."

"I see. May I ask why, Senor?" Juan Martinez studied the passport carefully for several minutes. When he was done, he handed it back to Gerlis and noticed a thick white envelope on his desk. With a casual motion, he covered the envelope and it disappeared into his top desk drawer. "I would be happy to accomplish your request, Senor Reid."

An hour later, Gerlis walked out of the bank with all that remained of Gerald Reid's money safely deposited into new, readily accessible accounts. The passport given to the banker would be discarded and in less than a day, Gerald Reid's money would be gone from this bank along with his own.

He glanced at his watch and noticed he had plenty of time before his next appointment.

◆

Omar Said watched from across the street as Asa Gerlis entered the small café. He saw no one following the man, but waited another ten minutes before entering himself. As he sat across from Gerlis, he narrowed his eyes. "What did you want to talk about?"

"You've shaved your beard." Gerlis sipped his espresso.

"I thought it wise after the incident in Barcelona."

Nodding, he handed the Iraqi sniper a folded piece of paper.

Said unfolded it, his eyes scanning the page. "What is this?"

"Your final payment."

"It is just numbers."

Taking another sip, Gerlis smiled as he studied the man. "Yes, the top one is an account number at Deutsche Bank. The next number is the user ID. The third number is the password and the bottom number is the amount in the account."

"Euros or dollars?"

"Euros."

"Very generous. Why is it my last payment?"

"Because you are going to find Michael Wolfe and, this time, make sure he is dead. Then you are going to disappear. Considering the sum of money in that account, you can retire."

Said studied the bottom number on the sheet. "What about expenses?"

"There is plenty there to cover expenses."

He looked up. "And how am I going to find Wolfe?"

"A woman by the name of Kendra Burges."

"Where is this woman?"

"New Zealand. She works at the US Embassy in

Wellington. She is CIA."

A small smile appeared on Said's lips. "What do I do with her once I know Wolfe's location?"

Gerlis smiled also. "Use your imagination."

"What if I just take the money and never find Wolfe?"

"He will find you."

The sniper laughed out loud. "He would never find me."

"Ever hear the name William Little?"

"No, why?"

"At one time Little was a general in the US military. He stole antiquities from your country during Operation Desert Freedom."

El Sombra frowned and silently kept his focus on Gerlis.

"He disappeared one day and later surfaced in Madagascar as a strong man using another name. He was untouchable by the US government due to the lack of an extradition treaty. He lived there for twenty years without incident until 2014."

"What happened in 2014?"

"Before I answer that, let me ask you how hard is it to make a 1600-meter headshot along a windy coastal beach?"

"I would say impossible."

"Little died when a .50 caliber bullet struck him in the head. The sniper who made the shot was Wolfe."

Said remained quiet.

"It took him twenty years to find Little, but he did."

"How do you know this story about Wolfe is true?"

Gerlis leaned forward, his forehead furrowed. "Gerald Reid and I were standing ten feet away when Little's head exploded. I helped his security guards find the sniper hide. Wolfe is relentless and he will not forget. He will find you if you do not find him first."

"Ahh—better to be the hunter than the hunted."

"Something like that."

"How does he know about me?"

"The fool in Barcelona."

El Sombra nodded slightly and stood. "You will know our association is over when Wolfe is dead. I will have fulfilled my contract and you must never contact me again." Without another word, he left the café.

Gerlis remained seated and finished his espresso. "Yes, when Wolfe is dead."

Kendra Burges returned to her small apartment after another boring and embarrassing day at the American embassy in Wellington, New Zealand. She was a highly trained CIA analyst who was now being punished by performing secretarial duties for the Deputy Chief of Mission. All because of her association with Gerald Reid.

Her frustration level increased daily amid regular thoughts of resignation interspersed with thinking of ways to jump start her stalled career. She paused before opening her apartment door and contemplated returning to the embassy to discuss it with her boss. The thought was quickly dismissed as unwise, so she unlocked the door and entered.

Before she could turn on a light, a strong masculine hand clamped over her mouth. Before thinking to utilize self-defense techniques—learned many years prior but never practiced—she felt a small prick on her neck. A feeling of well-being ensued and she stopped struggling as blackness engulfed her.

Lying on her bed she felt a sensation of cold air blowing across her body. The realization she was nude also crossed her mind. After trying to move her arms and legs, she discovered they were bound. Unable to open her eyes, she smelled the distinct odor of duct-tape. Her heart raced as she realized the gravity of her situation. She tugged her arms again, but they remained immobile.

"I see you're conscious."

The voice was male with a slight Boston accent. She turned her head toward it. "What do you want?"

"Information."

She felt fingers moving up the inside of her left leg toward her knee. "What information?"

"Where is Michael Wolfe?"

The hand progressed past her knee up her thigh. "How would I know? He's dead."

"Your old boss didn't think so. Oh, by the way, did you know he is dead?"

The hand was now at her crotch. She gasped. Shaking her head rapidly, she pleaded, "Please don't."

The hand remained there for a few moments before moving toward her stomach. "Where is Michael Wolfe? That is the last time I am going to ask nicely."

"I don't know."

"Sure, you do. Your boss sent someone to find him."

The hand massaged her breasts and then moved to her neck where it clamped around her throat and squeezed.

"Where is Wolfe?"

She managed to say as she gasped for air, "He never told me."

The pressure increased. "I think you're lying."

"No... Not lying..."

The pressure relaxed. "Who was the individual Reid sent?"

"Gregg Simpson."

"Where is he?"

"How would I know?"

The hand clamped around her neck again and squeezed. She managed to say, "I really don't know." She tried to breathe as she gasped. "I—was sent here—before—I could—talk to him."

The pressure relaxed again. "Is he CIA?"

She nodded.

All of a sudden, tape was placed over her mouth and she felt the bed sag as a heavy weight climbed on.

Fear engulfed her as she heard, "You are a very attractive woman, Kendra."

Three hours later, Omar Said closed the door to Kendra Burges' apartment. If found in time, the woman would survive. Even if she did, she would be unable to identify her attacker. If asked what he wanted, she would babble about him wanting to know where a dead person was.

He smiled to himself. No one would believe her.

CHAPTER 36

As the sun peeked above the horizon, Wolfe watched Nadia drive the Jeep west away from where he stood at the northern border of his property. He pulled the hood of his 3D forest camouflage Ghillie Suit over his green watch cap. After making sure his Remington 700 was securely strapped against his back, he entered the densely wooded area that was a half mile from the rutted turnoff to his house.

Progress was slow as he continuously checked for tripwires and other booby traps. He found none.

Two hours later, from his position within the tree line on the southeastern side of his property, Wolfe surveyed the entrance to his underground home with his Nikon 12x50 binoculars. He observed nothing out of the ordinary. With all the resources Reid used to find this particular spot, Wolfe would not assume they left it untouched.

He used the binoculars to survey the western tree line and caught sunlight reflecting off an object alien to his property. Focusing on the location of the reflection, he smiled to himself. A not-so-well-hidden GoPro camera powered by a solar panel. With the assumption it was motion-sensor activated, he proceeded to look for others.

Using the position of the camera on the west side, he estimated where one might be on the east side. Five minutes later, he spotted it. Wolfe sighted in on the western camera with his Remington 700 and dispatched it with one shot. He repeated the process on the eastern one. Concern about anyone hearing the rifle shots never crossed his mind—his property was too remote.

Wolfe approached the front entrance of his home with caution as he looked for trip wires or any other booby traps. The door looked untouched and after examining all four sides, he unlocked it and barely opened it. Extracting a small Maglite from a utility pocket, he quickly searched the opening looking for any thin wires. He found none.

The software on the security monitor only allowed anyone opening the front door thirty seconds to disarm the unit. He hurried to the main control panel in the kitchen and entered the proper code to disengage the system. Once this was done, he turned to scrutinize his long-time home. A sense of peace swept over him as he surveyed the interior.

Except for the slight musty smell and a chill, the house appeared untouched since the last time he and Nadia were here. He checked several markers, left in random locations, to see if anyone had opened a door or looked in a cabinet. All were in place.

Satisfied with the knowledge no one had gained entry to his home, he turned up the heat pump and went upstairs to the bedroom he used for his office. Since the security system was powered by solar energy, Wolfe never turned it off. He activated the monitor and proceeded to review various videos recorded by the numerous cameras around his home.

Because the cameras were activated by motion, the majority of the clips were of deer and other such creatures whose habitat surrounded his house. He found the recording of man driving a Jeep Wrangler within a few yards of his front door. He checked the time stamp, made a mental note and continued to watch.

The guy spent nearly an hour walking the perimeter of the house—looking for access points, Wolfe assumed. The clip ended as the man drove out of camera range to the south. The next clip showed the man returning and placing the two GoPro cameras he had dispatched in the tree lines facing the front entrance. As expected, the man then headed to the northern side of his home. Wolfe's security cameras followed as he placed two additional cameras within the tree line next to the access road. He finally returned to the Jeep and drove south and out of camera range.

He frowned as he tapped his finger on his lips. Wolfe replayed the video of the man placing the two cameras on the northern side of the house. He froze the video and zoomed in on the intruder.

As expected, he did not recognize him. He downloaded several still frames to a file on his security system and sent Nadia a text message with his phone. She was to avoid entering the property from the north. He had plans for the two remaining cameras.

"His name is Gregg Simpson. He's been with the agency less than a year, working for Gerald Reid."

"You mean *worked* for Reid, don't you, Joseph?"

"Yes, sorry, wrong tense. Where did the picture come from?"

"Security camera on my property. He was here while we were away. Any idea of where he might be?"

"I haven't inquired yet."

Wolfe was silent for several moments. "Who else would know he was snooping around my property besides Reid?"

"Probably Reid's assistant, Kendra Burges."

"Where is she?"

"Last I heard, she was transferred to the New Zealand embassy."

"That's one way to tell her she screwed up."

Joseph chuckled. "There are others, but this was meant as a teachable moment."

"Okay, I'm not flying to New Zealand. See if you can locate this Simpson person."

"I'll put my assistant on it."

Jerry Griggs looked up from his laptop when Joseph stopped in front of his desk. "Please tell me you're giving me the rest of the day off."

"On the contrary, I need you to do something for me."

"Is it legal?"

"Yes."

"Shoot, I was hoping for jail time to get out of this drudgery."

Joseph smiled. "I need you to find out where a CIA operative named Gregg Simpson is stationed."

A slight grin appeared on Griggs' lips. "At least when you ask me to do something for you, it's fun. What's he done?"

"He's been a naughty boy running an op inside the US."

The grin on Griggs' lips broadened. "Oh, dear. On whose orders?"

"Gerald Reid."

"Tsk, tsk. I hate it when my ex-comrades do stupid things."

Joseph took on a grave expression. "Jerry, I need you to do this with the utmost discretion."

The grin disappeared. "Okay, I won't ask why."

"Probably best."

"When do you need to know?"

"Yesterday."

Griggs grinned again, closed his laptop and stood. "I'm taking the rest of the day off, boss."

"Good, see you in the morning."

Both sets of Jerry's grandparents were sharecroppers from Alabama. However, his father and mother were the first generation from either family to graduate from college. His father retired from the army after twenty years and reaching the rank of major in the army. Afterward, he became the administrator of a small school system outside the city limits of Nashville. Jerry's mother taught at a high school in Nashville and over the years won various national teaching awards. The oldest of four children, Jerry dreamed of playing professional basketball.

He'd missed getting a basketball scholarship to a Division I team by three inches. At six-foot-two and above average skills, he had been heavily pursued by

Division II teams. But his heart was set on a Division 1 team. When his hometown school of Vanderbilt failed to come calling, he'd followed his father's footsteps and signed up with the Army, eventually becoming a Ranger. After the challenges he faced in the military, earning a degree at Vanderbilt was a snap and he graduated summa cum laude. During those years, he met his future wife Colleen.

With his military background and stellar grades, he caught the attention of a CIA recruiter named Joseph Kincaid. The rest, as they say, is history. He spent a decade overseas in some of the hottest locations the CIA could send you. Afterward, the then-forty-year-old ex-Ranger came home to a desk job and preceded to get reacquainted with his wife and two daughters.

Now after three years as an analyst at CIA's Langley Headquarters, Jerry jumped at the opportunity to be the assistant for the newly appointed National Security Advisor Joseph Kincaid

The bar resided in a less-than-desirable part of Washington, DC. A draft of generic beer sat on the greasy tabletop of the dark corner booth he occupied. His eyes continuously swept the denizens of the room as he waited for an individual to join him.

His wait occupied thirty minutes of his life before his contact opened the bar's front door. After stepping inside, he watched her hesitate as her vision adjusted to the smoky darkness. It took several moments for her to locate him, but she moved quickly toward the booth and slid in across from him.

"Where in the hell did you find this place, Jerry?"

"Google Earth."

She looked around the dark room and at the other patrons. "Charming."

He shrugged.

"How's the rarified air within the White House?"

"Stale. I saw a cockroach this morning."

She chuckled. "Regrets?"

"None."

"Good. Why the invitation?"

"I need information."

"You'll have to buy me a drink first, sailor."

"Not if you're going to insult me."

Carla Webb smiled. Her white teeth contrasted with her dark skin in the dim light of the bar. Pencil thin with short curly hair, she'd celebrated her tenth anniversary with the agency just before Griggs had left for the White House. She pointed at his glass. "What're you having?"

"Not sure. I ordered beer, but I don't think that's what I got."

"You always loved to complain. I'll have what you're having."

He looked at the bar and raised his glass. When he gained the bartender's attention, he nodded in Carla's direction.

She grinned as she gazed around the room. "I'll have to take a shower after I get home."

"Gripe, gripe, gripe."

As a waitress breezed by, she deposited a glass of foaming liquid in front of Carla. After taking a sip, she grimaced. "Better than what we had in Kabul, but not by much."

Griggs smiled. After she set the beer down, he said, "Do you know a guy named Gregg Simpson?"

Her eyes narrowed.

"Great nonverbal answer, Carla. Where is he?"

"Who wants to know?"

Griggs took a pull of his beer but did not respond.

Webb stared hard at him as she took another gulp of beer and grimaced again. She locked eyes with him. "Tell me who wants to know or I walk."

"I do."

"Why?"

He shrugged. "Inquiring minds."

"Not good enough."

His perpetual smile disappeared and he leaned forward. "Mr. Simpson's been a naughty boy and my boss is not happy."

"I'm not surprised. From what I hear there are more than a few higher-ups unhappy with Mr. Simpson."

"How so?"

"He fell into the orbit of Gerald Reid. Not a wise career decision, as it turned out."

"Where is he?"

She smiled and sipped her beer. "What do I get if I tell you?"

"The undying gratitude of your country."

With a shake of her head and a chuckle, she said, "You're so full of shit." She took another drink and paused. "He's in timeout. Assigned to a desk at Langley from midnight to eight."

"What department?"

"Pacific Rim."

"What's he doing there?"

She shrugged. "How the hell should I know?"

With a smile, Griggs nodded. "Okay, sorry I asked."

"You should be."

"Do you know where he lives?"

Tilting her head, she gave him an *are-you-kidding-me* look. "He's not my type."

"Sorry. Wrong question. How would I find out where he lives?"

She shook her head. "How long have you been gone?"

He chuckled and took another pull from his beer. "Touché. Guess I'm getting lazy."

"Sounds like it."

He stood and threw a twenty-dollar bill on the table. "Hate to drink and run, but the boss won't like it if I come back empty handed."

She watched as he exited the bar. With a shrug, she finished her beer and departed as well.

CHAPTER 37

WASHINGTON, DC

The Next Day

H e lives in an apartment complex in New Carrollton, Maryland. Works midnight to eight at Langley. My source tells me he's having to redeem himself after all the stunts he pulled working for Reid."

Joseph nodded, looking up at his assistant standing in front of his desk. He remained quiet as he listened to the recounting of the previous evening.

"If you ask me, he's really not cut out for this line of work."

Joseph tilted his head. "Why do you say that?"

"I found his address on Facebook."

"You're kidding?"

"Nope, wish I was. I drove by his place last night. If anyone is looking for him, they won't have a difficult time doing it. Not sure where they found this guy, but they need to rethink their recruiting skills."

With a sly smile, Joseph said, "Thank you for doing this, Jerry."

"Not a problem. Reminded me of why I took this job. I now get to associate with a higher class of creeps." He grinned, turned and left the NSA's office for his own.

Unconsciously tapping a pen on his desk, Joseph pinched his lips. Frustration set in as he realized, even though he was the National Security Adviser, his position no longer allowed him to do anything about someone like Gregg Simpson. Plus, he did not want to draw too much attention to his interest in the man. Utilizing Jerry was about as far as he could go within the ranks of government without raising eyebrows. He glanced at his watch. In the next twenty minutes, another busy day at the White House would begin.

After taking a deep breath and letting it out slowly, he realized he would need a little more time to think about his next steps.

The Next Day

New Carrollton Police Officer Marci Newton noticed a glow in the sky above the tree line while patrolling one of the city's many residential sections. The time approached one a.m. and her first fear was a house fire. She accelerated the Dodge Charger Pursuit toward the glow.

As she approached the fire, her worst fears were realized. She keyed the mic on her radio and said. "I have a fully-engaged fire at the New Madrid apartment complex. Alert FD and send back up." She screeched the car to a halt and ran toward the building to help with the evacuation of residents.

Three hours later, with the fire extinguished, one of the firemen rushed out of the building and approached his supervisor. New Carrollton FD Captain Harold Mendez turned to the younger man as he approached. "What've you got, Jesse?"

"Got a body on the second floor, Cap."

"Smoke inhalation?"

The expression on the soot-covered face of the rookie fireman told the Captain it wasn't.

"No, sir. Looks like it's where the fire started."

Jerry quietly leaned against the doorframe with his arms crossed as he watched Joseph read the multiple pages just laid on his desk. The older man removed his glasses and looked up at him.

"How did you find this out?"

"I heard about the fire at the apartment complex this morning on my way to work. The address sounded familiar so when I got here, I started making calls." He pointed toward the papers. "I received those in an email ten minutes ago."

Joseph pushed his chair away from his desk, removed his glasses and leaned back. He closed his eyes and pinched the bridge of his nose. "So, Gregg Simpson doesn't show up for work last night. He's later found burned to death in his apartment with four of his fingers cut off." Opening his eyes, he looked up at his assistant. "What does that tell us, Jerry?"

"Simpson knew or had something someone wanted and apparently didn't tell that someone fast enough."

Joseph leaned forward and picked up a single sheet of paper. "Kendra Burges was found in her apartment beaten and barely clinging to life in Wellington, New

Zealand. Both of these people worked directly for Gerald Reid, who was murdered on the streets of Barcelona."

Griggs nodded, "Care to tell me what all this means, boss?"

"It means someone is tying up loose ends left by Gerald Reid."

"Who's the someone?"

Smiling, Joseph didn't answer right away. Griggs titled his head. "Really, Joseph? After all these years?"

With a sigh, the older man folded his hands on the desk. "Come in and close the door."

Wolfe stood under the overhang outside his front door sipping coffee. The sun, not yet over the horizon, exposed the open field to the south in the soft glow of early dawn. Birds in the densely-wooded land to the east and west, serenaded the approaching daylight. A soft breeze out of the southwest carried the fragrance of dew-covered grass. Moments like this were the reason he stayed on this property. It was his oasis. Far from the chaos created by greedy businessmen, clueless politicians and power-grabbing despots. Now someone was on their way to bring disorder to his small out-of-the-way retreat.

Nadia wrapped her arms around his waist and pressed her body against his back. "Do you think he will come?"

"Yes."

"When?"

"Soon."

They were quiet for a while. "I love this time of day here, Michael. It is so peaceful."

"Yes."

Another period of silence passed between them as he sipped his coffee and enjoyed her presence.

She said. "What did Joseph tell you last night? You were quiet afterwards."

"The man we saw in our security videos was found burned to death in his apartment yesterday. Before being set on fire, someone cut off four of his fingers."

Nadia remained silent and tightened her embrace.

He continued. "It was El Sombra."

"How do you know?"

He paused and turned to put his arm around her. "Reid's assistant, Kendra Burges, was attacked also. Joseph didn't know her current condition, but she'd been beaten and raped."

"Could it be a coincidence?"

He shook his head. "No, it was him. He's done this before. Apparently, he likes it."

She took a deep breath. "Are we ready for him?"

Shrugging, Wolfe stared back out toward the south. "Without knowing when or how, we're as ready as possible."

Nodding, she remained quiet.

"You reprogrammed the low-light GoPro camera's Simpson left behind the house, right?"

"Yes."

"After you attached them to the cabin, you tested them to make sure we could see anyone coming from the south, right?"

She nodded again.

"Then we have eyes to the south. My current surveillance system will detect anyone coming from the north, east or west. We're about as ready as we can be."

"I am still worried, Michael."

His mouth twitched. "So am I. But you have to remember, you and I know this land better than he does."

"What happens when he is gone? What then?"

"We'll cross that bridge when we get to it."

She looked into his eyes. "Gerlis will not rest until we are dead."

"I know."

Omar Said studied the images provided by Google Earth on a Samsung tablet. The location given to him by the now-dead CIA man proved more difficult to find than he'd first thought. The time approached noon and the cabin, marking the southern boundary of the land he searched for, eluded him. The GPS device he'd purchased was useless as the roads were unmarked and barely passable. Plus, the earth shelter home Simpson mentioned did not appear on any of the satellite pictures from the website.

In addition, the concentration of trees in this part of the world unnerved him. At least in the deserts of the Middle East, you could see your enemy approaching. Here someone could be hiding behind any of them and he would never know until it was too late. Brushing this thought aside, he pressed on looking for the old homestead.

He found it mid-afternoon as dark swirling clouds rolled in from the northwest and a stiff wind rustled the trees. Unused to the sudden weather changes common in Missouri, Omar felt fear and dread, two emotions he seldom experienced. Taking binoculars with him, he skirted the structure and headed for the eastern tree line. This would be a reconnaissance trip to see if he had found the correct location and determine if the individuals he sought were here.

He stayed close to the wooded perimeter, using it

as a shield to hide his presence. After treading his way up the gentle incline of the property, he could see it peaked half a kilometer ahead. The land appeared just as the CIA man had depicted, after having three fingers cut off. The fourth finger was removed just to add to the man's discomfort.

When he approached the peak of the rise, he knelt and crawled to the top. The scene below him was as described. Off in the distance, he could see a large mound of earth out of place in the smooth pasture land. Trees surrounded the mound, assisting its blending into the natural landscape. Bringing the binoculars to his eyes, he surveyed it closer. From this distance, he could see the dark outline of what appeared to be a door located at the bottom center of the mound.

He judged the distance to be another thousand meters down the gently sloping field. After spending almost an hour observing the area and seeing no movement, he crawled back from the peak and stood when out of sight of the home. On his way back to his rented Chevy Equinox, the wind blew harder and thunder rolled across the land. A lightning strike not far from his location startled him as the immediate clap of thunder rattled his senses. A cold heavy rain fell, soaking him immediately. The combination of the thunder and the cold rain produced a reaction his body, so far, had never experienced. He started shivering.

Omar Said, a son of the Iraqi desert, felt out of his element and at a disadvantage. The feeling was followed by a premonition he would never see his homeland again, dangerous thoughts for a man in his line of work.

CHAPTER 38

SOMEWHERE IN SOUTHERN MISSOURI

Wolfe sat in front of the desk, studying the figure as it swept by the east side of the old cabin. "All I see him carrying are binoculars."

"That is all I saw, too."

He and Nadia were in the office where the large flat-screen security monitor showed multiple views from the various cameras placed strategically around his land. He pointed to the view provided by a camera high in a tree near the peak of the incline south of their home. "There he is, just outside the eastern tree line."

Nadia bent over to look closer. "Yes."

The fisheye camera lens distorted the view, but they could discern it was a man walking toward the peak.

She asked, "Can you zoom in?"

"Not with that one."

She continued to watch as the man crawled to the peak. "He is doing reconnaissance."

Wolfe nodded. "Smart."

As she straightened, she put her hands on her hips. "What now?"

"We know he's here. He doesn't know we know. Advantage us."

"For now."

"Yes, for now. We have to make sure we don't lose the advantage."

"How?"

"I'm going out and you need to watch the monitors."

She tapped her foot. "What if I go out and you watch the monitor?"

He turned to look at her. "Do you know where I placed the traps?"

She shook her head.

"Exactly. That's why I will be the one outside."

She closed her eyes and nodded. With a sigh she placed her arms around his shoulders. "I do not want anything to happen to you, Michael Wolfe."

He patted her hand. "Nothing will. We will be in constant contact with each other. You will tell me where he is at all times."

They watched the monitor for a few more minutes in silence. He looked up at her. "Why don't you get some sleep? It could be a long night."

She shook her head. "I no longer sleep well without you by my side. I will wait."

A small smile appeared on his lips. "Yeah, me either."

The storm lasted well into the evening. Wolfe felt it

would give him an advantage, but he did not know why. During the initial construction of his house, a deep ditch had been dug from the foundation toward a spot deep within the trees on the east side. Elliptical concrete pipe, wide enough for a man to crawl through, was laid and covered by three feet of dirt. Over the course of living in the house, Wolfe had made various modifications to the tunnel and now used it for egress and ingress from the interior without being seen. One of the modifications was waterproofing the interior with a rubber-based compound. Interior lights were not needed, as Wolfe knew the inside of the pipe as well as he did his home.

Wolfe pushed his Barrett M82A1 sniper rifle ahead of him in the tunnel while he dragged a black backpack behind. The black thermal heat retention underwear, he wore, would help him maintain body heat in the cold rain. The black utility pants, black hiking boots, black long sleeve T-shirt, a black utility vest, black watch cap and black face paint, would make him virtually invisible in the nighttime forest.

Before exiting the tunnel, he did a radio check with Nadia. "I'm about to leave."

"Be careful."

He smiled as he opened the exit door disguised as a tree stump. Once outside, he removed his Iris Gen 2+ Dual Tube NV Goggles from the backpack and slipped them over the watch cap. He felt his ankle to make sure his Black Ops Survival Knife was secure. After he secured the back pack on his shoulders, he lowered the NVG over his eyes. As the world took on a greenish hue, he patted his Glock 19 in a hip holster to make sure it had not fallen out in the tunnel. Taking the Barrett in both hands and keeping well within the tree line, he moved toward his rendezvous with El Sombra.

When he reached the highest part of the rise, Nadia's voice crackled in his earbud. "Michael. He is back."

Wolfe stopped and swore under his breath. "Damn. Where is he?"

"He just passed the cabin and is heading for the tree line."

"How's he dressed?"

"Exactly like you. All black."

"Could you tell if he has NVGs on?"

"I could not be sure. He was a blur as he passed, but to be safe, assume he does."

"Don't worry, I will." He paused as he stood still. "Okay, change in plan. Keep me posted on his position."

"Be careful."

Wolfe did not answer as he withdrew farther into the trees and underbrush.

Said's decision to approach the earth sheltered home after dark was fueled by his earlier unease. In a normal environment, he would wait until the early morning to execute his plan for finding his targets. But the storm, the trees and his subconscious desire to get this task behind him caused him to advance the timetable.

He carried a backpack containing an IED made from common household chemicals, a formula learned during his time with Saddam Hussein's Red Guard. This would be used to blow open the front door. Then, during the chaos inside from the explosion, he would sweep through the structure, shooting anything that moved. He carried two CZ 75 pistols and multiple spare magazines. The CZs had been purchased from a greedy Texas pawnshop owner whose eyes had grown wide when he saw the stack of one-hundred-dollar bills Said had lain on the glass counter.

It wasn't his best plan, but it would suffice for the moment.

He entered the tree line, staying close enough to the open field to keep track of where he was in relation to his target. An ancient pair of monocular NVGs adorned his head and allowed him to navigate in the darkness.

As he moved forward, his clothes became soaked from the constant drizzle and residual water left over from the earlier heavy rains. The cold night air penetrated his cotton pants and T-shirt. Halfway up the slope, he started shivering uncontrollably.

After finding a large white oak tree to use as a shield, Wolfe whispered into his radio headset, "Nadia, can you see him?"

"No, he entered the tree line several minutes ago."

"He'll stay close to the field."

"Why?"

"Because he's unfamiliar with the land. He'll get lost if he doesn't. Keep watching."

"Wait a minute..."

Wolfe stayed silent as he listened.

"I just saw something near the crest of the rise. I'm not sure, but it looked like him. Where are you?"

Wolfe did not answer as he caught a glimpse of movement through his NVGs to his right. As he shifted his position to get a better perspective, he heard another sound; the unmistakable sound of a slide being pulled back on an automatic pistol.

In the quiet of the forest, the following gunshot was deafening. With the sound bouncing off a multitude of trees, the muzzle flash became the only indicator of where the intruder stood. With a practiced move, Wolfe's Glock was out of its holster and firing less than half a second later.

Quiet returned to the secluded land as both hunters crouched behind cover. Not wishing to be in a standoff, Wolfe darted to his right toward a larger oak, firing his Glock as he ran.

Return fire ricocheted off the tree he just vacated.

A sound to his right caused Omar Said to train his NVGs in its direction. A slight movement was detected deep within the trees. He chambered a round in his CZ and fired. To his surprise, he received return fire and realized, after scrambling to safety behind a tree, he was no longer the hunter, but the hunted.

With this realization, Said pressed his back against a tree. Three more shots rang out as he heard them strike the tree he hid behind. He returned fire four times and ducked back behind the large oak. With his element of surprise gone, he decided his initial plan held no hope for success. With few options available, he unslung his backpack and removed the IED. After placing it on the ground, he set the timer, exited the tree line and ran toward the south.

Wolfe continued this trek away from the original gunfire, moving closer to the open field.

Nadia's voice came over the radio. "He just appeared out of the trees. He's running to the south."

His first thought was why. His answer came three seconds later as an explosion behind him brought trees down and a blinding flash in his NVGs. He flipped them up and ran toward the open field. After exiting the tree line, he lowered the goggles and saw a figure disappear over the rise heading south. He unslung the Barrett and followed.

As he reached the top of the crest, he fell into a prone position, cast aside the NVGs and switched on the night vision scope on his Barrett M82-A1. The figure could be seen running close to the edge of the trees, making a difficult target. Michael took a breath and let it out slowly as the crosshairs of the scope centered on the fleeing figure. Training and experience took over as he applied pressure to the trigger. Once again, the quiet of night was broken with the sound of a rifle shot.

The Barrett sent a .50 BMG bullet into the back of Omar Said. The round shattered numerous spinal vertebrae as it passed through El Sombra's body. Before exiting, it mangled the right and left ventricle and severed the descending aorta. With a separated spine and a non-functioning heart, the man collapsed forward, sliding on the wet grass for several yards.

A strong wind blew in from the northwest again and rain started to pelt Wolfe as he walked toward the fallen assassin. Flashes of lightning lit the sky and the continuous sound of thunder added to the surreal scene.

He secured the Barrett over his shoulder as he approached and withdrew the Glock from its holster. He trained the pistol on the prone, unmoving man. Kneeling several feet from the figure he waited. In the illumination of a lightning flash, he saw open unseeing eyes.

The intensity of the rain increased as Wolfe knelt

next to the figure. He felt no emotions—not relief, pride, contempt or sympathy, only emptiness. As water ran down his face, his mouth twitched as he stood. Weariness swept over him as he walked down the incline toward the cabin and El Sombra's vehicle.

CHAPTER 39

SOMEWHERE IN SOUTHERN MISSOURI

By the time the Howell Country Sheriff Harold Bright and EMTs arrived in the field south of Michael Wolfe's home, the rain had moved on to the east. The clearing sky exposed a full moon which allowed a dim light to the illuminate the scene.

Bright stood several yards from the dead figure as deputies searched the body and EMTs prepared to move it. He turned to Wolfe. "Do you know who he is?"

Wolfe shook his head. "Never seen him before."

"There's no ID on him, but there's a rental agreement in the SUV's glove box parked by the cabin."

No comment came from Wolfe.

"Indicated his name was Gregg Simpson. Ever hear that name before?"

As he maintained his neutral expression, Wolfe said. "No."

"How did you know he was out here?"

"I have security cameras everywhere. Most have low-light capabilities."

The sheriff nodded. "Where was the explosion?"

Wolfe pointed toward the north. "Just over the rise, inside the tree line."

"Huh. Wonder what that was about?"

"I believe he was going to try to gain access to the house with it."

"You think he set it off when you came after him?"

"Don't know."

"Well, I think this is a robbery gone bad."

Wolfe nodded. "That's what I thought."

"Hell of a shot in the rain and thunder."

"I don't like strangers threatening us."

The young deputy who had been searching the body stood and walked toward Bright. He held a CZ hand gun by the trigger guard. "Hey Sheriff, this guy's got two of these on him."

Bright smiled. "That makes this a righteous shooting, Michael. Maybe they will help us confirm his ID."

Wolfe knew different, but said, "Let's hope so."

After the EMTs took the body, the sheriff and his deputies left with a promise of a thorough investigation of the dead man. Wolfe knew they would never learn his true identity. El Sombra had traveled the world for years without anyone knowing who he really was. But telling the sheriff this did not seem like a good idea. The less said, the better.

Just after four a.m., dead tired and cold, Wolfe stood with his eyes closed under the shower, letting the scalding hot water career off his face. He heard the shower door open and felt gentle hands caress his back. Turning, he took Nadia into his arms and embraced her. They stood holding each other for several minutes as the hot water washed the tension from his muscles.

By noon, Michael and Nadia were up and driving to the condo in Branson. He needed quick access to the plane. As they headed west, he made a cell phone call to Joseph. He put it on speaker so Nadia could hear and he waited for it to be answered.

"Good afternoon, Michael."

"Hello, Joseph. We had a visitor last night."

"Oh. Anyone I know?"

"Only by reputation."

There was silence on the phone. Then a cautious, "How did it go?"

"A negative outcome for him."

"I see. Will he visit again?"

"No."

"Good. We can discuss it later."

"Yes. I need a favor, Joseph."

"Name it."

"I need to know the location of our visitor's employer."

"Do you think that wise?"

"Yes. Ask our friends across the pond. They might know by now."

"I'll see what I can do. Where will you be?"

"Ready to move when we know the location."

"I'll call you later."

The call ended and Wolfe glanced at Nadia. She was lost in her own thoughts as she concentrated on the highway in front of them. He reached into an inner pocket of his jacket, withdrew a cell phone and offered it to her.

"What is this?"

"El Sombra's cell phone."

She half smiled. "You did not give it to the sheriff? Why?"

"The cell phone will help us more than it will the sheriff. Besides, he will never discover who the dead man really was. His fingerprints will not be on file anywhere. I doubt even the Mossad have them."

She activated the phone and stared at the screen. "It's a Samsung Galaxy and it's locked. There is no way I am going to get into it."

Wolfe hit the re-dial on his cell phone. Joseph answered right away. "Yes."

"Is your friend still in Springfield?"

"Which friend is that?"

"The one who helped us two years ago."

"Yes. Why?"

"We have an electronic device we need assistance with."

"Oh, whose?"

"Our visitor left it behind."

"I see. Let me call him and see if he is available."

The call ended and Wolfe glanced at Nadia.

"Are you ready to get this nonsense over with?"

She stared ahead at the highway and nodded. After several minutes, she turned and took a deep breath. "I do not want to be on the sidelines for this one, Michael."

He shot her a quick glance then returned to watching the road. "By sidelines, what do you mean?"

"Gerlis took you away from me and then tried to kill me. I owe him."

Wolfe glanced at her again. "Are you sure?"

"Yes, very."

A slight smile came to his lips. "Then that's how we'll play it."

Wolfe parked the Jeep in an angled slot in front of a nondescript buff brick two-story office building on the southwest side of Springfield. It was mid-afternoon and the area surrounding the location was busy with pedestrians and automobile traffic. He turned to Nadia as they stepped out of the Jeep. "Are you sure this is the right place?"

"Yes." She pointed to numbers on the side of the building. "That is the address Joseph gave me when he called back."

"There's no name on the building."

She shrugged.

Wolfe stood on the sidewalk in front of the building and took in their surroundings. On the west side stood a high-end restaurant and to the east, an office with the names of four lawyers. Across the street was an urgent care facility and an expensive-looking daycare center. "Not what I expected."

Smiling, Nadia said, "What did you expect, Michael? The dark basement of a creepy old house?"

"I guess I did."

After entering the building, Wolfe approached a reception desk. The young lady behind it looked up from her computer. "Good afternoon. May I help you?"

"Yes, Michael and Nadia Lyon to see JR Diminski."

"Oh, good, he's expecting you." She pointed to a staircase to her right. "Second floor, you'll see a conference room when you get to the top. He's waiting for you there."

After they entered the room, JR shook both of their hands. "Good to see you two. What can I help you with?"

Wolfe was glad the hacker did not want to engage

in small talk. He handed him the cell phone.

Diminski looked at it, smiled and pried the back cover off. He expertly removed the battery and extracted the small SIM card. After placing the card in a slot of a black box attached to a laptop computer with a USB cord, JR used his mouse to click on an icon. The laptop screen immediately started scrolling data and computer code.

With a slight smile, he looked at Wolfe. "What exactly did you need to know?"

"I want to know what numbers the phone called."

JR nodded as his fingers flew over the keyboard. He was silent for almost five minutes. "The phone was purchased at a Walmart in Dallas, Texas. It has 852 minutes left of the original 1000 minutes purchased with the phone."

"What about calls."

"Uh—let's see." He typed for a few more seconds. "Ah, here they are. He called the reservation number for Choice Hotels. Numerous pawn shops in the Dallas-Fort Worth area and..." JR stopped and looked up at Wolfe. "An international number in Spain."

"That's the number we need to know about."

"Uri, have you had any luck locating Gerlis?"

Ben-David remained silent on the other end of Joseph's call. Finally, he said. "Unfortunately, no. He has vanished again. We suspect the cell phone number you gave us has been discarded by now."

"Don't bother looking for El Sombra anymore."

"You know something I don't?"

"He met with an accident here in the states."

"Fatal one?"

"Yes."

"Can you give me any details, Joseph?"

"Not at the moment. I don't have any. My source confirmed it earlier today."

"That just leaves Gerlis."

"Yes."

"Then we will find him, my friend."

Joseph set the hand set back in its cradle and mumbled, "I kind of doubt it."

JR pointed to the laptop screen. "He called the number four times—once in Dallas, once near Muskogee. Oklahoma, and twice near West Plains, Missouri."

"Where is the number located now?"

It took another five minutes before JR stopped and looked at Wolfe. "Madrid."

Wolfe leaned forward and placed his arms and hands flat on the conference table. "Where in Madrid?"

"Various locations, never one in particular."

Silence returned until Nadia broke the quiet. "JR, is there a way to give us a general idea of where in Madrid the phone was?"

Nodding, JR started typing again. "Looks like they are centered around a place called El Carrascal."

She raised an eyebrow. "I am familiar with this area. Lots of tall apartment buildings and cultural spots."

JR said, "Never been there."

Her eyes brightened, "I love Madrid. It is a beautiful city. I have been there numerous times both as a child and an adult."

"Is there a way to pinpoint where he lives?" The question came from Wolfe.

JR shook his head. "Not unless he makes a few calls from the location. If it's in a high-rise apartment building, probably not. But I could eventually determine the building location."

Wolfe stood. "Thanks, JR. We've taken enough of your time. This has been extremely helpful."

JR stood also. "Don't leave just yet. Let me give you something." He stepped out of the conference room and walked to a cubicle next to the glassed-in room. He returned and handed Wolfe a plain white business card with only a number handwritten on it. "You and I have something in common."

"What's that?"

"Joseph as a friend." JR paused for a second. "Eight years ago, he did something for me I will never be able to repay." He swept one hand toward the cubicle farm outside the conference room. "Because of Joseph, I was given the freedom to create this business. The only way I can repay him is to help his friends." He pointed to the number. "There are only a few individuals who know that. If you ever need help with anything, send me a text message. I will call you. Don't call, just text. Remember. I will call you."

Wolfe stared at the card for several seconds. He offered his hand to JR. As they shook, he said, "Thank you."

CHAPTER 40

WASHINGTON, DC

J erry, during your time overseas, were you ever in
Spain?"

Griggs turned and found Joseph standing in
his office doorway looking at him.

"It depends. Who wants to know?"

"Me."

"In that case, yes."

"Do you have any contacts there?"

"Yes."

"Who is he?"

"He is a she, who happens to work for The National
Intelligence Center."

"How well do you know her?"

"That's a little personal, Joseph. I don't kiss and
tell."

"Professionally, Jerry."

Griggs folded his arms. "She and I collaborated on
the Madrid train bombing in 2004. Why?"

"Is she still active?"

"I believe she has a desk job, a husband and two kids. Again, why?"

"Would she do you a favor?"

Taking a deep breath, Griggs shook his head. "You're dancing around something, boss. What is it?"

"A friend of mine needs to find someone in Madrid."

"You have a lead on Gerlis?"

Joseph nodded.

"Well then, it's time to impose on her sense of international cooperation." He turned to his computer and started typing.

An hour later, Griggs laid a piece of paper on Joseph's desk. Taking the page in hand, the National Security Advisor read it quickly. Looking up, he said, "She's in management now?"

Jerry nodded. "She wouldn't say which department, but I bet it is pretty high up."

"Will she help us?"

Another nod.

"What did you tell her?"

"I told her we had two US Marshalls traveling to Spain to look for a fugitive and we wanted to do this quietly without going through all the red tape."

"She agreed?"

"Not until I told who it was. Then she did."

Joseph frowned. "What did you tell her?"

"I appealed to her maternal instincts."

"Jerry, what the hell did you tell her?"

With a chuckle, he said, "I told her it was a rich American, charged with embezzlement, who had left his wife and kids without any financial means."

"Jerry..." Joseph closed his eyes and slowly shook his head. Finally, he said, "And she bought that?"

Griggs shrugged. "I doubt it, but she laughed and agreed to help without involving Spanish authorities."

"Okay, I'll let him know."

Griggs did not move, his face a mask of concern. "Why not let Mossad handle this?"

"Because if the CNI knows Mossad's involved, Gerlis will hear about it and vanish again. Besides, Michael can handle it quietly."

"Will he and Nadia come out of hiding after this?"

"Don't know. That will be up to them."

Madrid, Spain

Madrid Barajas Airport, along with Charles de Gaulle Airport in Paris, occupies the largest land mass of any airport in Europe. Located twelve kilometers northeast of Spain's capital city, travelers can connect to and from the city via rail and highway. Since both Wolfe and Nadia knew their way around Madrid, they rented a BMW Series 1 F20 hatchback. This would allow more flexibility with their search for Gerlis.

After checking into their hotel, Wolfe sent a text message to Joseph and received a reply five minutes later. He looked at Nadia and said, "Want to get a cup of coffee?"

"As long as it isn't American style."

He smiled. "You just used a contraction."

She stuck her tongue out and glared at him.

Ruda Café, located in the La Tina area of Madrid, maintained a reputation as one of the best coffee shops in the capital city by offering a variety of international styles. Wolfe and Nadia arrived thirty minutes before the scheduled appointment. Both sipped espresso as they kept a watchful eye on individuals entering and exiting the establishment.

At exactly 4:00 p.m., a tall slender woman with long black hair, round eyes and a professional demeanor entered the café. She swept her gaze around the room and immediately locked onto the couple.

Nadia gave a small gasp. Wolfe turned to her and asked, "What's wrong?"

"I know her."

With a frown, Wolfe returned his attention to the woman, who walked briskly toward their table. "How?"

Before Nadia could answer, Mariana Torres stopped beside them and offered her hand to Nadia. With unaccented English, she said, "Nadia Picard, what a surprise." Her attention turned to Michael. "And who is this handsome man?"

With a smile, Nadia said, "This is my husband, Michael Lyon. Michael, this is Mariana Torres."

Wolfe stood and shook the offered hand.

She said, "It is very nice to meet you, Michael Lyon."

"The pleasure is mine, Ms. Torres."

"Call me Mariana."

He nodded.

The three sat and Torres got right to the point. "Why are you here and why are you masquerading as US Marshals?"

Wolfe chuckled. "Very good, Mariana. I appreciate the candor."

She turned to Nadia. "Are you still with Mossad?"

Nadia shook her head. "No."

"Good, because I would have asked you both to leave my country. Now why are you here?"

"Have you heard of a man named Asa Gerlis?"

Torres' eyes grew wide for a few moments, then she resumed her neutral gaze. "Yes, he was killed by an ISIS terrorist. My agency was sent a copy of the video. Why?"

Wolfe shook his head. "He's alive and has been residing here in Spain under an assumed name for the past two years."

She stared at Wolfe before looking at Nadia.

Nadia placed her hand on Torres' arm. "He is why we are here."

"I see." She grew quiet as a waitress deposited an espresso in front of her. Taking her time, Torres sipped the beverage and set it down on the table. "I need details."

Wolfe leaned forward and spoke in a low voice. "Have you ever heard the name El Sombra?"

She blinked several times. "Yes, but I'm told he is a myth."

"He is not a myth, but no longer a problem."

She took another sip of her coffee and raised her eyebrows. "Oh."

"Gerlis has been dispatching him from Spain for some time. We believe he tried to kill Nadia and me in Barcelona two years ago and recently showed up near our home."

"You said he is no longer a problem."

Wolfe nodded.

"I see."

"His real name was Omar Said. He was responsible for the death of an MI6 operator named Geoffrey Canfield, and three CIA operatives, Gerald Reid being one of them. The Mossad claims he was responsible for the disappearance of several of their assets around the Middle East. They lost track of him eight years ago."

She tilted her head slightly. "I was told Reid suffered a heart attack in Barcelona."

Nadia shook her head. "Michael and I saw him in Barcelona, he touched Reid just before he died."

With a stern look, Torres straightened in her chair. "Why were you two in Barcelona?"

Wolfe smiled. "Sightseeing."

Torres glared at Wolfe as she sipped her coffee. "Yes, it is a lovely city. Now why is Gerlis responsible for all of this chaos?"

"Because he is eliminating anyone who knows he is alive."

"Does he know you know?"

Both Wolfe and Nadia nodded.

Taking a deep breath, Torres frowned. "Why? Why does he care if people know he is alive?"

"Operation Desert Shield and Desert Storm."

She blinked several times. "I beg your pardon."

Wolfe proceeded to tell her what they knew about Reid, Gerlis and General William Little. During his narrative, she stared at her espresso, taking a sip now and then. After he concluded, she remained quiet.

Finally, she looked up, "You just confirmed something NCI has suspected for a long time."

"What's that?"

"While it has never been acknowledged, Spain lost several NCI operatives during one of General Little's escapades. We thought we knew what Little was doing—the information you just gave me makes it clear we did not. How much do you think Reid and Gerlis got from Little?"

Wolfe shrugged. "Not sure, but it was enough for them to get nervous about others knowing. The Mossad and CIA believes the auction generated over one hundred million dollars in sales."

"My, my... No wonder Gerlis is nervous."

"I don't think it stopped with the auction after Desert Storm."

Nadia and Mariana Torres stared at Wolfe. Nadia said, "Michael, you have never mentioned anything about that."

"No, because I just remembered something someone told me not too long ago."

"What?" both women said in unison.

"When General Little met with his accident on the veranda of his mansion, Reid and Gerlis were there. Why?"

Both women shook their heads.

"Because they've never stopped dealing in stolen art and antiquities."

CHAPTER 41

MADRID, SPAIN

The small art gallery, located between a Senegalese and an Indian restaurant in the Lavapiés section of Madrid, fit in well with the multicultural neighborhood. The area catered to students, artists, and refugees—plus, it was one of the least expensive places in the city to live. With the high number of immigrants and tourists constantly milling around the area, the comings and goings of the shop's visitors went unnoticed by the neighborhood and the local authorities.

Asa Gerlis, in the disguise of Diego Luis, liked it that way. His store consisted of a display room in the front with a glassed-in office toward the back. Behind his office and closed to the public was his storage area. Sales from the display room barely paid the electrical bill. His real money came from activities related to the storage area and the internet.

His association with a former United States Army

General exposed him to the workings of a lucrative business: the brokering of stolen art. When General Little had an unfortunate encounter with a .50 caliber bullet, Gerlis took over the business. Contrary to the rumors he staged his own death to defect, the real reason was to divorce himself from the persona of an Israeli Mossad agent. He could now concentrate totally on this endeavor and increase his wealth. With Reid and Canfield no longer around, the fear of his two old partners developing a conscience disappeared.

Stolen works of art, as a rule, are seldom recovered. There are several reasons, one being specific pieces are stolen for a particular buyer. These pieces go into the private galleries of the ultra-rich around the world, both male and female. Possessed by a passion to own major works of art, those types of collectors will pay top dollar for famous paintings, sculptures, antiquities or any unique one-of-a-kind objects deemed irreplaceable.

Asa Gerlis enjoyed feeding those passions and made millions doing it. Through underground networks and dark web chat rooms, he knew what pieces of art were for sale and who might be in the market for them. Occasionally, he took possession of the piece, but typically he never touched it. He also knew the best art thieves. If someone contacted him about a certain desired work of art, he could easily arrange for it to be stolen.

The beauty of the system allowed him to accomplish these transactions without the need for face-to-face meetings.

Gerlis normally opened the shop around noon and closed between five and six. When he went out of town, the gallery remained closed. Today, he opened early. Rumors were floating around the dark web of a particularly sought-after painting coming onto the market. He wanted to be prepared if it did.

The meeting with Mariana Torres lasted two hours. At the conclusion, Mariana stood and turned her attention to Wolfe.

"Michael, if it becomes common knowledge that Asa Gerlis has been living in Madrid for over two years without anyone knowing, there will be serious repercussions for NCI. Plus, it will end the career of many of my colleagues, myself included."

Wolfe only nodded.

"What can I do to help?"

"Nadia and I are fluent in Spanish and French. We need cover while we search for him."

A sly smile came to her face. "I believe I can help you there. Where are you staying?"

Nadia told her.

"There is someone with the Policía Municipal de Madrid I want you to talk to. She is a Senior detective within their stolen property division."

With a frown, Wolfe stared at Torres.

"Don't worry, Michael. She specializes in stolen art. If Gerlis is still involved, like you think he might be, she will be instrumental with your search."

"Very, well." He turned to Nadia. "What do you think?"

"Without help, I don't see how we find him."

Wolfe smiled at the contraction used by Nadia, but did not comment. He turned back to the NCI agent. "What will be our cover story?"

"Expect a delivery in the morning. It will be self-explanatory after that. It was a pleasure to finally meet you, Michael Wolfe."

With this surprising statement, Mariana Torres

turned and walked out of the café.

Nadia put her hand on Wolfe's arm and looked at him wide-eyed. "How did..."

"She knew the whole time, Nadia." He paused and changed the subject. "Since we don't have anything to do until tomorrow, let's act like tourists and find a good restaurant."

She smiled.

The call from the concierge came at eight-thirty the next morning. "Senor Lyon, there is a package here for you at the front desk. Do you wish for someone to deliver it?"

"Yes, thank you."

Ten minutes later, Wolfe opened the padded manila envelope and tipped it upside down. Two wallet size booklets, a business card and a folded piece of paper fell out onto the bed. Smiling, Wolfe picked one of the booklets up and opened it. "Interpol IDs. This one is yours." He handed it to Nadia.

"Where did she get the pictures?"

"It's our Missouri driver's license pictures."

Nadia grimaced. "Oh, dear."

"Nadia, you of all people should know the capabilities of an intelligence agency."

"Yes, but still. That's a little scary."

He nodded. "These will give us a little authority. Not much, but it gives us a reason to be looking."

He looked at the business card. It had a name, title and a telephone number. Across the top was a handwritten address and a time. Wolfe said, "The detective's name is Sophia Lopez."

Nadia opened the folded page. She read silently for several seconds. "The detective will give us information on art galleries in Madrid. Michael, I know nothing about art. Particularly, stolen art."

"Me either."

He took his cell phone and sent a text message to a number recently given to them. The call came five minutes later.

"Didn't expect to hear from you this fast. What's up, Michael?"

"JR, we need a crash lesson in stolen art."

"Why?"

"We have a theory that Gerlis is still dealing in stolen artifacts—maybe art, too. I don't want to blow our cover if I'm asked an easy question."

Chuckling, JR was quiet afterward for several moments. "I know the FBI has a database on stolen art. I can send a link to you for that. Then, what if..."

Wolfe realized the computer hacker was thinking. He did not interrupt. He heard the faint sound of tapping on a keyboard in the background. Then, "I've got an idea. Give me an hour and I'll call you back."

The call ended.

Fifty-five minutes later, Wolfe's phone vibrated with a new call. He answered immediately. "Yes."

"Are you familiar with how to identify a fine art painting?"

"Not at all."

"I wasn't either, but here are a few tips. Paintings and drawings are referred to by the artist, title, media used to produce and on what, plus their measurements, and then sometimes the year it was produced. For example, the Mona Lisa would be described as Da Vinci, The Mona Lisa, oil on wood, 77 x 53 centimeters, 1503. It's not a hard and fast rule, but if you toss it around occasionally, you'll sound knowledgeable."

"Okay. Didn't know it was that small."

"I didn't either. Here is something else you might use. On May 20th, 2010, a guy named Vjeran Tomic broke into the Paris Museum of Modern Art and cut five paintings out of their frames. The theft was discovered the following morning by museum personnel when they found the frames still on the wall, but no paintings. No one knows how he got in without setting off the alarms, but he did. The five paintings stolen were Dove with Small Peas by Pablo Picasso, Pastoral by Henri Matisse, Olive Tree near l'Estaque by Georges Braque, Woman with Fan by Amedeo Modigliani, and Still Life with Candlestick by Fernand Leger."

"I won't remember all of that."

"It doesn't matter. Just remember Picasso. I'll explain in a moment. The five paintings combined were valued at over 100 million euros."

"Really?"

"Yeah, really. Here's where it gets interesting. The paintings have never been recovered. Tomic was caught and told the police he gave the paintings to an art dealer named Jean-Michel Corves. The art dealer was the one who ordered the theft for an unnamed client. When he heard the police were getting close, he gave them to another guy who claims he threw them into a trash bin when he got nervous. No one believed them. The paintings are thought to be in private collections scattered around the world."

"That part I was aware of."

"Good. Here's the other interesting piece for you to know."

"What?"

"There is a chat room on the dark web that discusses stolen paintings. Now, I don't know how authentic this information is, but there is a rumor the Picasso from that robbery is going to be available soon. The sale would be held via an underground art network since a legitimate auction of the piece would be impossible."

"Would we be able to monitor the room?"

"I don't know. Maybe. I need to do a little more snooping around before I feel comfortable answering your question."

"Get back to us."

"Will do."

The call ended and Wolfe looked at Nadia.

"We need to learn as much as possible about an art heist in Paris on May 20th, 2010."

At eleven a.m., they left the hotel room for their meeting with the police detective. As they walked toward the elevator, Nadia asked, "What happens if we find him?"

"That's a good question. Should we let the Mossad know where he is or should we let Torres know?"

She blinked several times before answering, "Either way, we will never be free as long as he is alive, Michael. If he is taken into custody by either service, there is always the chance he will escape. If that happens..."

"We're right back in the same situation we are now."

She nodded.

Wolfe pressed the down button for the elevator and looked at her. "Let's find him first. Then we can make a decision."

CHAPTER 42

MADRID, SPAIN

Madrid is an old city. While few of its earliest structures survive, central Madrid consists of architecture originally built in the 1500s. In a newer section of the ancient city lies a building built within the last decade. This building housed the office of Detective Sophia Lopez. Modern, clean and Spartan in furnishings, the structure stands in stark contrast to the Mudejar style of older Madrid. Wolfe and Nadia were escorted to her office on the second floor.

As they entered, the detective stood and walked around the desk to greet them. Lopez was a matronly figure and a study in gray. She wore her salt and pepper hair short. It outlined a round face with an ashen pallor. Pewter framed glasses sat on an oversize nose in front of steel blue eyes. Her conservatively-cut solid gray pantsuit completed the image of a black and white photograph.

Nadia shook the proffered hand as she presented

her Interpol identification.

Studying the document, Lopez smiled and handed it back to her. She spoke in Spanish. "A pleasure to meet you, Agent Picard." She turned to Wolfe and accepted his ID. After a quick glance, she returned it and said, "Thank you, Agent Lyon. Mariana Torres indicated you two were here on a tip."

Wolfe nodded. "We have credible evidence that a painting, stolen in the May 20th, 2010 robbery of the Paris Modern Art Museum will be the subject of an underground transaction at some point in the near future here in Madrid."

"I see. Which one?"

"Picasso, Pigeon with Small Peas, oil on canvas, 65 x 54 centimeters, 1911."

"Really? I thought it was destroyed."

Wolfe shook his head. "Apparently not."

"Who's the seller?"

"We do not know the name he is using at this time. We have a description, but no name. Have you ever heard of a man named William Little?"

Lopez's eyes widened. "Yes, I have."

"Our seller was associated with him until his sudden death in 2014. We think he might have taken over Little's business, but that is conjecture right now."

"What name has he used in the past?"

After a slight hesitation, Wolfe said, "Asa Gerlis."

Lopez appeared not to recognize the name. "So, what are your roles in this, agents?"

Nadia answered. "Since we know what he looks like, our task is to identify him and turn it over to local authorities. As you know, we do not have the authority to arrest anyone in Spain."

"Yes, I am aware of that. What do you need from me?"

"We know he has been in Madrid for the last two years. Our source told us he might operate a small art gallery as a cover," Wolfe replied.

"Madrid is the cultural center of Spain, Agent Lyon. We have hundreds of small art galleries throughout the various communities."

"We know. But we hoped you might have suspicions about a few of them."

A slight smile crossed Lopez's lips as she looked from Wolfe to Nadia. "Yes..." She paused. "We have suspicions about more than a few." Another pause. "When is this painting supposed to be sold?"

"We do not know. We were only told it would be soon."

She nodded her head. "We have not heard anything about it."

Neither Nadia or Wolfe responded.

Looking again at both of them, she gave them a bored expression and returned to her desk. They watched as she typed for a few moments at her computer. Seconds later they heard a laser printer spool up and spit out several pages. Lopez turned and retrieved them from the printer tray. She offered them to Nadia.

"This is a summary of galleries with questionable legitimacy. The owner and addresses are included. Will you need assistance in finding your way around the city?"

Shaking her head, Nadia said, "I grew up in France. I've been here many times."

Lopez nodded and stared at Wolfe. "Where did you grow up, Agent Lyon? I can't place your accent."

With a sly smile, he answered, "Military, Detective Lopez. All over."

"For what country?"

"Which one do you think it is?"

"Like I said, I can't place your accent."

"United States."

She frowned and gave them a stern look. "Make sure you inform me if you find him."

Both Nadia and Wolfe nodded before leaving the office.

When they returned to the rented BMW, Nadia turned to Wolfe. "I did not know your father was in the military."

"He wasn't. He was an accountant."

"Why did you tell her that?"

He shrugged, "It was information she didn't need to know."

"Maybe I should not have told her I was from France."

"Your accent gave you away. Since you didn't identify a city, you're good."

"Do you think she will check on us with Interpol?"

"I kind of doubt it, since Mariana Torres put us in contact with her. But we won't be getting back with Lopez anytime soon, if ever. We got what we needed and are now officially on our own."

Nadia kept her grim expression and studied the list of galleries. "There are twenty-three locations on here, Michael."

"I thought there would be more."

She shook her head. "About half are in the Lavapiés district."

He glanced at her. "What's that?"

"It is the bohemian section of Madrid. Lots of students, artists and immigrants. Very unconventional."

His mouth twitched. "Let's start there."

To speed up their search, they split up, each scrutinizing separate galleries. They started early and worked late, watching as the proprietors opened the shop for the day or locked up after hours. On the first day of their quest, they cleared four galleries. On the second day, only two. Their third day produced a possibility, but fell out of contention when the person of interest turned out to be a customer.

On the fourth day their search ended.

Nadia sat inside a small café sipping espresso and nibbling on a pastry. The gallery she watched was sandwiched between a Senegalese and an Indian restaurant. She checked the time on her cell phone and noted it was approaching eleven in the morning. Wolfe was on his way to meet her after clearing the shop he watched.

A middle-aged man approached the small gallery she had under surveillance. As she raised her espresso for another sip, she stopped and lowered the cup to the table.

A man, shorter than the average male, walked toward the gallery across from her. There was something familiar about his gait as he approached the shop's front door. His bald head possessed a ring of short clipped salt and pepper hair above his ears. A beard, trimmed to the same length, adorned his round face. At this distance, she could not see the color of this man's eyes but she knew them to be sky blue. The primary feature identifying this individual was the prominent Roman nose. This was Asa Gerlis, of that she was sure.

Memories of their last encounter and his disgusting proposal made her shiver. She did not worry about him recognizing her. She sat inside the café and wore her hair tied up. Dark sunglasses kept anyone interested from seeing her green eyes.

After the man entered the shop, she sent a two-word text to Michael. *Found him.*

Fifteen minutes later, Wolfe sat next to her, placing an espresso on the table. "Are you sure?"

"Yes, it is him."

He sipped his drink and stared at the shop door. "What is the name of the owner on the list?"

She referred to it and answered. "Diego Luis." Looking back at the shop, she asked, "What now?"

"My first inclination is to go over there and shoot him, but we both know that's not a good idea. Too many people know we are looking at art galleries. If the police find one of the owners dead..."

"Yes, probably not our best move. There is another option, Michael."

"I'm open for ideas."

"What if we lure him to a secluded spot and he just disappears?"

Wolfe blinked a few times and a small smile appeared on his lips.

The text message to JR occurred the second they returned to their hotel room. He called a few minutes later.

"What's up?"

"We found him."

"Cool. What name is he using?"

"Diego Luis. He owns an art gallery called *Pequeño Prado*. It means, Little Prado."

"Kind of pretentious."

"Considering how famous the real Prado art gallery

is, yes, very."

"If we wanted to contact him via the dark web, how would we do that?"

"What have you got in mind?"

Wolfe proceeded to tell him.

CHAPTER 43

MADRID, SPAIN

At five p.m., Diego Luis locked the front door to his gallery, turned off the *open* sign and retreated to his office. The lack of foot traffic to his business on this particular day did not concern him at all. It gave him more time to work on more profitable endeavors.

An encrypted message from one of his rich clients intrigued him. The individual, who happened to be the wife of a Chinese billionaire, requested he start the process of finding a particular Andy Warhol production. While he did not personally care for the artist's work, the money being offered for the individual's Pop Art did create a sense of professional caring. In 2016, seven prints of the iconic Campbell Soup cans had been stolen from an art museum in the central United States and never recovered. This meant they were either in storage somewhere waiting for a buyer or in a private gallery somewhere on the planet.

Gerlis knew who to contact. He sent an encrypted message to the individual and would receive an answer within a week.

Just before he closed his laptop for the night, another encrypted email arrived. The sender used the correct encryption protocols, but was unknown to him. He opened the message. *Are you interested in acquiring Picasso, Pigeon with Small Peas, oil on canvas, 65 x 54 centimeters, 1911?*

Greed overcame caution as he smiled. The rumors were apparently true—the painting existed and apparently available. He replied to the email: *Yes.*

A response did not arrive for ten minutes. *How soon can you be in Toulouse, France?*

Blinking several times, Gerlis stared at the message on the screen. When his surprise ebbed, he consulted Google Maps and found the town to be a little over 800 kilometers from his location. He typed his response—*Will need to physically examine, otherwise, no interest.*

Five minutes later: *Agreed. When?*

Day after tomorrow, must have location prior to travel.

His reply came back fifteen seconds later. *Details will be provided tomorrow. Be prepared to send funds via electronic transfer IF negotiations are successful.*

With a smile, Gerlis closed the email program and shut the laptop down for the night.

Toulouse, France
Thursday

Gerlis walked up to the reception desk at the

Crowne Plaza in Toulouse. An email on Wednesday had instructed him to check into the hotel around five p.m. A room would be reserved for him and dinner arrangements, in the hotel's dining room, would be secured. Instructions for Friday would be in the room.

When the art dealer approached the check-in desk, a young female greeted him.

"Bonsoir, Monsieur."

"Good evening." Gerlis spoke in accented English. "My name is Diego Luis. I believe there is a reservation for me."

The pretty clerk smiled and nodded. She typed his name into the computer and read the screen. Responding to him in excellent English, she said, "Ahh... Monsieur Luis, we are so glad you have arrived. Your room is ready. Plus, please tell me when you wish to dine and I will make the reservation for you now."

Gerlis returned the smile. "Can I dine in my room?"

"Of course. Just contact room service and let them know what you want and the wine you prefer."

"Excellent."

"Would you like help with your luggage?"

He shook his head. "No, thank you." He accepted the key and headed toward the elevator pulling his small suitcase behind him. The fewer individuals he encountered, the better.

When he arrived in the room, he found a fruit basket and an envelope on the small desk. He withdrew the contents of the envelope and read, *Looking forward to our meeting on Friday. A map to guide you is enclosed.*

His original apprehension about the arrangements started to subside. The accommodations were first class and, so far, he did not see any red flags. He settled in for a pleasant evening.

Michael Wolfe watched as Asa Gerlis checked into the hotel, having followed him from the parking garage. He now knew the make and model of the car the ex-Mossad agent drove and where he would be for the next twelve or more hours.

Ten minutes later, Wolfe rode the elevator to the fourth floor and walked by Gerlis' door. A *Do Not Disturb* sign hung on the doorknob. He walked back to the elevator and rode it to the first floor. After exiting the hotel, he returned to Gerlis' SEAT Leon hatchback. Once he checked to make sure no one was watching, he placed a GPS tracker unit within the driver's side rear wheel well. With his task completed, he walked to the opposite side of the parking garage and slipped into the passenger seat of their rented BMW.

He turned to Nadia who sat in the driver's seat. "He's all tucked in for the night."

She half smiled, started the engine and took a deep breath. "Why do I think tomorrow will not be as easy?"

"Because it won't. Always plan for Murphy's Law."

She frowned and looked at him. "Murphy's Law? What is this Murphy's Law?"

"If anything can go wrong, it will."

She did not move for several moments. "I have never heard this, but it is true."

"Yup, it is." He gave her a sly smile. "That's why we have this planned like we do."

She nodded and drove out of the parking garage.

Nadia and Wolfe arrived at the meeting site after sunset. Michael would stay there while Nadia returned to follow Gerlis the next morning. The location, chosen for its isolation, was owned by a bank, currently vacant and for sale. Nadia had found it with a Google search of properties looking for buyers. Located in the rural countryside of southern France, the farmhouse provided an out-of-the-way spot for the events of the next day, whatever they might be.

The night passed slowly for Wolfe. During his career as a sniper, he could block out the passing of time by slowing his heart rate, controlling his breathing, visualizing the shot and waiting for the right moment. This was different. There was nothing to do except pace and worry about Nadia.

The preparations for Gerlis' visit took a little prep work. Earlier in the day a cheap print of the Picasso painting was purchased at an art gallery in Toulouse. The imitation painting was the correct size and after being placed in a simple black frame, resembled the original. But it would only fool someone from a distance. The print now sat on an easel facing the front door in the otherwise empty farmhouse living room.

Gerlis' instructions were to enter the house, examine the painting and if satisfied, send a text message to a number. Instructions would be given on where to transfer the money. There was one warning—if Gerlis tried to leave the farmhouse with the painting before transferring the funds, he would never find his way back to Madrid alive.

Wolfe stood at the front window of the house watching the sun rise as night turned to dawn and eventually morning. He expected Gerlis to realize the picture was fake from halfway across the room. With this expectation as his guide, he prepared for that moment.

He parked the SEAT Leon beside the small farmhouse per his instructions. Gerlis stared at the front of the old structure. It looked abandoned with a front yard of weeds and uncut grass. Uncertainty crept back into the back of his mind. He retrieved a Sig Sauer P225 from under the driver's seat, checked the chamber and then charged the weapon. He placed another magazine in his front pant pocket.

Holding the pistol in his right hand, he exited the car and slowly walked toward one of two front windows of the house. There were no drapes or curtains, allowing a clear view of the inside. What he saw allowed him to relax. In the shadows of the room against the back wall resided the Picasso, Pigeon with Small Peas, oil on canvas, 65 x 54 centimeters, 1911 sitting on an easel. He almost put the gun behind his back in his belt, but caution kept it in his hand.

The unlocked front door opened easily allowing him to step into the dimly lit front room. The interior smelled of dust and neglect. With only the light of two windows, details of the painting could not be distinguished from across the room. He squinted and waited a few moments before approaching the picture. Once his eyes grew accustomed to the light,he frowned.

Rushing toward the painting, he felt the surface. It was smooth, lacking brushstrokes and texture. Enraged, Gerlis raised the Sig Sauer and fired point blank into the picture. He turned and walked rapidly toward the front door.

Wolfe made his appearance as Gerlis presented his

back to the kitchen.

"Not what you expected, was it, Asa?"

The seething ex-Mossad agent whirled around and fired the gun in the direction of the voice.

Wolfe, anticipating the move, ducked back behind the wall. Gerlis ran out of the house toward the car and turned. Aiming the gun at the front door, he waited for whoever was in the house to emerge.

From inside the house, he heard. "You're not going anywhere, Gerlis. Look at your car."

Gerlis glanced at the front and rear driver side. Both tires had long knife gashes in the side wall. The car was going nowhere.

"Put the gun down."

Gerlis pointed the Sig Saur at the front door and yelled, "Who are you?"

"A man who's been dead for two years."

"Wolfe?"

"Very perceptive."

"Where's Nadia?"

"Doesn't matter. Throw the gun down and put your hands on the car roof."

Gerlis laughed hysterically. "No way." He fired the Sig Sauer at the front door and through the front window. He pulled the trigger until the slide slammed back and froze. His left hand reached into his front pocket and extracted the extra magazine. After pressing a button next to the trigger guard, the empty magazine fell to the ground. He rammed the full one into the gun and started firing again. When the slide slammed back for the second time, he stood quietly next to the car, breathing hard.

Wolfe appeared in the front doorway. "These old farmhouses are well built, Gerlis."

With a wild animal scream, he threw the gun at Wolfe and charged. Before he got three steps, a bullet slammed into his chest, spinning him around. He collapsed face-up, staring at the sky. As blood oozed from his wound, he blinked several times and his breathing became even more labored.

Wolfe walked over to him. He smiled as he looked down.

Gerlis glared at the ex-sniper and saw Wolfe without a weapon. "Who?"

"We decided Nadia should return the favor after you tried to have her killed in Barcelona."

Gerlis shook his head. "Not—my—idea."

Chuckling, Wolfe knelt down. "Nice try. Was it, Reid?"

Gerlis stared at Michael, his eyes starting to glaze. He coughed as blood gurgled from his mouth. With great difficulty, he said, "No—it—wa..."

The next sound from the dying man was more of a gurgle than a word, but Wolfe recognized it. The chest of the ex-Mossad agent deflated one last time and remained still. His sightless eyes locked on Wolfe.

Nadia appeared next to Wolfe, a Remington 700 fitted with a scope in her hands. She stared at the now-dead Asa Gerlis. "Is it over?"

"Unfortunately—no."

CHAPTER 44

GRAND CAYMAN ISLAND

Three Weeks Later

Wolfe sat at the table where he had met Geoffrey Canfield what seemed like an eon ago. The conversations he heard were low and murmured using a generous dose of the Queen's English. He sipped from a glass of beer, his eyes glued to the front door.

At exactly, 4:00 p.m. Canfield entered the bar and waved as his mates raised their drinks to him. He strode purposefully to the bar, leaned over and spoke to the bartender. When the man handed him the gin and tonic, his head nodded toward the ex-MI6 operative's regular table. While taking a sip, Canfield turned to see what the bartender indicated.

Wolfe raised his glass but did not smile.

Canfield hesitated, took a large gulp of his drink and walked slowly toward the table. "You're sitting in my chair, mate."

"Tough shit. Sit down."

Hesitating, Canfield looked toward the door, shrugged and sat. "Didn't expect to see you again."

"I can't imagine why."

"How much do you know?"

"Most of it." He raised a laptop from the chair beside him and placed it on the table. "Nadia is becoming quite adept with computers. This one used to belong to Asa Gerlis."

Canfield stared at Wolfe, then the laptop. With a quick gulp he emptied his glass. "Where is the lovely lass?"

"Having a chat with your lady doctor friend. By the way, was she the woman who sent Nadia to Barcelona?"

He nodded and took a deep breath. Letting it out slowly, Canfield said, "Hopefully, a pleasant chat."

Wolfe's mouth twitched. "For now. Who did she work for?"

"MI6. She was always on call for us." Canfield caught the bartender's eye and raised his empty glass. "I suppose I owe you an explanation."

"Depends."

The older man tilted his head. "Depends on what?"

"How truthful you are."

"Ahh..." He remained silent until a fresh drink was placed in front of him. "Yes, there is that." Holding the drink in both hands, he studied the tiny bubbles as they rose to the top. "I was the one who introduced William Little to Reid and Gerlis."

"When was this?" Michael took a sip of beer without looking away from Canfield.

"Operation Desert Shield. Everything I told you before is true, except one small detail."

Wolfe did not respond.

After another long pull on his drink, the older man

looked up at Michael. "I'm the one who put the idea of appropriating antiquities into their heads. Reid and Gerlis were the planners, General Little merely acted as the muscle." He drained his glass again and set it back on the table. "Actually, in all fairness, General Little was a lazy sod."

"What do you mean?"

With a sly smile, Canfield looked at Wolfe. "I found him to be dead from the neck up."

"Go on."

"The six officers who helped William Little were really the brains. Especially Major Nathan Tucker."

Wolfe glared hard at his ex-controller.

"Without Tucker, the general would have been worthless."

"Who hired the assassins that eliminated them?"

Canfield watched as another gin and tonic appeared in front of him while the waitress breezed by. He did not respond to the question.

"You?"

The ex-MI6 operative nodded. "All of them, except for the man who got Tucker." He looked up at Wolfe. "I understand it was as difficult a shot as the one in Madagascar."

Wolfe did not respond.

Canfield continued, "Tucker was actually the brains of our little conspiracy. He also helped the general escape to Madagascar."

"Why?"

"The sorry sot had too big of a mouth. It would only have been a matter of time before he said something to the wrong individual." Canfield looked over the top of his glass at Wolfe as he took a sip of the new drink. "You know anything about who shot Tucker?"

Michael focused on Canfield's eyes, but said nothing.

"Now who's not being truthful?"

"This isn't about me, Geoffrey. This is your confession."

"Oh, yeah. Forgot."

"Who was the man I killed in Turkey?"

"Oh, him. He tried to sell us a Warhol forgery. We had to set an example, you know, to keep the others honest."

"Right. What about the job I refused in Russia?"

The ex-MI6 operative shrugged. "That one was Reid's idea. He never explained."

"Who made the arrangements in Barcelona?'

Canfield stared at his drink for a long time before he answered. "Me."

"Why?"

The older man took another deep breath and let it out slowly while staring at a rotating ceiling fan. "Not proud of it."

"Geoffrey?"

"Gerlis asked me to do it."

"Again, why?"

After a long silence, he said. "The original idea was for you to be the only target. Gerlis was jealous. He wanted Nadia for himself."

"He was married."

A smile touched Canfield's lips. "He wanted her as his mistress. His ego was such, he thought if you were out of the way, she would fall into his arms."

No response came from Wolfe.

"Anyway, he tried numerous times—she rebuffed all of his advances. Finally, he realized it wasn't going to happen so he decided both of you needed to go. That's when he contacted me."

"Why did you agree?"

Canfield let out a hard sigh and closed his eyes. "Because you scare me."

"Keep that in mind, Geoffrey."

With both hands gripping his drink, the older man nodded.

"I'm curious about the video showing Gerlis' supposed death by an ISIS jihadist. Who made it?"

Canfield grinned. "I was proud of that one."

"Who made it, Geoffrey?"

"A very talented young lad I found in London. I told him it was an audition for a job."

"Was it?"

"Yes, he's working as a CGI technician for an independent film studio in London."

"Is the kid aware of what he was actually doing?"

"No."

"How did you get it distributed?"

"I have no idea. Gerlis handled that part of it."

Wolfe pushed his chair back and stood.

Looking up at Wolfe, the old man frowned. "What are you going to do?"

The ex-sniper hesitated, "I'm thinking."

Canfield drained his drink.

"Geoffrey, here's the deal. You will never know when you will experience your last breath. It could be in an hour, or it could be years from now when you're dying of old age. I've never acknowledged I made the shot in Madagascar on Little, but I did." Wolfe placed his palms on the table and leaned closer. "It was an easy shot. Sixteen hundred meters with a soft breeze out of the east. Simple. One second, the General is alive, the next, he isn't. I can promise you the same fate. However, General Little didn't know I was there. You, on the other hand, will never know if I am or I'm not.

"Never try what you did in Barcelona again. Even if you relocate, I'll find you. Keep in mind, it took me over fifteen years to locate William Little and you saw what happened to him. I don't think your lady friend would like to see your head explode in front of her, would she?"

Canfield shook his head.

Still leaning over the table, Wolfe said in a low whisper. "Welcome to your new nightmare, Geoffrey."

With those words, Wolfe walked out of the bar. Canfield closed his eyes and felt a warm sensation spread in his crotch.

Washington, DC

Jerry appeared at the office door of the National Security Advisor. Joseph looked up. "Yes."

"Call for you on line one."

"You could have used the intercom."

"I could have, but I want to hear the conversation."

"Who is it?"

"Uri Ben-David."

"Shut the door and sit down."

Griggs smiled and did.

Placing the phone on speaker, Joseph touched the key with the small blinking light. "Good Morning, Uri."

"I wanted to thank you for the tip, Joseph."

Frowning, Joseph looked at Griggs whose response was a shrug and a shake of the head.

"Refresh my memory, Uri. What tip?"

"Where to find Asa Gerlis."

"Really? Glad we could help. When did you find him?"

They heard a chuckle. "You have no idea what I am talking about do you?"

"To be honest, no. What happened?"

"We received a tip through the proper channels about the location of Gerlis—or I should say, where his body was. We found him on the seventeenth of last month. It was a Saturday, I believe. It took us several weeks to get his body back to Israel. DNA tests confirmed it was him."

"Where did you find him?"

"Abandoned farm in southern France. He was obviously ambushed. The tires on his car were slashed and he had a gaping hole in his chest. We found a Sig Sauer next to him with two spent magazines. Lots of holes from the Sig Sauer, only one from the opponent."

"Huh."

"One other thing. There was a poster of a famous painting in a frame inside the house. It had one bullet hole through it."

"Huh."

"Can you enlighten me about anything, Joseph?"

"We know he was dealing in stolen art—maybe it was a deal gone bad."

"Maybe. Did your CIA have any assets in France at the time?"

"Now, how would I know that?"

Another chuckle. "Joseph, you and I have known each other for over two decades and you expect me to believe you?"

"While I am sure they have assets in France, as far as I am aware, the CIA did not have anyone searching for Gerlis."

"Well, whoever sent the tip, we want to thank them. The questions about Gerlis are now answered. We have officially closed our inquiry."

"Good."

"Talk to you soon, Joseph."

The call ended and Joseph stared at the now-silent phone. "Jerry, find out when Wolfe and Nadia left Spain."

"Yes, sir."

Two Hours Later

"They flew out of Madrid on the fourteenth to Paris and then on to Atlanta."

Joseph stared at his assistant. "That's good to hear."

"I spoke to Mariana Torres."

"Oh..."

"She told me they stopped by early on the fourteenth to thank her for her hospitality, but their search did not produce any results and were flying out at noon."

A small smile appeared on Joseph's lips.

"What are you thinking, boss?"

"Michael has always been good at creating plausible alibis. What is my schedule for the next few days?"

"Normal stuff. The president is going to Camp David this weekend. You're not scheduled to accompany him. Why?"

"I need to check on my house."

"I'll make the necessary arrangements."

"Thanks, Jerry."

Griggs turned to leave the office but hesitated a few moments. "Ah—boss?"

"Yes"

"Can I take the weekend off, too?"

Joseph smiled and nodded.

Once his assistant left and the door to his office closed, Joseph took his cell phone out of a drawer in his desk and dialed a number. The call was answered on the fourth ring.

"I haven't heard from you in a while, Joseph. How are you?"

"I'm good, Michael. How are you and Nadia?"

"We're fine. You seldom call unless it's important."

"I'm going to be at my place in Christian County this weekend. Would you and Nadia like to join Mary and me?"

There was a short silence. "I would have to check with Nadia, but I'm sure we can. When?"

"Saturday evening, let's say around four. We'll cook out and have a nice meal."

"We'll see you then."

Saturday

As evening fell, Joseph and Wolfe retreated to the back deck by themselves. Each held a crystal tumbler with a few ice cubes and twelve-year-old Glenfiddich.

Wolfe smiled and sipped his drink. "You never told me why we're here."

"The right opportunity hadn't presented itself, Michael."

"There appears to be one now."

Joseph nodded. "Asa Gerlis was found dead near Toulouse, France about four weeks ago."

"Good."

Turning to the ex-sniper, he asked, "Know anything about it?"

"Why would I?"

"Because it happened three days after you left Spain."

"Well, see, there you go. I wasn't even on the continent."

Another smile appeared on Joseph's face. "You and Nadia spent a week looking for him and three days after you leave, he's found dead."

"We went to Spain, Joseph, not France."

Joseph nodded. "You've done this before. Who used your passports?"

With a grin, Wolfe looked at his old controller. "Trade secret you taught me years ago."

Joseph chuckled. "Who contacted the Mossad?"

"Nadia."

"Figured. She would know the correct protocols."

Wolfe nodded.

"Is it over?"

"Yes, I believe it is."

"Are you going back to your old identities?"

"We're not sure. Now that you're the National Security Advisor, we can't work for you. So, we really don't know what to do."

"Think it over, I might have a solution for you."

EPILOGUE

SOUTHERN MISSOURI

Two Months Later

A re you sure this is what you want, Michael?"

Wolfe nodded as he signed the listing agent contract. He looked at Nadia. "I want a place you and I design together."

She smiled and put her hand on his arm.

Handing the contract back to the real estate agent, Wolfe said, "How long do you think it will take to sell?"

Ronda Blankenship accepted the contract and placed it in her leather portfolio. "Not long. I already have several inquiries. When the rumors started floating around West Plains you were going to sell, well..." She smiled. "I anticipate a bidding war, to be honest with you."

Wolfe remained quiet.

Nadia stood and offered her hand to Blankenship. "Thank you, Ronda."

358

"You are welcome. If I were you, I would start looking for a new place. Know where you two want to go?"

"Michael mentioned a plot of land near Ozark. I haven't seen it yet, but he says it's beautiful."

The real estate agent smiled. "Better make an offer. I'll be in touch."

Wolfe and Nadia walked out of the real estate office and stood on the sidewalk in front. Located in a busy strip mall on the south side of the small city, the parking lot was full with numerous cars searching for empty parking slots. He stuck his hands in his jean pockets and lifted his gaze toward the cloudless blue sky. "Not only do I want a new place, I want to put our old lives behind us."

She nodded and hugged his left arm. "How do we do that?"

"Break all ties to the past."

"Start over?"

"Yes. Start over."

"Using what names?"

He chuckled. "Michael and Nadia Wolfe."

"We have never officially been married."

With a sly smile, he looked at her. "We'll have to correct that."

She smiled and placed her head on his shoulder as they walked toward the Jeep.

Neither spoke for the next twenty minutes while Michael drove out of town. As they passed the exit for the airport ten miles north, Nadia turned to him. "Where is this land Joseph told you about?"

"West of his place about fifteen miles."

"When can I see it?"

"We can head there now if you want."

"Yes, I want. What's so special about it?"

"Joseph told me it used to be a private airport.

There's an abandoned hangar and fueling station already present. It will take a lot of money to restore, but the proceeds from the sale of my land will be more than enough."

"You can keep your plane there."

He nodded. "The runway needs to be resurfaced, but other than that, it's in good shape."

She smiled. "What about a house?'

"There's one on the property built in the 1940s. It would give us a place to live while we build."

"I believe I will like this, Michael."

He glanced at her. "I hope you do. If you don't, we can find somewhere else."

"I see no reason why I wouldn't like it."

"Have you listened to yourself recently?"

She frowned. "Why? Do I sound silly?"

He laughed out loud. "No, your accent is almost gone."

"Really?"

He nodded.

The silence of two individuals comfortable around each other, filled the Jeep for ten minutes. Nadia broke the silence. "I am curious—what are we going to do with all the money we found in Gerlis' bank accounts?"

"Pay cash for the property."

"That will only take a small portion."

"Yes, I know. I thought we could give some of it to Martin and Jana. After all, they had to disrupt their lives because of Reid and Gerlis."

"Another idea I like."

"Have you heard from Jana?"

"Yes. They are married and she is pregnant."

"Good."

Nadia's smile disappeared. "Do you believe Martin shot his half-brother?"

"I don't think he executed him, if that's what you mean."

"What do you think happened?"

"I believe Martin took his drunk half-brother out into the woods and helped him end his life."

"Why would he do that?"

Taking a deep breath, Wolfe hesitated. "It's hard to explain. Martin was in real bad shape when I started helping him. We now know it wasn't PTSD, but a fear of the people Bobby associated with. In a way, I think he looked at me more like a brother then his real one. When Bobby showed up and started threatening the people he cared about, well..."

"You think he did it for you?"

"No, not so much me, but to protect Jana."

She nodded. "That makes sense."

Another lengthy quiet period filled the interior as the Jeep moved west on Highway 60. As they passed the last exit for the small town of Mountain Grove, Nadia asked. "What are we going to do after the house is finished?"

"Glad you asked. Joseph made a proposal to me the other day."

"And you chose not to tell me?"

He smiled. "I chose not to tell you until I had a few days to think it over."

She crossed her arms, a frown appearing. "How thoughtful."

Chuckling, he glanced at her. "My first inclination was to turn him down. Now that I've thought it over a little, I'm not so sure. It would involve both of us."

"I see. Care to enlighten me on my future?"

"Nadia, why did you join the Mossad?"

The only sound he could hear was road noise as the tires turned rapidly over the highway. She lost her frown and stared out the front windshield. "I did it to help my country."

"As did I when I joined the Marines and the CIA. But what is the underlying motivation for doing that?"

"I don't know. I haven't thought about it before."

"To help people."

"Okay."

"You and I have specialized training. Training most individuals haven't even thought about."

"True."

"What if we put our specialized training to good use instead of all the international intrigue and bullshit we used to get caught up in?"

"How would we do that?" Her frown returned.

"During his work as the National Security Adviser, Joseph discovered a problem both the government and society have ignored."

She rolled her eyes. "Just tell me, Michael?"

"What do I do best, Nadia?"

She thought about it for several moments. "Find people who don't want to be found."

"Exactly. What do you do best?"

Smiling, she straightened in her seat and raised her chin. "I am French. I do many things well. Why?"

He chuckled. "Yes, you do, but what is your specialty?"

"I was trained to blend in..." Another smile appeared. "I am good at changing my appearance and blending into a crowd."

"Exactly."

"Okay, so what does this all have to do with working for Joseph?"

He glanced at her. "Joseph wants us to find missing persons. People who have disappeared, either by their own accord or at times, with the help of others."

"I do not wish to chase delusional faux jihadists anymore."

"Neither do I and I told Joseph that. He replied they are still working out the details, but if we are interested, they'll start figuring out the specifics."

"Will we work for Joseph?"

Wolfe shook his head. "No, he might be involved, but we would get our assignments and any needed assistance from Jerry Griggs."

"Who is he?"

"Good guy. Ex-Army Ranger who spent a decade or so overseas with the CIA. I met him a few times when I worked for Joseph."

Quiet returned to the Jeep. Nadia turned her head toward the passenger window and watched the countryside pass. Five minutes lapsed before she turned to Wolfe. "Tell Joseph I am interested."

He nodded. "As am I."

"So, Michael, when do we get married?"

"Glad you asked." He opened the Jeep's center console, removed a small black box and flipped it open with one hand. "I believe this is the one you've been eyeing on the internet for weeks. I bought it the other day."

Wolfe heard a gasp as Nadia's eyes grew wide. She stared at the wedding ring nestled in the cushioned box.

"Oh, Michael..."

ABOUT THE AUTHOR

He is active with numerous writing groups and serves on the board of the Springfield Writers' Guild.

J.C. has previously published five novels, *The Fugitive's Trail* (2015), *The Assassin's Trail* (2016), *The Imposter's Trail,* (2017), and *The Cold Trail* (2018). His fifth installment of the Sean Kruger series, *The Money Trail*, was released on February 4th, 2019. All are available on Amazon.com and Audible.com. His sixth novel, *A Lone Wolf* is the first in a new series. Sean Kruger will return in a new adventure early 2020.

The Sean Kruger Series has won numerous awards. All five novels have been presented with the Literary Titan Gold Book Award. In addition, *The Imposter's Trail* was awarded Best Mystery/Thriller at the 2017 Ozark Indie Book Fest, and in 2018, Readers' Favorite announced *The Fugitive's Trail* won a Silver Medal in the Fiction - Suspense genre.

He lives with his wife, Connie in southwest Missouri.

Visit his website at www.jcfieldsbooks.com.

Made in United States
North Haven, CT
21 September 2022

24372332R00205